RACHEL LOUISE DOVE is a wife and mum of two from Yorkshire. She has always loved writing and has had previous success as a self-published author. Rachel is the winner of the Mills & Boon & *Prima Magazine* Flirty Fiction competition and won The Writers Bureau Writer of the Year Award in 2016. She is a qualified adult education tutor specialising in child development and autism. In 2018 she founded the Rachel Dove Bursary, giving one working-class writer each year a fully funded place on the Romantic Novelists' Association New Writers' Scheme.

Also by Rachel Dove

The Chic Boutique on Baker Street
The Flower Shop on Foxley Street
The Long Walk Back
The Wedding Shop on Wexley Street
The Fire House on Honeysuckle Street
The Second Chance Hotel
Meet Me at Fir Tree Lodge
The Forever House

Someone Like You

RACHEL DOVE

ONE PLACE. MANY STORIES

This novel is entirely a work of fiction. The names, characters and incidents portrayed in it are the work of the author's imagination. Any resemblance to actual persons, living or dead, events or localities is entirely coincidental.

HQ
An imprint of HarperCollins*Publishers* Ltd
1 London Bridge Street
London SE1 9GF

www.harpercollins.co.uk

HarperCollins*Publishers*
1st Floor, Watermarque Building, Ringsend Road
Dublin 4, Ireland

This paperback edition 2022

1
First published in Great Britain by
HQ, an imprint of HarperCollins*Publishers* Ltd 2022

Copyright © Rachel Dove 2022

Rachel Dove asserts the moral right to be
identified as the author of this work.
A catalogue record for this book is
available from the British Library.

ISBN: 9780008481001

This book is produced from independently certified FSC™ paper
to ensure responsible forest management.

For more information visit: www.harpercollins.co.uk/green

Printed and Bound in the UK using
100% Renewable Electricity at CPI Group (UK) Ltd

For all the Hannahs

At any given moment, you have the power to say: This is not how the story is going to end.

Christine Mason Miller

Refuge Against Domestic Violence –
Help for women & children.
https://refuge.org.uk

Chapter 1

You'll never do it on your own. You'll never survive without me. You're all front. If I left, you'd be a complete wreck. You're nothing without me, and you know it.

The squeak of the pram wheels as they switched from pavement to polished tile floor was the only herald to the two women's arrival into the busy train station. Kate walked slightly in front of her friend with the squeaky pram, looking around her and back to her pal. They were both still wearing their hoods up, despite the fact they had left the rain outside. Water dripped from the clear plastic rain cover on the pram onto the floor, leaving a trail of raindrops in their wake.

'The departure boards are over here.' Kate pointed. 'Don't lose your tickets. I put some extra cash in there for another too. If you need to get away again, you'll have that.'

Kate pushed a long cream envelope addressed to Hannah into her changing bag, zipping it up and checking her watch. 'I hope there's no delays.'

Hannah checked the board, holding the hoodie strings tight to her chin. She shook her head. A tiny wisp of red hair poked out from the material around her neck, and she swept it back into hiding.

'Nope, it's on time. I'd better get to the platform.' Her words sounded cut off, clipped.

The two women came around the pram, hugging each other tight. The few other commuters passing by walked around them, taking no notice of a goodbye that meant more than many others on the platform that day. This goodbye was one that they'd fought hard to get to. Even with their success, it didn't make parting ways any easier for these two women.

'Oh God,' Kate half sobbed into her friend's shoulder. 'I can't believe we got here. I didn't think I would feel like this.' The two women pulled back, still holding each other tight. 'I'm going to miss you both so much.'

'I'm really gonna miss you.' Hannah was clinging to her friend, even as her eyeline kept drifting to the entrance doors every few seconds. 'I have to go. Thank you, Kate. I love you.'

Kate's eyes swam with tears, each little pool threatening to spill over the edge onto her cheeks, but she brushed them away. The pair of them were used to hiding their emotions now when it came to the other. Survival mode. They knew how to protect each other. They had become fiercely close in their short few months together, but their friendship was forged from something hard. Solid.

'Not half as much as I am going to miss you, and your little girl.' Her voice cracked but her face was determined.

Hannah tried not to cry. She didn't want that to be the last thing Kate saw before they parted. This was a happy day. She tried to remind herself of that often, but now it was here, all she felt was loss, and fear.

'But we stick to the plan. It's not forever. Just till we can figure it all out. Okay?'

'You just be safe back home. He might—'

Kate cut her off, her voice sounding like steel. 'I don't care what he might or might not do. I'm not going to let him win. He won't win. Today we win, right?'

She could only nod to Kate. There was no other way. It was a moot point anyway. Hannah knew it would just feel mean to point that out now, especially after everything they'd done to get her here. To this point. He'd already won though, hadn't he? Isn't that why she was standing in a train station, with the only three bags of possessions to her name slung on her pram?

'Right?' Kate pressed, locking eyes with her.

'Right.' She had to push hard to force the certainty of her answer into her tone. 'Today, we win.'

Kate sounded certain, but the truth was that she had tried to talk Hannah out of it for months, not that Hannah didn't understand her fear. It was madness, really. She was standing here, ready to go with her baby, but she still didn't quite believe it herself. Going alone was a big step, but it was really something that she needed to do. She *had* to do it. Kate understood that now, after the last beating it had been made crystal clear. Hannah didn't think he was going to stop. She had Ava to think about now. What if he hurt her too? What if next time, he didn't stop?

At the women's next meeting, Hannah bruised and sore, Kate stopped talking about trying the police again. Or trying to go to a local shelter, and Hannah didn't want to put Ava into that situation. When Kate had examined her, the boot prints left on the skin of her back added to the other marks and blemishes. Added together, her body read like a road map of her marriage. What Victor didn't realise at the time, was that his beatings had made his wife a new friend.

A secret friend. One he didn't know about, so she was allowed to keep her.

A midwife friend. Who didn't know him, or his temper. Kate wasn't afraid of standing up to him, but his wife knew better than to try now. The time with Victor had almost taught her not to even hope for good things.

Since that first appointment, the two women had been bonded.

They'd both stood in that room, looked at the pregnancy in her belly, the bruises and scratches on the body surrounding it, and made a plan.

'How long has this been going on?' Kate had asked, that fateful day, once Hannah was up on the table, the doppler on her growing stomach. The room rang out with the sound of the baby's heartbeat, and the lie already primed to fall from her mouth didn't come. In fact, she swallowed it in favour of the truth. Perhaps it was that heartbeat that changed things. Made her bolder somehow. The terrified mother-to-be on the table didn't know what it was but listening to that strong, determined little piece of her and the strength of the heartbeat, she caved.

'Too long,' she'd said to the midwife. They'd only met once before, when her pregnancy was confirmed. Victor had been there, the epitome of the loving husband. 'Too long.'

She'd never expected the woman to do anything. Anyone who met her husband was bowled over. And if he got a sniff of anything suspect, she'd never be able to go to her appointments alone again. It was only his work schedule that had saved her this time. He kept a close eye as it was, but he thought he was pretty safe. Arrogant with it even. Once, he'd broken her finger by holding it too tight at a dinner for his company. He'd not liked the way she'd laughed at one of his colleague's jokes. Too flirty, he'd said. Gripping her hand so tight her finger bone snapped. She'd had to sit through the rest of the dinner in agony, trying not to show how much pain she was in. He'd watched her the rest of the night, along with his colleague.

She'd lain there on the table as Kate listened to the heartbeat, off in her own desperate thoughts. Kate had removed the doppler, and the heartbeat went quiet.

'I can help,' Kate said to her, wiping the gel off her belly with one hand and holding her other tight. 'Let me help you both, okay? We have some time.'

Now there was no more time left. This was it, no turning back.

She'd got through the rest of Christmas and got the hell out of there the first chance they could get to enact their plan.

Silencing the negative thoughts in her head for once, she smiled at her best friend. 'Yes, we stick to the plan. We have to. I love you, Kate, thank you.'

'Love you too. Both of you. Now, get gone, girl.'

By the time Hannah had reached her destination, emotional and exhausted, her baby daughter sound asleep in her pram, all thoughts of going home were far from her mind. She had made her decision, and she had a new life to lead. She just hoped that everything she had done would be enough.

That first cold January night, she slept on the floor of the living room of a strange new house, her daughter sleeping on a thick pile of blankets next to her. Fireworks were still going off, people making the New Year festivities spread just a day or two further. She used to love fireworks. Now the bangs and pops jarred in her skull, and she jumped at the shadows they cast through the bare windows. She touched her sleeping child's chubby little cheeks, pulling a smile from her lips as she slept. She knew how hard it was going to be. They had each other though, and that would be enough for now. It had to be. There would be no going back. Not again.

The park across the street was one of the biggest selling points to renting the little terrace Hannah had saved for. Kate had shown her the details for the house, and she'd had a good virtual look at the area on her phone. She needed to feel secure, safe. The park looked so beautiful, so normal. She'd imagined walking with Ava there, in her pram. Watching her from the window when she was older, playing there with all her school friends. Waving to people as they passed by, a normal mother and daughter out for the day. It had helped to calm her terror, thinking of that park. This was the first time she'd had the courage to go, and she hated herself for waiting so long. Being so shut down. Still under control.

Being here now seemed surreal, like a dream come true in a way, but like a living nightmare in others. It took her two days to really take in the fact that she was here, a new mum, in a new place. The house was nice, luckily. A contact of Kate's had really come through, having a tenant-free house that they didn't mind taking a little cheap rent on for a while. She had her start, thanks to Kate, and in between the sleep deprivation, worrying about money and feeling utterly alone, she got to know her new home, just a little. Kate had sent money through the landlord as well, and it was sitting in an envelope on the fireplace when she arrived. She'd been to visit the local charity shop, and the owner had a little van for deliveries.

The locals who were in the shop had all fallen in love with baby Ava on sight, marvelling at how happy and inquisitive she was for her short time in the world. It was true; Hannah had seen it herself. Ava *was* happier here. She laughed and smiled more; she didn't sit quietly as much as she once did. That thought cut her to the quick, and she pushed it away. She was so tiny, surely she wouldn't be tainted by the horrors of what they'd left already? The thought made her more determined never to have to return. Her little house might be sparse, and a bit cold, but it was theirs. It was a happy house.

Her new house was overlooked by neighbours, but not too overlooked. An odd distinction, but Hannah had learnt to tell instantly the difference between the two. Ava loved the colours, the muted greens and yellows of the grass, the hedges lining the streets here. Hannah noticed little changes in her every day, little differences and things learnt for the first time. Experiences she cherished and committed to memory to keep her going on the dark days. And if the days were dark, the nights were truly black. Isolated. Days turned into weeks. But then Hannah stopped jumping at every little sigh her new home made. She got used to the click and whoosh of the boiler as the heating turned on every evening. The way the roof seemed to sigh late at night, as if this little abode of hers was settling in for sleep too.

Once Ava was settled and the little terrace was clean, Hannah would end up in bed before nine at night. She'd managed to pack a few books to bring with her, but they weren't going to last long. She couldn't afford a television, although she would like to get one before Ava got much older. She wouldn't want her to start school feeling different from the other kids – not that it was a concern right now. The area was quiet, a great relief to Hannah when she arrived.

They'd been there in the sleepy Yorkshire village called Leadsham a couple of months now, March just beginning to make its presence known in the weather. Which is more than Hannah and Ava had done since their arrival. Aside from the odd supermarket shop or charity shop, she'd hunkered down with her baby. No visitors, other than a couple of doorstep sellers. She didn't even open the door to them. The thought of a random man in her new space overwhelmed her.

The furthest they had been was on the bus to the next town. Hannah had registered them both at the doctor's surgery there, and headed straight back home. She didn't feel right being outdoors yet, she realised. It made her teeth clench. She still wasn't free. She still felt alone.

They'd even seen Ava's first birthday in alone. Poor Ava. A homemade cake and a new outfit and toy. No family. No friends. Kate sent a card and some money through the post, but it wasn't the same. Everything Hannah had bought Ava was from the supermarket reduced aisle. Hannah knew she wouldn't know about it. She wouldn't remember her first birthday at all, but Hannah still resolved to be in a better position when the terrible twos came to call.

Now though, money was on her mind. When another Monday rolled around, she decided it was about time she got out of the house and venture out further. Ava had slept later than usual, Hannah managing to grab a cup of tea to take to bed as she gave her daughter a sippy cup of milk. Kate had shown her the

9

ropes with breastfeeding back when Ava was born, but of course it was something else she'd been denied trying by Victor. Another piece of control she'd lost. Jealousy was a twisted thing, and it fuelled her husband. Even though it was never warranted. Ava had taken to the bottle like a champ though, and weaned like a dream, which was a good thing, especially given the price of formula milk and Hannah's tight budget. It was a relief that she was on cow's milk now. Cheaper, even at the rate she drank it.

Food still wasn't cheap, and nappies added in meant Hannah lived on basic ranges and coupon clipping. She needed to eke her money out as long as possible. She'd paid for six months up front on the rent, but after that her plan needed to be fully in place and her life in some kind of routine. She had no other option. Kate had been great, but she couldn't help her anymore now. The two women had to keep their distance for a while. She could hardly go visit her – Victor was tenacious. He wasn't going to let her walk out with his child and not look back. She wasn't stupid. She just wasn't going to accept the alternative either. Kate had her own life, and she didn't need him on her case trying to cause trouble. She was on her own, and that was probably the most daunting thing about the last year.

It had taken her by complete surprise, the feelings of not being enough. How could she think any different though, given the last few years? She was here though. She had to remind herself of that every morning, when she jerked awake in the early hours, drenched in sweat, looking around wildly for the man in her bed who wasn't even there. She had to sit and will her heart to settle down, listening for any and every noise in her creaky house. Her bed was basic, but a double, and Ava was in a cot in the other room. Another bargain from the local charity shop. The manager was looking out for other things for her too. She would lie in bed and make lists of things she needed and counted them off in her head till her brain stopped screaming. Ava was sleeping well, but Hannah still felt like a zombie half the time.

When she finished feeding Ava breakfast, she got the pair of them dressed and ready to go out. She looked in the fridge for something to fill her empty stomach till she could do a food shop, but things were pretty bare. She hunted around for another few moments and gave up. Putting Ava in her pram, she readied the changing bag.

'I think that your mother needs to get outside today and start this new life we want. What do you say, Ava?' Her adorable daughter looked back up at her, a happy grin on her cheeky chops. She really was beautiful. She didn't scream the house down every night, and she seemed to be a happy baby. She had her father's eyes; there was no mistaking that. Every so often she would look at her daughter and it was like she was looking at him. It took her breath away every time.

The hair was all her though, a little crop of red hair on top of her sweet-smelling head. Kate had nicknamed her Fireball, because of her swift arrival into their lives with her shock of red hair. Fireball sounded about right. Hannah found herself wishing that for her daughter. She nurtured the thought of her growing up strong, with a voice of her own and a conviction steely enough to use it. Experience enough to tell her to run the hell away from any man remotely like the man who'd helped create her. She wanted all of that for her daughter. It helped keep the overwhelming feelings at bay. She would be strong, for Ava. To give her the life she deserved to live. Not in fear. In hiding. A fireball didn't hide. It burned instead.

Hannah wrapped Ava up and wheeled the pram out towards the front door. Remembering about the food, she nipped back into the kitchen and knelt down on the tile floor. She was wearing one of Kate's long, smart dresses, the thin material allowing the cold to seep into her bones through her thin tights. She could barely afford the heating on a night, so during the day was out of the question, even in the cold March weather they had been experiencing. She always made sure that Ava was warm enough, and that would be enough for now.

She leaned down close to the corner of the units and pulled at one of the wooden kicker boards. It had been loose when she'd moved in, a discovery that made her feel like this house was welcoming her too, in its own little way. Helping her to keep her secrets hidden away, and her daughter safe from harm. After pulling the piece of board away she put her hand in and pulled out a purse and a large yellow jiffy bag. She counted the notes in the bag, got enough out for shopping and put the rest away. The purse in her hand felt alien, part of her old life. She never usually carried it with her here, but something made her today. She didn't open it, putting back the jiffy bag of cash and making sure everything was back in place. Pushing the kicker board with her foot, she was satisfied when it didn't move.

After tucking the money into her changing bag, in the secret side pocket she was so accustomed to using, she smiled down at Ava, who was sitting wide-eyed in her pram, looking at the reflection through the glass-window-panelled front door. There were glass roses intertwined on the panels, the sunlight throwing off red and green patterned shards of light onto her daughter's face.

'Come on then, Ava, let's go try and get our new life started, eh?'

Ava babbled along happily in response, and Hannah's heart soared once more as she took her in. She was so perfect. She couldn't imagine how, given her start, but here she was. Happy, eating well, growing. Safe. She leaned in, dropping a kiss on her daughter's little cheeks, and they headed outside. She pushed the pram over the threshold of the front door of her rental, clicking the brake on and turning to lock the door. The wood was swollen from the recent rains, and it didn't fit snugly into the housing. She had to really push at the door to get the key to turn, and her panic grew by the second, her palms clammy. She'd have to get it fixed. She didn't want to bother the landlord, considering the cheap rent. Plus, it was all arranged through Kate, so she didn't have the details, and they didn't have hers. She'd have to get a joiner in, and God knows how much that would be. Another thing on her list of being an adult that she couldn't quite get her head around at the moment.

She'd never have to do these things normally. It was the kind of thing Victor just . . . took care of. If something needed doing, it would be taken care of, no questions asked. He did nice things at first. Putting up a shelf. Making her a coffee she hadn't asked for. She'd relinquished control, one tiny piece at a time. Pieces so small she didn't notice them falling away from her. From the woman she was before she met him. Before she met Victor and he tried to destroy her. What good would this door do against Victor's might, if she couldn't even get it to lock properly? Her heart was beating wildly in her chest, fast, scary. It was like it was trying to free itself from her ribcage and run. Trauma, she knew. She'd read up about it enough to know that her body was still on edge. Always waiting for a noise, a fist. The sound of a voice that turned her insides to liquid with a mere comment. *He's not here. You're safe, heart. Don't give up on me now.*

Trying to quell the panic rising within her, she gave the stubborn door another hard shove and the wood finally joined up. After locking it and triple-checking it, she put her keys into her dress pocket and gripped firmly onto the pram handles. *You did it. You can do this.*

Fenchurch Street looked beautiful in the morning sun, the muted green of the park beckoning to her across the road. She found herself hurrying to the paper shop, picking up a copy of the local news and a soft drink to quench her thirst. Ava was soon asleep. Hannah was halfway through the park when she decided to take the opportunity to sit on a bench and read the paper. It was mild out, and even with her thin clothing it felt good to be outside. Out of the bubble that was their bare little hideaway. She turned to the job section, which was a little on the thin side. Dismissing everything almost as soon as she'd read it, she turned to the last page with a part-time and temporary section. Everything was the same, either zero contracts with working hours she couldn't rely on or full-time. Most of the shift patterns of the jobs on offer ruled her out instantly, she had no childcare and most of these jobs didn't even fit into day care hours.

Hannah tried to stop the sharp pain in her chest by closing the paper and checking on Ava, who was still dozing. They were shaded against the weak sun's rays by a large oak tree, the bench she was sitting on rough on the back of her legs as she sat back and looked up to the sky.

Calm down, it's okay. You can do this. You knew it would be hard. This is it. This is what you worked for. She opened her eyes slowly, trying to ground herself in the moment, to stop her flapping. A dark streak passed her eyeline, and the next second, there was a man standing in front of her. He looked around him in an easy way, taking in the people living their lives around them. Hannah was frozen to her seat. *Leave, please. Why are you here?* The man looked into the pram at sleeping Ava, a smile spreading across his lips.

'Cute kid,' he said, and before Hannah could move a muscle, his hands were on her changing bag, and he was pulling it away from the pram. Hannah's surprise turned to fear.

'Hey!' she shouted, scrabbling to her feet and taking hold of the pram handle. Ava stirred at the jostling.

The man glared at her. 'Don't make a scene; I just want the bag.' He went to pull it again, and Hannah's heart hammered in her chest. He was going to take it. He was going to take the bag, with her money in, her purse. Her purse! Ava's meagre possessions were in that bag. He was going to take their stuff, right here in front of everyone. She felt her heart hammer in her chest, as though fear itself was taking a sledgehammer to her ribcage. She could feel the thud thud thud of the blood pumping around her body, ringing in her ears. She felt like she was at home, just for a second. Right back in her old life, willing her heart to keep beating and her hands to stop shaking, her legs to work. Willing her body to do anything but shudder, panic, and even shut down. *Ava. Ava. Fight, Hannah. Fight!*

'Help!' she shouted, going to try to get Ava out of the pram. The man shoved her hard and grabbed for the bag once more. 'No, no! Help, please!'

The man, noticing the attention he was getting, tried once more to make a grab. His fingers closed around the strap of the bag, but Hannah gripped his hands in hers, and dug her nails in as hard and for as long as she could. She waited for a blow to come, shutting her eyes as he screamed in pain.

'Arrgghh! Get off me, you crazy woman!' He tried to throw her off, freeing one hand, but when she wouldn't stop, Ava now screaming blue murder in her pram, he grabbed for the pram handle instead.

'Let go now, or I'll throw this pram. Don't mess me about!'

Hannah looked at Ava, screaming her head off, her little face red with panic and fear, and she gripped tighter. Dug her nails in as hard as she could while she tried to get to Ava.

'I'm not letting go till you get away from my daughter! Help me, please!' She looked around wildly and felt relief when she saw people coming their way.

'Hey!'

'Hey, someone call the police!'

'Get your hands off her now!'

'Hey! Stop him, someone!'

Some of the people in the park were running now, one man on the periphery of the line of trees on his phone catching her attention as she clung on for dear life. He was running differently than the others, faster.

'Bullet! Bullet!'

This man was shouting something too as he ran, his hand at one ear as he spoke rapidly into a mobile phone. Hannah tried one more time to get to Ava, and the man's hand disappeared from the pram handle the second she lunged for her daughter. Unclipping her at lightning speed, Hannah grabbed her child and her bag, running in the other direction, towards the benches. She

15

could hear people behind her, angry snarling noises over high-pitched, rapid-fire voices.

'Arrgghhh! Get it off! Get it off!'

Hannah could hear the would-be thief struggling behind her, immobilised, and she frantically undressed Ava a little, trying to look for any sign of injuries. *He never touched her. He didn't hurt her.* The thought hit her brain, and she stopped. She was comforted now by the words of truth she'd told herself before, in a different place. About a different man. Ava was screaming her head off, her whole body shaking with the violence of her terror. Hannah tried to pull it together. There was quite a scene forming at the park now.

'Ssshh, ssshh, it's okay, Ava. Mummy's here, I've got you, I've got you.' There was nothing, no tears in her clothing, no marks, not a scratch on her bright puce face. She was fine. The relief flooded through Hannah's system, reducing her to a blubbering, grateful wreck. 'You're fine, baby. You're fine.' She was fine, her hot little cheeks red and angry-looking, but full of blood, full of life. A woman came running towards her, a pack of baby wipes in her hand.

'Oh my God, are you okay? Is your baby okay? Do you need any first aid?' She offered the baby wipes to Hannah, and she took them with a very shaky hand. The plastic packaging rustled against Hannah's fingers as she held the little packet and her baby in the other. 'I brought these in case; my kids are just over there. Well, they're not *all* my kids. We're childminders in the village. That's my partner.' The woman, a rather short lady in a pair of faded dungarees and cream T-shirt, pointed over to the grass, where another woman sat on a blanket, surrounded by toddlers, looking their way with a concerned expression on her face. 'I'm Martine; that's Ruby. Are you okay?'

The would-be mugger was laid on the ground, the man with the large brown dog sitting astride him, one knee either side of his body. He was shouting at the man to calm down, to stop fighting, and the dog still had him pinned by one leg. Every time the man moved even a toe, the dog gripped a little harder, a deep low grumbling growl emitting from his throat, which could be heard from their position. Martine looked at the two men and back to Hannah. Ava was now silent, her little body shuddering with the aftershock of her sobbing. Hannah held her close. She had the shivers herself.

'I'm okay, we're okay, thank you.' She took a few wipes from the packet and offered them back to the woman.

'Oh no, you keep them. We have loads.' Martine gave her a little smile, and then pointed back to her companions. 'Listen, I'd better go help my mate wrangle the kids, but we run the parent–toddler group at the community centre, if you fancy it. Tuesdays and Thursdays, ten till twelve. Come see us if you are at a loose end.' She dropped a business card onto the bench. Hannah nodded dumbly, tucking the card away into her bag. She'd barely taken Martine in. Cradling a now quiet Ava close, she watched a police car pull up and the police scramble to get out. Two officers, both huge dark-haired men, were running towards the two men on the ground. As they got closer, Hannah's fear grew. She needed to get out of here, now. Too many people, too many questions. Too much exposure.

Martine was looking at her intently, her gaze flicking from her party, to the melee of arms, legs and paws, and the approaching officers. 'You sure you're okay? You have far to walk to get home?'

Hannah took her eyes off the officers just long enough to try to convince the concerned woman that she wasn't having a mild heart attack and didn't need any assistance.

'No, I'm fine, honestly. I'm just over there.' She pointed in the opposite direction to her house, and the woman nodded in reply. She was biting her lip, looking back at her own kids who were just starting to grumble and moan. 'Honestly, I'm fine. I'll see you at the group thing, okay?'

That seemed to placate her, and it was all Hannah could do not to grab her baby and run as she watched the woman wrestle with the situation. Finally, she smiled at Hannah, and turned to leave.

'Okay, listen, I'd better get back to the rabble. You'll be there though, at the group?'

Hannah tried to form her panicked body into a halfway relaxed pose, willing the fear cascading through her body to subside, so she could stop everyone looking at her, and get home.

'Yeah, we'll be there. And thank you, again. Please, thank your friend for me too.' She gave her a winning smile, before looking down at Ava and busying herself with settling her on her lap. She daren't look at the policemen.

Clutching Ava to her chest, Hannah felt their two hearts beating together, so fast. As fast as a stampede of horses. She shushed the tot, grateful that her terrified screams and wails had subsided to an occasional exhausted shudder. She'd need lunch soon, and now there was no chance of Hannah getting to the shops. The job hunt was dead in the water too. Another day with no money coming in, not to mention the fact that she'd nearly lost her bag and everything in it. She thought of Ava, sitting in that pram while the man wrestled with the handles, and felt her throat constrict in a way so familiar to her. She gasped to catch her breath when a pair of green-flecked blue eyes filled her vision. *Kind eyes*. She didn't know why that particular thought had crossed her mind, but that was what had been her first instinct.

'Hello? Can you hear me?'

She frowned at the eyes, nodding her head slowly. 'Yes, I can hear you. Sorry.'

He held out a hand towards her, palm down, but he didn't take a step closer.

18

Chapter 2

She's scared. Softly does it. Brody, now hands free from the mugger, tipped his hand slightly in Bullet's direction. Bullet sank to his belly beside him, not taking his eyes off the woman and her child. The gathered crowd were leaving the park now, the occasional backward glance in their direction. People always surprised Brody, both in good and bad ways. His colleagues had bundled the offender into the van and taken him back to the station. Brody had elected to stay behind, to check on the woman, take some details. His colleagues on the force had been keen to check up on them both, but something about the woman had made something in him hold them back, to give her a minute. Looking across at Bullet, who was still staring at the pair intently, told his partner everything he needed to know. Everything that he was feeling himself. Instinct.

'I'm Andrew Brody. I'm an off-duty police officer. I'm sorry if Bullet here startled you, but he never did like days off. You going to be okay?'

'I'll be fine. I don't think he got anything in the end.'

'Where do you live? Are you local?'

She nodded her head but didn't meet his eyes. Her shoulders were scrunched up, curved like wings as she held her baby tight. The little one was the spitting image of her mother.

'She yours?'

The flinch that jolted from the body of the woman before him shocked them all. The little one stirred, crying for a half-minute before settling down again. He clocked the woman's shaky hands. Bullet whined once at the side of him, and Brody nodded to him in response. Leaning in a little closer, squatting in front of her, he tried a different tack.

'She's beautiful. What's her name?'

'Ava. Thank you.'

He leaned in, just a half-inch closer to take in the baby's face fully for the first time.

'She's your daughter?'

'Yes. I'm Hannah.'

'Hi, Hannah. I need to ask you a few questions, if you will.' She opened her mouth, a look of panic on her face. 'Later, of course. I would like to get you and Ava checked over medically first.'

'We're fine. I've checked her over. I just really want to get home.'

'Where's home?'

That look again, like he'd asked her for her inside leg measurement.

'I'm sorry. I have to ask these questions. You've been the victim of a crime, and we need details.'

'I don't want to press any charges. You have him, don't you?'

Brody said nothing, waiting for her to fill the space in conversation. She didn't; instead, she was up on her feet, heading towards her belongings. Her back was ramrod straight as she turned away from him, departing with steady steps across the grass. Bullet was still sitting down just behind Brody, watching the whole scene in his usual easy way. She stopped in front of him abruptly, and Brody watched Bullet look up at her. After a moment, she walked back and bent down and stroked the dog behind the ears.

'Thank you,' Brody heard her say softly to the hound, and Bullet, being the ever-stoic dog he was, looked up at her in his customary calm way. Brody always wondered what the dog was

20

thinking when he did this, but then Bullet surprised him. Leaning forward, he sniffed at the baby, and then licked Hannah's hand before sitting back down in front of them both.

'Good boy.'

She continued to walk to her pram, checking the interior for damage or scuffle debris, before strapping her now calm baby daughter in. Brody approached her slowly, taking his time to stand next to the dog. She looked across at him, flashing him a little tiny smile before looking away again. *She's pretty when she smiles.* The thought popped into his head just as quickly as he dismissed it. He wasn't in the habit of checking out members of the public, let alone a woman with a baby who had just endured a very scary mugging. The perp was on the way back to the station now with his colleagues, no doubt pleading his case very loudly in the back of the police transport vehicle. He'd have to file a report on the crime when he got to the station for his afternoon shift, and he needed further details, but something about this woman made him drag his feet.

'Do I have to make a statement?' She was looking at him, pram handles in hand. She still appeared flushed in the face, her movements fast, jerky. 'I did have things I needed to get done today.' She checked the bag on the back of the pram, unzipping and zipping it back up tight.

'You can come to the station, make one later this afternoon? The mugger is known to us, so I can't see there being much trouble with the charge.' He looked around at the people in the park, waving one of his arms in their direction. 'Plenty of witnesses, my colleagues who attended took their details. I do still need to take yours though.' He reached into his pocket and took out a little notebook he kept with him. 'If you ask for Brody, I'll be around.' He looked up from his pad at her, a gentle smile playing across his features. 'That okay with you?'

Hannah looked from the pad, to Bullet, and back to him. 'I really don't want to get involved; I'd just like to forget to be honest.'

Brody understood, but he frowned anyway. 'Your choice. We are here to help though, and this guy has a record. You could stop him from hurting someone else.'

Something flashed in her eyes, silencing the rest of his usual pep talk. The one he trotted out to the victims, who were normally in shock and just wanting to get home, get over their ordeal in private. No one liked being reminded how dark and ugly the world could be.

'What makes you think that?' Her voice was stronger now. A sharp edge to her clipped tone.

'Think what?'

'That me making a statement will prevent a guy like him from doing this all again tomorrow.'

Brody was taken aback for a moment. The change in her; it startled him. She was watching him with the embers of fire in her eyes, waiting for his reply.

'Well, we have him in custody. We have a lot of witnesses. And your statement if you choose to make one. The thing is . . .'

She'd never given her last name and he didn't feel comfortable calling her Hannah in this moment.

'The thing is, madam, we have the opportunity to deal with this crime. I wouldn't be doing my job if I didn't have the public's best interests at heart.'

'I can't make a statement, and it's Hannah.'

'It doesn't have to be today.' He could tell by her face that she'd made her mind up. Given that the last thing he wanted to do was harass a stressed mother, he didn't really know what else to do.

'I have to go.' Her hands gripped the pram handles a little tighter, signalling her departure. Before he could register his actions, his contact details were in his hand.

'Please, if you do change your mind, my details are on there or you can come to the station. We're based just off the magistrates' court in town.'

'I won't change my mind,' she said, a little less forcefully this time. The two of them stared at each other for a moment. Brody was given the distinct impression that she was sizing him up just as much as he was her. His gut was practically roiling as he watched her, his arm still outstretched, the paper in his hand.

'I really don't want to get involved.'

The supermarket was more of a local store, rather than one of the chains. Hannah strapped her daughter into the baby seat, taking the trolley and heading down the first aisle. After the day she'd had already, looking at everything she didn't have at home wasn't helping. She thought back to her last home. Neatly painted walls, cupboards full of food. The gadgets that had sat on the kitchen worktops were worth more than the cash she'd brought with her. She marvelled at how life could change in a moment, and then pushed herself back into the present. She'd never needed all that stuff anyway. It was just the gilding on her former cage. She had no need of it.

She picked up the basics, staples for the cupboard, bits she needed for Ava, enough to stock her up for a few days. She needed to keep a low profile, given that her outing for Operation Get a New Life had gone from a quiet morning in the park to a very public mugging, and the aftermath. Plus the rather inquisitive off-duty officer. The image of his doubting features sprang into her head. She'd piqued his interest, which was a disaster in the making. The last thing she needed was to have the local law enforcement asking questions.

She was halfway along an aisle perusing the discount shelf when she caught a woman and man looking at her intently. The woman frowned, looking at her whilst talking out of the corner of her mouth. Her husband had his eyes set on Hannah now too, but he was shaking his head at his wife. Hannah put her head down, busying herself in the shelves, looking for the cheaper snacks to fill her cupboard. She reached for a pack of rice cakes, and accidently caught the woman's eye.

'Hi,' the woman said, and she could see her husband rolling his eyes behind her. 'Is it you?'

Hannah plastered her best smile on her face and laughed a little. 'Is what me?'

'Leave her alone, love. It's not her.'

'It is!'

Hannah wanted to grab Ava and run. Did the news of the mugging get around already? Surely not. Did this woman know who she was? Hannah found herself looking around for Victor, her heart pumping. Did he have people looking? What if he had gone to the police? Was her face on some poster somewhere? She swallowed hard, trying not to look terrified. Trying to stay as calm as the surface of a mill pond, while her legs frantically paddled beneath to keep her afloat.

'I'm sorry,' she told the couple. 'I guess I must just have one of those faces. I don't think we've met. Have a good day though.' She put the packet in her hands into the trolley behind her daughter and made to leave.

The woman put a hand on the trolley handle, very close to Hannah's own, and Hannah glared at her.

She was in no mood for talking to her anymore. She didn't like this one bit. She didn't recognise either of them, and it wasn't like she had been going to many places since she'd arrived. What was the deal with this woman? She found that the anger and fear swirling within her had given her a stronger voice than usual.

'If you could take your hand off my trolley.' She looked pointedly at the hand still holding the trolley handle, and the woman blushed and removed it.

'It's not you, is it,' she said sadly, and her face fell. 'Harold?'

'Come on, Joyce, it's obviously not her. Leave the poor woman alone.' He came to put his arm around his wife, his face a poster for awkward apologies. 'Our daughter lives in Australia now, with her family. She looks like you, that's all.' He gave his wife a look of sad reproach and steered his trolley away from Hannah's. 'Joyce's not been well lately, forgetful.' Hannah looked at the tired man's face and wondered what it was like to be so loved and cherished by someone. 'She was convinced our window cleaner was one of her old school mates a bit ago. Nearly scared him off his ladder.' He laughed, just once, but Hannah could tell it was a reflex.

Hannah let go the urge to run and gave the man her best understanding smile. 'I understand.'

'Sorry again.'

'But . . .' Joyce was still not ready to move on, but her husband tucked her into his arm.

'No buts, Joyce, it's not her. Carolyn's in Australia, remember? We'll talk to her later, on the computer. Come on, let's get out of here.'

The pair of them walked away, deep in conversation. He was rubbing his wife's arm, and Hannah watched them leave. Once they had left her sight, and she could breathe again, she looked at Ava. She was sitting placidly in the trolley seat, playing with a discounted bath book she'd picked up for her from the baby aisle. She went to move but found that her legs were shaking uncontrollably. That felt too close for a moment. She had to keep a low profile. It was a mistake this time, but it didn't mean that she was feeling any safer. *Not now, not so soon.* She had thought that she might get more time, but she felt a sting of shame envelop her. She'd failed already. She'd come here and thought it would be okay. It would never, ever be okay.

She finished her shopping on autopilot, before heading home and locking the door behind them both. When she put Ava down later that night, she went to bed with her. She felt like she wanted her daughter close by. Safe. She dreamed of red-eyed wolves that night, snarling and nipping at her heels. She was in the park again, Ava screaming in her pram. There was no mugger this time, no man and dog coming to her rescue. This time, the mugger was an animal, and he never stopped till he'd found his prey.

She awoke panting, slick with sweat. Ava cried beside her, her little body shocked by the sudden commotion, before settling back into a restful slumber. Hannah watched her daughter breathe in and out, until sleep finally reclaimed her. She didn't dream again that night. She had hoped the nightmares would be gone forever, but she realised she was kidding herself. There was no way to keep the wolves from the door. She'd already tried.

Chapter 3

The next morning, Ava was playing with her toys on the floor. Or picking them up and throwing them, which meant there were plastic bricks scattered across the surface. Hannah had relished not having to worry about a little bit of mess. She was sitting at the table, reading yesterday's paper, when the doorbell rang. She had one hand on the page, the other cradling a strong coffee. She felt like she hadn't slept a wink, but she'd been up with the dawn anyway. The birds at her bedroom window didn't give a toss how ratty or hemmed in she felt. She envied them, being able to sing and fly wherever and whenever they wanted. The minute her eyes opened she knew that even trying to sleep was going to be a waste of time. Now it was barely after nine, the sun just starting to shine through the thin cotton curtains draping the kitchen window.

She rose from her seat at the table and looked at the front door. She could see a shadow of a man standing there, and her breath caught in her throat. The doorbell rang again, just once, and then she heard a deep voice.

'Hello, Hannah?'

She didn't utter a word, just held back from the door. Ava was watching her, half interested. She begged her in her head to stay quiet.

'Hannah, we met yesterday. At the park – the officer?'

It took her a second, but she placed the voice behind the hulking shadow. It was Brody. Her heart started working in her chest again, but her hands still shook while opening the door on the chain. She opened it just enough to look through, and there he was.

'Good morning.'

He was without his dog this time, but that wasn't the first thing she noticed. His eyes almost pinned her to the spot, something about his face seemed to do that. It wasn't his eyes that she was focused on though. It was the police uniform he was wearing. He looked official. She bit the inside of her lip, hard. She was doing with needing a policeman at her door. Where were they before, back home? When she needed protection from Victor? Nowhere. Now some attempted mugging had occurred, she was a victim again, and they were relentless in their pursuit. *Too late, PC Plod. I don't need a thing from you and your ilk.*

'Hello,' she managed to utter back, flashing him a short smile. 'How did you find me?'

He looked a little embarrassed for a second, his cheeks throwing out a hint of pink beneath his hat.

'I figured you lived local; it didn't take much asking around about new arrivals.'

Shit. So much for a smaller town, a quiet life. She'd have been better drowning herself in a bigger city by the sound of this rumour mill.

'Okay. What's this about?'

His lips pursed, and he looked down the street for a second before returning his gaze to hers.

'We still need to take a statement. I was expecting you yesterday, but I thought it might be better done out of the station. May I come in?' He reached behind him and produced a little soft toy version of his dog. 'I come bearing gifts.'

'I don't need gifts, and I'm rather busy this morning. I don't want to press charges either, so the statement is pointless.'

28

She pushed the door shut, and he made no move to stop her. He knocked again, a couple of short taps.

'I'm not trying to bother you; I just wanted to take a statement. This guy had been a nuisance for a while. I understand, I apologise for disturbing you.' Hannah listened, but she didn't hear him leave. 'The toy is for Ava. We give them out to kids at the station. You have my card in case you change your mind. I left one with the dog.'

Hannah hid behind the door for a second, trying to catch her breath and slow the strong drum of her heart. She listened for the gate to click shut, but nothing happened. Checking that Ava was still occupied, she slowly took the chain off the door and opened it.

Brody was standing outside the gate, looking at the house. The gate was slightly open, his hand on the metal clasp. The soft toy dog was sitting on the doorstep, looking at her like a hopeful stray. Brody met her eye and she looked right back at him warily. He was younger than she first thought, but then again, she had been rather distracted by the mugging. And the quiet, rather nosy policeman who was now staring at her so intently made her head spin. It made her think of another man's stare. The polar opposite of Brody's, but the effect still pinned her in place in the same head-swirling way. She recalled a colder, threatening gaze, one that filled her with dread each time.

She blinked rapidly to cleanse the memory from her eyes and looked again. He'd closed the gate now and turned to walk back to his police car. In the back, she could see Bullet. His big black eyes were also focused on her, and she nodded awkwardly at the hound, who barked once in response. Brody looked at him, and then back at her. When he saw her still standing there, he sighed and rested one hand on the little fence at the front of her house.

'Hannah, are you sure you're okay?'

She opened her mouth to dismiss him, as she had learnt to do with some degree of skill over the last few years. She had perfected the carefree smile, the pain-free body movements, even though sometimes she had just wanted to curl up under the covers of her prison and cry till she was nothing but a pool of tears and regret. She was great at deflecting, an expert in excuses too. She would have been a good solicitor she fancied, in another life. It came so naturally to her now. Editing the facts and history of her life to suit the agenda she needed it to. She opened her mouth again, trying and failing to think of something to say to get rid of this man.

'I will be,' she said instead, and she found herself smiling at her own words. 'I will be.'

Brody nodded, the corner of his mouth lifting slightly. 'Good,' was all he said, and then he was gone. She watched the car pull away, and Ava started to cry indoors. On her front step, the cuddly dog was sitting on a piece of paper. She picked them up, looking to see if anyone was watching first. The street was quiet and serene, as usual. After locking the door behind her, she went to get her daughter fed and dressed.

She had a hell of a lot to get through today. The paper from yesterday was still sitting on the kitchen table, but it made for grim reading. Long gone were the days when you could spend half an afternoon ringing around for vacancies, full of possibilities. Jobs were sparse where she could go undetected, and with Ava in tow, it was near impossible. She'd already rung a couple of the adverts, but with childcare, she would end up out of pocket before she started.

You can't do this. There it was again, the familiar old voice. It drove her mad, haunted her dreams. Scolded her inwardly for every celebration she had ever notched up. Every time Ava smiled, or gurgled in her cot, he was there. In her head. The things he used to spew at her were coded into her brain now. She was so gaslighted that even her own thoughts had his agenda. But in her own voice. *You won't be a good mother. Bad wife, bad mother.* She gripped the corner of the table, her knuckles turning white as she pushed him out of her head.

Once the silence returned to her ears, she gathered her things together. Checking the leftover cash was still zipped in the inside of her bag from yesterday, she settled Ava in the pram and headed out of the door.

The first job she'd seen was through an agency, a small red-windowed building situated between a nail salon and a comic book shop. After dragging her pram in while three people sitting at desks in the open-plan space stared at her, she knew it was a mistake the second she'd sat down.

'So, you don't have a driving licence?'

'No. Well, yes I do, but I would prefer a non-driving job anyway. It's not necessary then, is it?'

The woman sitting behind the cheap chipboard desk stared at her, her heavily kohled eyes squinting as she looked from her to the baby.

'No, I suppose not. We will need references though.'

'Well, as I said, the movers lost a box. It's been a nightmare. Everything was in that box.' She looked down at the desk. Someone had written *help me get out of here* on the surface in red biro. Her fingers tingled to touch it.

'Well, I know that's a problem, but I'm afraid without paperwork we won't be able to match you with an employer.' The woman picked at her nails, the pale pink shellac half gone and in clumps on her half-bitten trotters. 'I'm sorry.' Looking down at Ava in her pram, she raised a smile. 'Cute kid. If I were you, I'd just enjoy your time off, try again in a few months. You should have replaced all your ID by then. These bureaucrats take their time anyway.' She flashed her teeth and picked up the ringing phone on her desk. Hannah's leg muscles twitched, but she didn't move off the seat. She found herself staring at the woman. When her finger went to press a number on the keypad, Hannah slammed down on the cut-off lever.

'Some of us don't have that luxury. And we don't need people like you looking down at us either.'

She waited till she had wheeled the pram around the corner of the road before she allowed one single tear to drop. The rest of the afternoon was much the same. One sandwich shop with a 'Help Wanted' sign looked promising until she mentioned that she needed to organise childcare and couldn't start before eight of a morning. The man's face fell quicker than a lemming off a cliff, and so had her hope of working in there.

Ava started to stir as she left defeated, and she headed away from the crowds to look for somewhere quiet to attend to her. She saw a sign for the library, and something in her pulled her feet in that direction. Libraries had always been her safe place, a building filled with peace and words and wonder. She left the pram just inside the main doors, out of the way of other visitors, and pushed the library doors open with her free arm. They welcomed them in with a quiet swish, her bag over one shoulder, Ava in her arms.

The second she walked in, her body relaxed. Ava, fussing in her arms, seemed to subside a little, and Hannah stood there for a second, taking a lungful of the air around her. It was an old building. Heavy wooden doors with metal handles giving way to high ceilings with ornate ceiling roses and coving. Bumpy white-painted walls, posters of movie adaptations and books placed around the room. The reception desk was in the centre of the large square room, doors off to each side. It was quiet, the lull before lunch that she knew so well from her old job. There were a couple of people using the computers, but the reception desk was quiet. One man was talking about the latest book he'd requested, telling the librarian the bare bones of the plot. Hannah found herself smiling, enjoying the relaxed to and fro of their conversation.

'Hello.'

A deep voice behind made her jump, and she whirled around. 'You again!' Her voice ricocheted around the space.

'Er . . .'

'Why are you here?' she demanded.

Brody, dressed in his uniform, raised his hands in surrender. He had two fiction books in one of his hands. He raised a brow in their direction, keeping his arms in the air.

'I came in peace. I have a library card, if you'd like to see that. Just don't laugh at my picture.' His lips formed a short smirk.

'Oh, sorry. I just wasn't expecting to see you.' Ava chose that moment to decide she couldn't wait any longer and let out a shrill wail. 'She needs changing. I'm a bit stressed.'

Brody nodded once, lowering his arms and walking around her to the reception desk. Hannah jiggled Ava in her arms, trying to shush her. He was back in a flash.

'Here.' Brody held a key aloft. He kept his distance. 'Family room in the back. Anyone is welcome to us it when they need to.'

He tipped his policeman's hat at her like some kind of gallant cowboy and strode back over to the desk. Hannah locked herself into the family room, which was a large room consisting of benches, a changing table, changing supplies, and a nursing chair. She left the key in the door and changed her daughter. Once Ava was all cleaned up, she gave her a bottle of juice from the bag. Ava sat playing with Hannah's necklace in one hand, the juice bottle in the other. Hannah took the moment to sit in the chair and shake off her day. She found herself relaxing for once, away from prying eyes in a peaceful building.

She tried not to think of Brody. The PC Plod of this village seemed to get around a lot. He had helped her though. That's all that he seemed to want to do. It was rather annoying, but there was something about him that she liked. He was calm, even cutting such an imposing figure. Especially in the uniform. She knew that some women loved a man in uniform, but it had never done much for her. Even on him, it evoked unwelcome feelings in her gut.

Reaching across to her bag, she pulled her pay-as-you-go phone from one of the pockets. She dialled the only number in her call log saved as a contact. It picked up on the second ring. Hannah waited for the other person to speak before she did.

'I'm here. Talk.'

'It's me,' she said quietly. 'I'm good. Still job hunting. Any news?'

They kept it short, not wanting to have the calls tracked. Kate's idea. In case things got bad. Hannah teased that she'd watched too much true crime, but she'd agreed anyway.

'Nothing official. I heard he's taken some time off work.' One of her college friends worked in the same company as Victor. Kate delivered his twins last year, so he owed her a favour. 'He's telling the office you're all going away on holiday.'

Hannah's breath caught. She ran her fingers over the back of Ava's head, the soft downy hair was growing fast. She was looking like a real little person now, growing out of her babyhood.

'He's looking then. I had a couple of people staring my way the other day; a woman thought she knew me . . . It was a misunderstanding, but it made me think. You seen anything weird?'

'No, nothing. As far as I can tell, he's playing it off as happy families. I can't see why he'd do anything else round here. Putting flyers up or calling the police would just serve to contradict himself. You safe?'

Her friend's voice was strong, but Hannah could still hear the waver behind it.

'I'm fine. I told you, he won't go to the police. He's just going to keep looking. You concentrate on you. Be careful. Time's up.' They didn't want to say goodbye but keeping it short was safer. Safer for Hannah. She didn't want to break down on the phone.

'Love you.'

'Love you.'

The line went dead. Hannah turned the phone off. She wasn't surprised, but it still filled her with dread to hear it. It's not like she didn't know how he would take her leaving. It wasn't allowed, after all. She knew he wouldn't phone the police. He knew that she'd already called them. He was in the system, even if they did nothing but make it worse. He wouldn't risk it. He just planned to take back what he owned.

She felt her throat constrict at the thought of it, that feeling of knowing that there was nothing she could do. It wasn't an unfamiliar feeling, which made the fear and anxiety far worse to live with. *Something's changed, and now this is my life.* That's what she'd thought for months. Till the line on the stick turned pink. That feeling was far more powerful. She felt it now, looking down at her daughter who was trying to launch herself off her lap in search of the next thing to explore.

'You listen to me, Ava. We're going to be just fine, me and you. I'll see to that.'

Ava's responding babble made her giggle.

'I'll take that as a yes.'

Chapter 4

After locking the family room door, she headed to the desk to hand the keys back. She could hear children giggling now, loud carefree laughs and a deep voice laughing right along with them. As she neared the desk, she noticed the library's children area. Bullet, Brody's partner, was sitting on the carpet in the middle of the reading corner, a wicker basket full of books hanging from his mouth. The woman who was working on the desk was standing nearby, and Hannah tapped her on her arm. Brody was talking to the children, Bullet sitting by his feet and looking every inch the efficient police dog in his police vest.

'Thank you,' she said to the woman.

The woman turned to take the keys, and instead wrapped her hands in a warm grasp.

'Doreen please. Come here any time, love, it's nice to have somewhere to see to the little ones; helps the mums out shopping round here.' Another ripple of amusement came from the kids, and Hannah's eyes slid to find Brody. He was saying goodbye to the kids. Bullet dropped the basket handle right into his hand, and he gave it to a small girl next to him. She beamed back up at him, and high-fived his hand when he held it out to her. 'Isn't he great? The kids love Brody and Bullet. They're like celebrities round here. He does such a lot for the community.' Doreen's eyes were focused on her now, and Hannah turned to face her. She didn't want Brody to see her still there. He might push for that statement again.

'I bet he does,' Hannah agreed. 'Anyway, thank you again.'

Doreen waved her off, beckoning to Brody with her other hand.

'Oh don't go just yet! You can meet them!' Ava was already reaching a pudgy hand out towards Bullet. She loved that bloody stuffed dog too. Hannah was suddenly glad that she'd hidden it under the pram seat. 'Brody, come over here a minute, love?'

Brody rose from his kneeling position, and Hannah noticed how tall and muscular he was. He wasn't muscle-bound, but she could tell that he worked out. *Why am I even looking?* He filled the space in the room, but it wasn't a dark shadow he cast. The uniform shocked her every time but looking at him in this environment, she realised that it suited him well. Bullet's eyes clocked her, and with the children all being ferried off by their teacher back to the local primary school, he padded across the carpet and sniffed at Hannah's hand. A second later, he gave her a big lick and a bonus sniff at the bundle in her arms.

'Well, would you look at that?' Doreen remarked, looking agog at Brody. 'I've never seen him act that way.'

Hannah reached out her hand and petted the soft fur on the dog's head. He panted happily back at her, sitting down at Brody's feet. Now out of the two, she liked the dog far better. She trusted him.

'We've already met, haven't we, Bullet.'

Doreen looked at her, the confused look on her face turning to a gasp.

'Oh no, you're the mum from the park!' She patted Hannah on the shoulder, giving it a little rub for good measure. 'And to think, I was here about to introduce the pair of you to each other, and you already had a meet-cute!' She laughed at her own librarian joke and practically shoved Brody into her face. 'Well then, I'll leave you two to chat. Alison, nice to see you again!' She headed off to deal with her next customer, leaving the four of them alone.

'Well,' Hannah said, feeling her cheeks blush. She felt like her face was on fire. 'I'd better be off. She's getting heavy.'

'Lead the way.'

Brody whistled to Bullet, and Bullet rose to walk with him. He opened the library doors for her, waiting for her to strap her daughter in. She kept her eyes on him the whole time. He looked right back, his gaze not giving anything away.

As he opened the main doors for her to leave, he lifted the front of the pram over the doorframe and set it back down gently. Hannah eyed him, frowning, but he shrugged as if it was normal. Nothing.

'Er . . . thank you.' She looked back at the library doors, rather than look at him again. He felt too close, but he made no move to leave.

'You're welcome. What's a meet-cute?' he asked. He had a daft, confused expression on his face that almost made her laugh. She rolled her eyes at him to cover it.

'A meet-cute is where two people meet in unusual or funny circumstances, usually. Lots of great romance books out there have characters meet and it's not plain sailing.' Her smile dimmed a little, but she brushed it off. 'Librarian joke.'

'Oh yeah?'

'Yeah, I used to be one myself.' It just slipped out, and she couldn't take it back. *This guy makes me forget myself. Dangerous eyes. He distracts me.* 'Years ago.'

'What do you do now?'

They walked from the library back towards the park, his steps falling in with hers without being asked. Bullet walked alongside the pram, like a direwolf protecting a Stark babe. *Too much late-night reading, Han.* She did feel safe though, with him around. Not the usual thought of a skittish mother around a highly trained weapon of a dog she supposed, but something in the

38

canine's manner calmed her. She trusted him. Looking at Brody, she wasn't sure she could say the same about him. The librarian slip was careless.

'Do you not have to get back to work?' She countered his question with another.

He raised his brows before he answered. *Did he notice my deflection?* 'Not today. I do some outreach sessions in the community. This was my day off. It's not exactly hard – Bullet charms the kids for me. They learn a little about being safe out there, and my bosses are happy. They learn to trust police dogs.'

Hannah didn't reply; she just kept walking. If she didn't talk back, he would leave.

'I live near the park, like you. In case you wondered why we were heading the same way.'

She side-eyed him. *That explains it. And why he and Bullet were in the park that day.*

She didn't want to ask how near to the park he lived. Asking questions made refusing to answer his less easy to do. She didn't need to know about him. He told her anyway.

'The other end, corner of Beverley Street.'

The other end of the park, and just at the other end of her street. She had thought he had to live close, given their meetings. Strangely, the thought didn't terrify her like she'd thought it would.

'Bullet live with you?'

'Yeah, he lives with me.'

The park gates stood before them, and they strolled along the neat, gravelled path, Ava's pram wheels throwing the odd chip out as they walked in silence. The sun was obscured by the shadows of the trees, but the air felt warm and fresh. Bullet went off towards the trees to sprinkle some trunks. There were only a couple of dog walkers milling around, a few other people on the fringes heading to the playground area with their little ones in tow. People nodded to Brody as they passed, casting an interested eye her way. She kept her head turned in the direction of her feet, wishing she was already back in her little safehouse.

They walked along in silence, Brody close enough to brush an occasional arm against hers. She flinched the first time, but he didn't react. Perhaps he didn't notice. The jolt of human contact fired her nerve endings, turning them to confused little goose bumps on her skin. She rubbed at the arm closest to him before returning it to the pram handle. He continued walking next to her, his strides matching hers. He didn't brush her arm again, and he walked a step further apart. Bullet panted at the side of him, Ava watching from her pram as they slowly walked along.

It was getting less scary to be in his proximity somehow. She didn't feel the panic crushing down on her as they strolled together, saying nothing. He himself seemed quite carefree today, less serious than usual. He never said much, but she didn't find herself wanting to fill the silences. It was quite nice. She was just starting to think that she'd perhaps misjudged him, just a little, when he spoke again.

'So, what are you up to today?' His eyes fell on the pram, the newspaper stashed in the basket under Ava was poking out. She could see the circles from her pen on the pages. 'Job hunting?'

She looked away, watching a little grey terrier chase a stick across the grass in the distance. There was no point denying it. Especially to an observant copper.

'Yeah,' she admitted. *He doesn't miss a trick. Watch yourself. Don't get comfortable.*

'How's that going?' He waved back at a little boy walking with his mum.

He didn't say anything else, and she turned her head to gauge his expression. He had no expression, which was something she'd noticed before, she realised. He didn't have the blank-faced expression you might expect from a sociopath, his face was just . . . neutral. Giving nothing away. She guessed she wasn't the only one who kept herself to herself. He turned his head towards her, and their eyes locked. The green flecks in his eyes matched the leaves on the scrubs nearby today. They changed, she noticed. Victor's used to change. From human to dark shark-like eyes. *Stupid*. She hated that she'd noticed that detail about Brody. She was supposed to keep her damn eyes on the ground. She kept her answer firmly behind her closed lips.

A woman pushing an elderly gentleman in a wheelchair walked past, and Brody stopped to say hello to them. She kept walking, but Bullet followed her, and Brody caught her up. Bullet headed to sniff the borders of the park.

'I know of a job. On Marion Lane, there's a bookshop café. They just expanded.'

'What – no, you don't have to do that. I wasn't asking for help.'

They were headed towards the houses now, and Brody let out a short low whistle. Bullet bounded out of the bushes, stopping right in front of him with an elegant bow of the head. Brody nodded back at him, and she felt herself smirk at their relationship. The two of them were bonded – that was plain to see. It softened Brody somehow, even with his six-foot-odd stature and rather burly voice. That was why she wasn't terrified to speak to him. The dog. They were alike, she mused. Bullet and he communicated the same way. Very few words and lots of body language.

She found herself idly taking in his uniform once more. He didn't look so bad, she could admit. Not such an ogre. He seemed to care about his job. People stopped to say hello to him. *Victor was popular,* she reminded herself. *Everyone likes him, but they didn't see the monster behind the veneered smile.*

'I never said you did. They need staff, saw the sign myself as I drove past. Have a good day, Hannah. Miss Ava.'

He tipped his hat as he walked away, giving her a wave with his meaty hand as man and dog went on their way. She found herself staring after him for a moment in shock, before turning her pram towards Marion Lane, and her next uncomfortable job rejection.

Chapter 5

Marion Lane was just about the cutest place she'd ever seen. Compared to the other streets in Leadsham, which were nice enough, this little corner of the Yorkshire village looked like it belonged in the country magazines she used to see in the supermarket. The ones he'd wanted her to read but which had left her cold. There was a florist, full of colour with green-painted wood windows, a little café with a few tables and chairs dotted around outside. Up the lane were other shops, a law firm, and opposite she noticed, at the end, stood the police station.

She turned to look, pulling the pram away from the kerb. Brody worked there. She waited for the panic to grab at her throat, but she breathed easily. He'd seen the sign going to work. It made perfect sense. She thought it over every which way in her head, but she couldn't see why he would have bad intentions. It was just good luck, him seeing the sign and her mentioning her need of a job. If anything felt iffy, surely there would be signs?

She didn't owe him a thing. If she got the job, it would be on her merit, right? It didn't make them friends. It wouldn't, she resolved. Taking a deep breath she pressed on.

Hey.

The voice in her head spoke over the sound of her steps. Her voice, his words. Like always. She didn't hear him anymore. Just his control over her showing it still had a few tendrils clinging on.

What are you doing?

She ignored it.

Ha-ha.

I can't hear you. You're not here.

You can't do this without me. Brody could be a tracker. He's a policeman. He knows where you live. Why can't you be smarter?

She told the voice in her head to shut the hell up and squared her shoulders. She needed this job.

Turning back to the row of shops, she scanned each one. And there, next to the florist, was the bookshop café. The building was cream, with a huge bay window at one side of a red wooden door. The window frames were painted black. Full hanging baskets dripping with water hung from painted wrought-iron hooks. The window was full of new releases, some with reviews pinned to the plinth fronts. Hannah walked over to the window, scanning each title and not recognising any of them. She hadn't gotten much reading done of late, aside from neurotic late-night googling of every sniffle and fart Ava emitted. As she stepped slowly closer to the door, she saw the sign.

PART-TIME HELP WANTED

ENQUIRE WITHIN

Looking from the sign back to the window, she wondered whether this could be the one.

Glancing down at Ava, who was staring right back at her, the cuddly dog in her arms because she'd cried at the loss of Bullet. She knew she had to try anyway. She'd come this bloody far, right?

'Right, Ava, no kicking off in here, okay? We'll go to the park after I promise.'

Turning the pram around to park it outside the shop neatly, she heard the door open behind her.

'No need, love, we have a little area for prams. Come on in. I'm Lola.'

Hannah turned to face the woman, and was confronted by a cute, freckled face surrounded by a shock of dark brown curly hair. The woman looked like Nicole Kidman but wearing an apron bearing the name of the bookshop café.

'Er . . . thanks. I was here about the sign.'

The woman beamed again, reaching for the front of the pram and hoicking it over the threshold.

'Ah, even better!'

Inside, it was as though a Tardis unfurled before her. Her eyes were everywhere as she followed the woman towards a little fenced-off area away from the main doors. They stashed the pram in there, and Lola clapped her hands together.

'Right, coffee?'

'So you just moved here?'

'A little while ago yes.'

'What do you think of the place so far?' Lola took a sip of her brew, nodding in a motherly way for Hannah to do the same. She took a sip, Ava sleeping in her pram now. God, she forgot how much caffeine could perk a girl up. She'd been good at avoiding it, but with the insomnia it was a fine line some days.

'It's nice. I like it.'

A tall, thick-set man placed two plates of carrot cake on the table, winking at Lola and heading back off to serve a customer.

'That's my other half. Don't feel obligated to eat the cake either. He's had a bit of a *Bake-Off* thing going on lately. Since we decided to add the café, he fancies he's Paul Hollywood, I think. Keeps him busy. Anyway, I won't bore you.' She pushed her hair out of her eyes with one hand while drinking coffee with the other. She licked at her lips and straightened her shoulders.

'Right, so the job? What we are looking for is someone to help on the bookshop side of things mainly. Business is getting really busy now, especially with the online orders. We did think that after the initial excitement on the website and delivery side was over it would slow down, but it's taking up a lot of time now and only getting bigger. The locals are hardcore book lovers, I can tell you! We need a hand, someone who can deal with the customers, maybe help with locating the orders in the shop and putting them to one side. The stock levels are a bit hit and miss at the minute with everything going on. I keep getting behind with ordering the stock in time. Scattered brain. Christmas was brutal.'

I can relate. Hannah shuddered inwardly at the memory. She physically shook herself, laughing awkwardly. Hannah smiled, enjoying the chat with another person. Lola was looking at Ava now, a smile across her lips.

'Sorry,' she began again. 'I tend to overshare. Pregnancy hormones.' She rolled her eyes theatrically. 'And I just did it again. Another reason for needing the help is the fact that we're expecting, and I know I won't be able to keep up this pace then. So that's it in a nutshell.' She talked about the flexible hours, and the pay was more than Hannah was expecting too. As they talked about the job, they got onto the subject of books and reading. The cake and coffees were long gone by the time they'd finished, and Hannah found herself relaxing. Which she already knew was usually a big mistake.

'So, if you want the job, it's yours. I think you'd be great here!'

'That's fantastic!' Hannah beamed back at her, willing her hands to stay steady. 'I'm thrilled, really – the thing is, I don't really have any references that you could check. The library I told you about closed down.'

'Okay, no worries. Could you ask another past employer maybe?'

John, Lola's husband, came and collected the plates then, putting the used crockery onto a round wooden tray.

Hannah kept her head up.

'Not really. I would need to be paid in cash too, if that's possible. I don't have access to my bank account.' She threw in a nonchalant shrug. *It's hot in here.* She rolled her sleeves up her arms, something she used to do pre-Victor. Pre-bruises. She shoved them down again, but Lola's eyes were all over them. 'I lost a couple of boxes in the move. It's been a nightmare.' She paused. 'Bit of a klutz, too.'

Lola was looking at her differently. *She's not buying it.* She'd seen the look before, but no one ever followed up. Over her shoulder, Hannah noticed that John was listening now, not that you could tell from his body language. He flicked his eyes in her direction and took the tray back towards the kitchen. Lola's face told Hannah that it wasn't washing, and she knew it sounded weak, even to her own ears. *You can't do this without me. I told you so, stupid.* Hannah put her hands on her lap under the table, moving her right arm down her leg to squeeze at the flesh with her fingers. The pain centred her, snapped her awake. It kept her from falling into a dark hole. There was nothing there for her but his cutting comments.

Leaning forward across the table slightly, Hannah swallowed and looked Lola right in the eye.

'I'm a really hard worker. I loved working at the library, and I really think I could help you here. I've already got a childminder lined up for Ava, and I can start this week.' Lola pursed her lips, but before she could speak Hannah rushed to fill the space. It was crunch time now. She needed this. 'I'm not in any trouble . . . I haven't done anything wrong. I just moved here to make a good life for me and my daughter.' She looked pointedly towards Lola's tummy. 'That's all I want for my baby. A good life. I just need to lay low.' She whispered the last part, but Lola's look wasn't one of pity, or shock. She looked like she cared, for some reason. Her eyes kept sliding behind Hannah, and she knew that she and John were having some kind of secret conversation.

'Well, I'm . . . just let me speak to John a minute, okay? Can you wait?'

Lola flicked her hair back, looking across towards John, who was busy stocking shelves now, or pretending to. Hannah felt her hope slide away the second Lola made to get up. It was mere seconds, but it felt like hours. She could feel the sting of tears in her eyes, and her body tingled. The urge to run out of there was so strong, all she could do was keep fighting to stay upright. She knew how to play a little dirty; she'd seen it enough times to play the role herself for once. She didn't want to miss out on this job.

Lola had seen the lingering ghosts of finger-mark bruises on her arms. Unmistakable. She was getting comfortable, forgetting to hide everything about herself. She couldn't go back. She didn't want to let this moment go. Lola wavered between standing and sitting, and she took her shot.

'Brody told me about the job. I'm sure he'd vouch for me.'

That got a raised eyebrow from Lola, but the sounds of books being dropped broke the conversation off short. Lola sat back down.

'Andrew Brody?' she checked steadily. 'Andrew Brody spoke to you, and sent you here about the job?'

Hannah nodded, holding her breath and praying she hadn't just overstepped. Lola seemed surprised about Brody, but she clearly knew him. Hannah had counted on it. She was playing the small-town angle and it was working. She took no pleasure from it. She wasn't used to this, feeling free like this. It had been a long while since she'd not bitten her tongue to keep the words she wanted to say in. And now she was free to speak, and she was using her words to lie to complete strangers, to bend them to her will. It sickened her, but she had to get this job. Her money was running out. Her rental wasn't forever. If she didn't get some sort of semblance of normality, when he found her, she would have no option but to go back. She could sort everything else, given a bit of time. She was due to visit Martine and Ruby today to discuss them childminding Ava. They'd jumped at the chance of

47

taking her on. She just needed the job. Victor had access to her bank account; she couldn't use it.

'Yes, the police officer? He told me about the position.' She pressed her hands onto the table in front of them, tapping it in frustration. Tap. Tap. Tap. 'I'm desperate,' she whispered, and she hated herself for it. All she could feel was her skin tingling with the absurdity of it all. She laughed, despite herself, and then the tears started to fall. She sat back in her chair, still laughing like a strangled drain and trying to stem the flow of tears. They felt hot on her face, and she could feel them against the chill on her skin. She felt ice cold and red hot all at the same time, and she wanted to pull her skin off and run for the hills. To just disappear.

'Forget it,' she said, standing angrily and going to leave. 'I'm sorry I disturbed your day.' She turned to look at the shocked woman and nodded to her bump. 'I am really sorry.' Lola tried to follow her, moving awkwardly around the stack of books by her desk.

'No, don't go! Hannah, we would love to have you! You misunderstood.'

She was halfway out of the door, wrangling the pram and Ava, when John spoke from behind her.

'Start tomorrow, nine o'clock.' She turned to look at him, and he was watching her now from the office doorway. 'If Brody sent you, we're good. The job's yours, cash every Friday.'

Hannah cleared her throat, swallowing hard and forcing the tears to stop leaking from her eyes. She clenched her fists, using the pain of the digging of her nails on her palm to centre her.

'What about the paperwork?' she checked.

John looked at her for a long moment.

'For now, we'll just keep it informal.' He met her eye, giving a slight nod towards the pram. 'Till you get yourself sorted.'

She nodded mutely. She would have to come clean soon, but for now she had work, and money coming in. Hopefully Lola wouldn't tell John what she'd seen. The bruises would be gone eventually. No more to cover up. She was almost there. One piece of her new life at a time. She knew that it would be an issue that would keep coming up. Kate had offered up her own ID one appointment, when they were frantically planning her escape, but it was too risky and she had to use her own anyway. She wasn't some Soprano, getting fake identities on the black market. She needed her ID; she just couldn't use her old accounts. Besides, borrowing ID was too easy to check up on, and what the hell would Kate do if she needed it in an emergency? She was biting her lip now, hard. 'It might be a while before I can do that.'

John waved her off, but he didn't take his gaze from hers.

'We'll work something out. Down the line.'

'Thank you,' she said, a little less fear in her voice now.

She smiled all the way down the street, singing along with Ava's musical toy as they headed to the park. That afternoon, the voices were eerily quiet in her head.

Chapter 6

The next day, Hannah stopped to take a breath and remember that triumphant feeling when she got to the bookshop door. She was child-free for the first time since Ava was born, and she felt naked without her. As though she'd casually left a limb hanging over the chair at home like a forgotten bag. It had been a shock of a day yesterday, first the job, and then Martine and Ruby's house. She'd signed Ava up on their books, and had to bend the truth once more to get what she needed. That night, when she'd returned home and finally gone to bed, she'd slept like a log. Their identities were safe for now. Life was clicking into place. She just had to keep her guard up, keep saving, and keep moving forward.

She'd caught sight of herself in the mirror that morning, nervous about her first day. Wanting to be herself for the first time in months, but knowing that she'd have to conceal parts too. She didn't even look right; the alien form of herself staring back like she had for so many months. As her body had changed shape as she grew Ava, so too her face had changed. She was starting to slim down a little now; all of the stress, and then the walking around Leadsham was helping to shed the baby weight. Not that she cared. Not anymore. The alien in the mirror might feel a world apart from the real her but she was still a big improvement on the woman she'd been. She looked a little like the person she wanted to be, and that was enough. It had gotten her here, to the door of her new workplace.

She'd dressed in her best black slacks, a black and white spotted blouse tucked in, and her comfiest ballet shoes. She felt good for once, happy that she had something that made her feel comfortable. She was looking at her reflection in the shop window when a man's face appeared right next to her own. She caught sight of the eyes watching her and jumped half a foot back in shock. The door opened a second later.

'Sorry, I didn't mean to startle you! Come on in – Lola's just in the back.'

John Tucker was an imposing man up close. Not as tall as Brody, but no slouch either. She carefully looked him up and down before entering the bookshop. He seemed to shrink from her a little, taking a couple of steps back before offering her his hand across the space.

'I didn't introduce myself properly before. John Tucker, Lola's other half. It's really nice to meet you.'

Hannah took his hand with a smile but didn't hold it long.

'You too. Looking forward to getting started.'

'We really need some help around here; you might regret saying that.' John led her through the bookshop to the back. Lola was sitting at her desk working on the computer. Around her, on shelves and in piles, were books of all varieties – some with paper invoices tucked into the pages, the printer firing off many more behind her. Lola's face lit up when they walked into the room, and she was out of her chair and across the room before Hannah could blink.

'Hi! Oh God, I can't tell you how glad I am that you're here! Baby settled okay at the childminders'?'

'Fine thanks. She was having pancakes when I left.'

'Brilliant. Martine and Ruby are great. They'll look after her so well. I've already booked a place for this one, for when we need it.' She laughed and pointed at her little bump. 'Do you fancy a coffee before we get started?'

John coughed behind them, and Lola rolled her eyes at him. 'Ugh. Decaf tea then. The caffeine police are here again.'

John laughed, heading out of the office into the shop. Lola kept up a steady stream of chatter as she made their drinks, telling her about the job, and some of the characters in Leadsham. She didn't ask any questions about her life before coming here, and Hannah found herself relaxing into the chat. It felt so nice, after the last couple of months of only having a baby to talk to. Ava wasn't great with conversation yet, after all.

'So, that's about it really.' Lola led her through to the shopfront, where John was just opening the doors. 'Today I was thinking we could get the online orders in the back under control, and then maybe once we get that sorted, we could get you on the till maybe?'

Hannah was too busy looking at the books all around her.

'I'm happy to help wherever. This place is beautiful you know. Even the shopfront really doesn't do the inside justice.' She thumbed one of the books on the table next to her, feeling at home for the first time in a long time. She missed some of her old life, the library job she'd had especially. 'I'm really grateful to be working here.'

Lola beamed back at her, taking a couple of books off the table and thrusting them into Hannah's hands.

'Perk of the job. We want to start doing more reviews for the fronts of the shelves, compete with the chain stores from the larger towns a bit more. Fancy taking these home and doing a few?'

Hannah looked at the new books in her hands and felt like she had been handed a lifeline.

'I would love to. It's a bit dull once Ava's down on a night. No TV yet.'

'Oh, right.' Lola nodded to the books with a smile, adding another two to the pile in Hannah's hands. 'Well, my friend,' Lola touched her shoulder in a sisterly way, and Hannah thought of

Kate, and how the two women made her feel. 'It's all trash on the box lately anyway. We've got you covered.' She dropped her voice. 'I mean that, Hannah. Just ask if you need anything.'

Hannah nodded, not trusting herself to speak. She was really beginning to like Lola.

The pair of them laughed together over their drinks, and the rest of the morning went just as well. Before Hannah had even had a chance to look at the clock, it was lunchtime, and she was more than halfway through her first shift.

'Hannah, you go get something to eat if you want. Take your lunch hour; the rush has passed. We get busier again once the schools are out.'

Hannah finished wrapping the order in her hands, sticking on the address label and putting it into the bulging post bag in the back office. She was just gathering her things when the door went again, and Hannah felt the atmosphere in the shop change. Looking up at the customer coming through the door, she found herself staring straight into Brody's eyes.

He was standing in the shop doorway, John talking to him in quiet tones. She couldn't hear what they were saying, but she wasn't trying. He flashed her a smile. All she could do was look at him, talking in hushed tones to John, but his eyes never left her face. *What is it about this quiet man?* She felt her body grow hot and looking at a man that way again made her whole world tilt on its axis. She turned away, breaking the connection.

'Look at the two of them, thick as thieves.'

Lola had come to stand next to her, and she hadn't even noticed. 'Er yeah. Are they friends?'

Lola looked across at the two men, a look of love crossing her features.

'They used to be partners, before John left the force to help me here. The business was getting so busy, and John . . . well, he had a bad experience.' She paused but didn't offer any details. 'It stayed with him. It was time for him to go, but it was hard on them both. They're like brothers, and Brody is a loyal man. They both are.' A frown crossed her features. 'I worry about him sometimes.'

Hannah didn't know which man she was talking about with that last statement, but she wasn't in a position to be asking. She did want to know about Brody though. Every time they met, she was left wanting to see more of him. It was as annoying as it was surprising. As usual, she was adept at keeping her cards close to her chest. Trouble was, so was he.

Hannah was about to ask more about Brody and John's bromance, but Brody was looking at her again. He strode over to the two women. His damned absorbing eyes zoned in on hers. She heard Lola whisper something under her breath, but she couldn't focus on anything but him.

'Hi.'

'Hi.'

Lola tapped Brody on the shoulder.

'Hey, Brody. I'll let you get on with things, Hannah – orders to get to the post office. Enjoy your lunch break.'

She looked at her behind Brody's back, and Hannah felt her face explode with colour at being left alone with him here. She looked at Brody, and he seemed just as ambushed. He was more amused than she was too.

'Where's Ava?'

Her heart beat just that little bit faster. It was unusual to hear him say her name. To hear anyone say her name really.

'Childminders.'

'Ruby?' he asked, but then his face fell. 'Don't answer that – I shouldn't have asked.'

'Don't worry, it's fine. I don't think it's a village secret. It's nice that you asked about her.' She didn't want to answer his question, but the fear on his face after he'd said it told her that it was an innocent question. He was normally so poker-faced; it was a definite tell. 'She loves that dog you gave her too. She calls him

Bub-bub. She can't say Bullet yet. I tried to teach her.' She blushed at how fan-girly that made her sound, but he looked delighted. His smile was wide, and it made him look more handsome. His slightly stubbled cheeks were filled with colour. He was quite goofy for his size. It made him look less . . . threatening. Victor wasn't a huge man, but as the saying went, size didn't have to matter. It was what you could do with it.

'That was quite a lucky day then, all in all. The day in the park, I mean.'

Wow. Hannah felt her stomach do a three-sixty. 'Yes, I suppose it was. Aside from the crazed mugger.'

'Of course, sorry. I didn't mean to be rude.' His jaw clenched.

'You weren't being rude. I was joking.' He looked back at her, a slight frown on his face that made her want to laugh. 'I feel like Mindy here, Mork. Are you always so serious, questioning everything?'

Shit. Where did that come from?

'Not always.' His lip twitched. 'Are you normally this defensive?'

'Yes, and that was another question.' She huffed, trying not to raise her voice. Somehow she didn't seem scared to argue back with him. He seemed to find it amusing. Another thing to add to the list of annoying things that made her curious. 'How come you didn't tell me your mate owns the bookshop?'

His brows lifted. 'I came to tell you today.'

'After I took the job.' She lowered hers in response. His rose higher as a counter-move.

'You wouldn't have gone for the job if I'd told you, and I wanted to help.'

'Me? I don't need any help.' She poked herself hard in the chest. It made her glare all the harder at Brody. They were having a near-silent disagreement, which was another first for Hannah.

'Lola and John.' He glanced around, but John and Lola were not in sight. 'I wanted to help them. You have a love of books, experience, and they needed staff. Why don't you like being helped?'

He looked genuinely interested in her reply, the lift of one dark brow giving him away. The man with all the questions.

'Another question. I don't need it, that's all. Anything else you'd like to know?'

'Well, maybe one thing, but I'm starting to think I already know the answer.'

Her heart stopped, like it had shushed itself to listen in.

'You can ask.' She folded her arms. 'I might not answer.'

'Fine,' he replied with another lip twitch. 'Will you have lunch with me?'

The answer was out of her mouth before she could even think about engaging her brain.

'No.'

'Okay.'

'Sorry.'

'It's fine.' He looked over her shoulder. 'See ya, John,' he called out.

Hannah felt awkward, wanting to fill the silence. She hated the silence more than she hated the decibels of chaos with Victor she'd left.

She hadn't expected him to say that. She couldn't. Wouldn't, anyway. A policeman? It would be madness. Even if she liked him enough to try. Still, she felt the need to fill that silence as he walked away.

'I have something to collect.' She said this to Brody's retreating back. He stilled, turning to eye her over his shoulder.

'Oh yeah?'

'Yeah,' she echoed. 'New TV.' Now she had a job, she wanted to treat herself. Kill more silence.

He nodded once, pulling his keys out of his pocket.

'I'll give you a lift. See you at the car.'

Only the ring of the shop doorbell heard her protestations. Everyone else had seemingly gone deaf.

* * *

56

'I didn't need a lift,' she sulked from the passenger seat of his car. 'I could have managed. It smells like dog in here.'

He pushed a button, and her window went down halfway. He turned on the radio, filling the car with low-playing chart music. She glared at him, but his eyes never left the road. He'd winkled the destination out of her when she'd halted his exit. She'd been planning to pick up the TV, taxi it back home and race back to the bookshop. Annoyingly, when she stomped out of the bookshop, irritated and confused by their exchange, bag in hand, he was standing there. One hand on the open passenger seat door of his car like a limo driver to the Oscars. She'd rolled her eyes, muttering her thanks as she sank into the seat. It didn't take long thankfully, and she was soon standing in front of the counter at the charity shop.

'Hi.' She smiled. 'Hannah? I came to collect the TV you found for me? I got a text this morning?'

The woman behind the counter took her name and ticked it off a list on her clipboard. 'It's in the back.' She thumbed behind her as she took Hannah's money with the other. Fifty pounds for a little colour flatscreen. A bargain. Brody had followed her like a hulking shadow, and when she was finished talking to the woman, he was standing behind her with a bag full of his own purchases.

'Bargain hunter,' he supplied easily when she raised a brow at him. 'Jan, I'll get it.' He walked into the back room, returning a moment later with the television and a plastic bag of wires and the remote. Jan gave him a motherly look, adjusting her glasses on her nose.

'Thanks, Brody love.' She looked back at Hannah, pushing a receipt from the till in her direction. 'There you go. How's the little one?'

Hannah felt a pang of panic at the mention of Ava, before remembering that Ava was safe with Martine and Ruby. Her heartbeat was drowning out the ability to form words. 'She's great, thank you. See you later.' Brody dipped his head in Jan's direction.

When they got to his car, he put everything into the boot. She got into the car before he could repeat the door-opening saga, checking the time on the dashboard. She'd still have time to eat when she got back. She could have done it herself, but she had to admit, it was easier with her own personal mountain to carry things around for her.

'Thanks,' she offered reluctantly. 'It was easier with you there.'

He nodded once, indicating right and smoothly turning the wheel onto the road.

'For telling me about the job, too. That was nice of you.'

Another nod. He turned the radio down, just a notch. She waited for his lips to move.

'You don't talk a lot, do you?'

He looked her way then, his jaw tightening. 'I've been told that. And I thought you didn't like questions?'

Half a song went by. Her stomach gurgled. Another look. She covered her tummy with one hand.

'I've got lunch at work,' she felt the need to explain.

'Good. Eat it.' He swallowed, slowing down as they reached her house.

'I won't be a minute.' When the car came to a stop, her hand was already on the handle. She met him at the boot, but he passed her the bag of wires and scooped up the rest. 'You want to put this inside?'

She didn't think of that.

'The hallway will be great, thanks.' She could do the rest herself. She didn't want a man over her threshold.

Chapter 7

Lola was working on the computer in the back office when Hannah arrived the next morning, heading straight to put her lunch in the fridge. Brody had put everything in her hallway and then headed off after he dropped her back at work. When she'd got home that night, done everything she needed to and settled Ava, she'd lugged the TV and bag inside her living room and got to work setting it up. Brody had left his own shopping bag there too, and when she looked, there was a second-hand DVD player in there, with some DVDs. The usual early years DVDs of funny animals, songs and primary colours. On a Post-it Note, he'd written a note. Short and to the point. Which was what she'd come to understand about him. He was a man of few words, not one to use flowery prose or filler words.

Thought Ava might like these. She remembered the shifty way he'd taken her bag. He'd known she wouldn't have accepted it. She tried to feel annoyed, but looking at Peppa Pig, smiling out at her from one of the cases, she was touched by the gesture. She could offer him the money, given that it wouldn't break the bank being second-hand, but she knew she wouldn't. She wouldn't be rude like that. He'd been a help to her. She could let this one slide, and not worry about the repercussions so much. He'd asked her to have lunch with him again before he left, but she'd declined again without reason. To his credit, he'd just shrugged and waved her goodbye. The novelty would wear off soon. Once she was settled in a bit more, less of a new face.

'Decaf?' she asked, waggling the coffee jar in Lola's direction.

'No ta, just had one.' She yawned loudly. 'Oh God sorry. As you can see, it doesn't quite hit the spot.' She looked longingly at the Kenco in Hannah's hand. 'I miss coffee. And runny eggs. I swear, John vetoes everything I like. Runny eggs aren't even on the list of pregnancy no-nos.' She shot Hannah a triumphant look. 'I googled it.'

Hannah took her coffee to the other desk, making a start on the online order slips before the shop doors opened. 'He's sweet. It's nice he cares.' She thought back to when they were out with Victor's friends one night. He'd made a fuss of her all night, checking the menu. The other wives were fawning over him. That night, when they'd got home, he'd pinched the skin on her elbow tight. Just once. Like he was reminding her that he was still nasty under the nice. 'You shouldn't let him dictate to you though.'

A look of understanding passed between the two women. Lola was sharp, she decided. This wasn't the same thing. This wasn't Victor.

'Sorry, I didn't mean . . . I just meant . . .'

'I know what you meant,' Lola replied softly. 'Do you want to talk about it?'

Hannah shook her head automatically. 'No, no. John is just being nice, I know.'

'I know.' Lola let the conversation drop. Hannah really did like her. 'Speaking of caring, was Brody a help yesterday?' Hannah's hand almost dropped her cup, two sploshes of hot, dark liquid falling onto an order for a rather long list of books for a local villager. 'I heard he took you shopping.'

'He just gave me a lift,' Hannah retorted, plucking a tissue from the box on the desk and wiping ineffectually at the blobs.

Shit. She squinted at the order. She could still make out the titles. They were classics; she'd read most of them.

'Still, it was nice of him. Brody doesn't do things like that for just anyone.'

Hannah rolled her eyes, but when she saw Lola she regretted it. She'd clocked her.

'Sorry, I'm a bit grumpy.'

'Ava okay?'

'She's fine. It's not that. I just . . . nothing.'

Lola returned to tapping on the keyboard, and Hannah stood, coffee and printed order sheets in hand. She was halfway out the door before she turned back.

'What did you mean?'

Lola finished typing and eyed her evenly.

'About what?'

'About Brody. Not doing things for just anyone.' She looked at the floor. 'He's a copper. And every time I see him he's helping people.'

Lola's mouth twitched.

'It's nothing special. I just don't really need the help.'

'Right,' Lola turned her head to one side. 'What I actually meant was that he likes you. He doesn't . . . warm to people too easily. He hasn't got a big circle of people around him, never had really. The force, Bullet, John – they're his family. He's good at his job, and yeah, he helps people. He's a damn saint sometimes, but he doesn't act like he does around you.'

Hannah mulled on her words, processing this information pretty slowly too. Lola's amused expression told Hannah she was watching for her reaction. Hannah also knew that she'd probably already read a reaction on her usual poker face: confusion.

'Act?' She threw the word out there, bait for her fishhook of a question.

'He doesn't talk to people, or about them. It's just not him. He can speak when he wants to, but with you . . . it's different.'

Hannah's brows furrowed, her breath huffing out of her nostrils like dragon smoke. Her tight lips had sealed off her air.

'I think John sees it too,' Lola said. 'Not that he'd rat out a mate.'

'Who's ratting on a mate?' John approached the doorway slowly. Hannah noticed he was always careful that she knew where he was. He gave her space, without her having to ask. In his job he'd probably learnt to recognise damaged people. She made a mental note to watch herself around him.

'No one, love. It's from a book I read last night.'

'Oh really? I thought you were reading about piles in your pregnancy book?'

Lola banged her open palm on the desk. 'Git.' She glared at him, but he just laughed in response. Hannah's own lip curled a little to stop her titter. 'I think that deserves a proper coffee by way of apology.'

John's smile dropped, and he looked like a comical drill sergeant complete with commando stance. 'No dice. What were you—'

His phone stopped him mid-interrogation, and his face was serious when he saw the number.

'Yeah.' His voice was different than his normal easy way. It was official. Clipped.

His eyes widened.

'Fuck! How bad? Where are they?' He walked over to Lola who was trying to get up from her seat and settled her down with a gentle push of his hand on her shoulder. 'Okay, okay. Hit me up when you know.'

'What?' Lola demanded, one of her hands over his now and one on her bump. Hannah headed out of the doors, things still in her hands. It sounded urgent, private and none of her business. She got to work, pulling the relevant books from the shelves, packaging them for postal delivery and filling the order basket for John's van. A couple of police cars shot past towards the station, a police transport vehicle between them. Sirens blaring, lights flashing. The people on the street turned to watch them, and instead of hiding amongst the shelves, she was nose to the window. She wondered if Brody was with them.

Two hours later, she overheard her answer. It did involve Brody, and he was hurt.

Chapter 8

Hannah managed to get through till the end of the day, busying herself with working in the shop. In the afternoon, she sat in the window, writing the reviews of the books she'd read and loved so far ready to go on the bookshelves. Now that she had a TV, she had worried that she'd just be glued to that. She hadn't really watched it so far, other than the odd DVD with her daughter. She thought of Brody again, and his gift, and she looked once more up the street towards the police station.

She hadn't wanted to ask John or Lola how bad it was, but she knew it was enough for him to go to hospital. In an ambulance. Hurt. The thought of him hurt didn't sit right with her. She didn't like the fact that she cared either, but she'd been in hospital before. Battered, bruised. Lying her arse off to get home for more of the same. She remembered pain, and she thought of Brody, big and hulking, hurt. It was hard to digest. She wondered what had happened to Bullet. She couldn't imagine the dog would have wanted to be parted from his owner, or Brody him.

It was still light enough outside to see the near-deserted street, and she blinked her eyes a couple of times to wake herself up. She'd really gone to town on her distraction technique. She'd done everything from clean the toilets to dust the shelves and organise the till rolls. She was tired. Bone-tired.

'You get off, Han – you should have knocked off ten minutes ago.' John was standing there, his coat over his arm. 'I can walk you.' Lola had gone home earlier in the day, driven home by John to put her feet up. Hannah had near choked her out of the office with the smell of polish.

'Thanks, I'm good,' she muttered, distracted. She did need to get to Ava. She grabbed her things and, as they were walking out, she caught the look on John's face. She pushed out the question.

'Where are you going? Home?'

The jaw flex was just like Brody's. Subtle but obvious when you knew how to interpret it.

'No, I have to pick up a mate.'

He reached his car and she waved him off. As soon as she got round the corner, she halted and reached into her bag. It wasn't till she didn't find what she was looking for that she realised. She'd wanted to call Brody. Was he even awake? He might be really injured. She just wanted to hear his voice. She couldn't deny that. If she could just hear from him that he was okay, hear in his voice that he was still in there, then she could stop thinking about him and go back to avoiding him. She hadn't even stored his number. She'd got rid of the card. *What would I have said anyway? Something's off with John? I saw the cars, heard the call? Are you okay? How bad is it?*

Not her concern. She walked to pick up Ava in record speed, and Ruby and Martine were their usual jovial, happy selves. Hannah was bundled off with cookies they'd made that day. The smell of chocolate and sugar made her realise how hungry she was.

Ava was grumpy on the way home, coming down from the highs of the childminders' and getting to that 'hour of the day'. The hour of the day when kids threw tired tantrums before bath and bed. She'd read about it online, and some parents called it 'the witching hour'. Given that her daughter was growing, she had been waiting for her personality to come out in full force – now that the patterns of her new life were forming, and she was growing into her own person. And her attitude was starting to make itself known. Her little fireball. She was protesting loudly in the pram now, tired out.

'Nearly home,' she trilled soothingly. *Please, Ava. Give me a break.* She was about to walk past Brody's house, not that she'd taken that way on purpose. Well, she totally had. Normally she avoided going down to the corner of the street that he lived on. She avoided the whole area and walked the other way home from the childminders' or from the supermarket. She walked a lot too, through the park. Even after the incident with the mugger, she still felt pretty safe there. Out in the open.

She was on his street now, Ava still giving the occasional high-pitched screech to remind her that she wasn't happy. She saw John's car, right outside the house on the corner. Two men were halfway across the pavement between his car and the house. Brody was unmistakable even with his back to her, and she recognised John, who was helping him go inside. Brody's gait was off, limping. Bullet was barking in the back of the car. She kept her head down as she walked past.

That dealt with the witching hour. Hannah's brain went onto full autopilot. After a very loud bath time, a bottle of warm milk and a story, Ava was settled and drowsy on her lap. She'd leave the housework till tomorrow. She couldn't stop thinking about Brody. He'd been hurt, and she was pretty sure he didn't have anybody at home. A housemate would surely have picked him up. No girlfriend, she'd already assumed. He'd asked her out for lunch, for a start. Twice. Lola had said that John and Bullet were family. No mention of any real family, or a partner. Why would John need to take him home, if he had someone? She'd have been on the other side of him, propping him up. It was just the two of them. If she existed, she'd have been there, surely.

It was getting dark now, and she packed the changing bag, put it next to her handbag on the pram handles, and headed out. She'd got changed into a pair of jeans and a black top, Ava in the pram in her sleepsuit and bundled against the cold. Hannah's first-aid kit was sitting underneath in the basket. After putting her phone in her bag, she locked up and headed out into the night.

Chapter 9

'Lola, please stop fussing. You need to rest. John will rip me a new one if you freak out. I'm fine.'

Lola tried to start up again, but Brody jumped in. 'I think I'm going to sleep now, Lola. The meds are kicking in. Yes, I'm sure. Okay. Bye.'

She hung up, and he dropped the phone onto the couch next to him.

'Jesus Christ. I hope John takes her phone away.'

She'd called four times. Four times, and John had only left an hour ago. Brody had not moved from the couch since then. He wanted to be in bed, but he wasn't sure he could get back down the stairs. Going up would be bad enough. He reached for his drink, wincing as a blinding-hot flash of pain reverberated around his body. The hospital staff had been pretty pushy, wanting him to stay in, but he had Bullet. He could let him out into the garden from down here, and he had the downstairs toilet for himself. He could wing it for a couple of days. He didn't want Bullet in kennels, and he had no one else. With Lola being pregnant, he didn't want to put on John. He'd not even wanted the lift home, but he'd soon realised that he needed the hand getting inside. He'd not let on of course. John needed to be home with Lola.

Brody was used to taking care of himself. It wasn't the first time he'd been attacked on the job.

They'd been working on taking down an illegal puppy farming gang that was causing issues in their area. Their head guy was a huge, rotund dude called Big Pete, and he was a big hitter in every sense. Drugs, guns, stolen goods. All funded by overbreeding puppies in warehouses and selling them through fronts. He'd taken a fair few kickings along the way. Big Pete had introduced him to Bullet. He was one of the farmed puppies. Instead of running away terrified like the rest of the dogs the scumbags released, Bullet chose to fight. He'd come right to Brody's aid, just a pup. Stinking and matted, too thin for his age. They'd saved each other. Teamed up, and now they both had Big Pete's scent in their nostrils.

It wouldn't be the last time Brody would be hurt, either. Fuckers on this job had even taken a swing or two at Bullet, but he'd dodged them. Managed to take a couple of them down, but the whole thing was off. Obviously word was spreading. They'd been surprised on the early morning raid, and it was all he could think about. They were getting close to smashing the gangs apart, stopping the traffic they were producing with the dogs and the drugs. They'd even had dogs of their own this time, trained to attack. Brody had a feeling that he and Bullet were a hot topic of discussion tonight at Camp Scumbag.

Bullet growled, padding to the hallway and sniffing the air near the front door. He wagged his tail, sitting down on the mat. Brody looked across at him from his couch viewpoint. His big dark brown eyes told him they had company. He heard the footsteps coming up his path, a low rhythmic squeak providing a backbeat. There was a knock at the door, and Bullet stood. He barked once, moving to Brody.

'I heard it.' He slowly rolled himself off the couch and into a standing position. Well, he was standing, but his stooped stance took a fair few inches off his height. 'Coming.' He shouted louder.

He motioned for Bullet to get back out of the way and unlocked the door.

'Hannah.'

What are you doing here? Oh God. Look at the state of me. He ran a hand through his hair ruefully, instantly regretting the motion when his broken ribs screamed at him. He wobbled a little in the doorway. She looked beautiful standing there, but her eyes showed her concern. He knew what he looked like. He'd clocked himself in the mirror of John's car.

'Hi.' She looked around, up and down the street. 'I came to see if you were okay.'

'How did—'

'I passed by on the way home – I saw John taking you inside.'

Shit. She'd seen him half dragged in. The car ride had been a nightmare. He'd never felt pain quite like it, not that he showed it. He'd gritted his teeth so hard he thought they might crack in half. She looked behind him, her eyes a little wider now. She had such soulful eyes. He forgot what he was saying half the time when she really looked at him. He wondered where Ava's father was. Not for the first time. Did he ever feel like that when he'd looked at her? He felt his jealousy bristle deep within him. Even in his battered state, his mind was still very much in commission.

'Do you have company?'

'No, just me and Bullet. John left to get back to Lola.'

Hannah nodded once, looking over her shoulder at nothing. It was dark and quiet, like every night in this small corner of England. She glanced at Ava, who was now fast asleep. 'Do you have anyone coming?'

'No. Why did you come? You look nice.'

He leaned forward a touch, resting his back against the door-jamb. His pain lessened a little.

'I came to check on you. You're hurt.'

'I'm fine.'

'You can barely walk. A couple of ribs gone at least, I'd say. From the blown vessels in your eye, you took quite a blow to the head. I'm surprised you weren't kept in.' Bullet whined from behind him.

'I'm fine,' he said to them both. Neither gave an indication they believed him. 'Listen, you can't stand on the doorstep. Come in.'

He stood back slowly, partly because he always acted that way around her. Partly because he couldn't move fast to save his life. He'd keel over. The pain meds were wearing off, and he was feeling the long day.

She hadn't moved, but she was contemplating it. It was all over her face. The question kept swirling in his head.

'Why are you here?' *Well, I asked.*

She straightened up, slowly pushing the pram to the threshold.

'I told you. I came to check on you.'

She went to take Ava out, to collapse the pram, but he leaned down, veerryyy slowly, and took the footrest in his hands. He started to lift and with raised brows she lifted the pram handles. The door closed behind them as the pram wheels hit the wood floor.

He gave her a moment to look around her. He didn't miss the jolt of her shoulders when the door clicked shut. He made no move to lock up, although given his day, he probably should. He didn't fancy being a sitting duck.

'I won't stay,' she muttered. Her eyes fell on a photo on the wall. Him and Maddy.

'My half-sister,' he offered. 'She lives in Ireland, with her husband.'

'She's pretty.' Hannah smiled. Her shoulders lost a little of their slump.

Not as pretty as what I'm looking at.

'Thanks,' he said instead. 'Do you want a drink? Ava need anything?' He tried to lower himself down to Ava's eyeline, but he didn't get far before he gave up. 'Actually, I need to sit for a second. The kitchen's just through there.' He walked to the lounge, and Hannah followed him through not long after. Ava was in her PJs, her little cheeks flushed pink from the short walk in the night air.

'Hey, little one.' He said it softly, not wanting to wake her up, but it did anyway. He was rewarded with a smile though. She was adorable.

'She was tired.' Hannah went to get her out of the pram when she lifted her arms to her.

'Please, sit down.'

Hannah looked at the easy chair, Bullet in front of the fire next to it. She surprised him by bypassing it and choosing the opposite end of the couch to him. Ava grizzled on her knee to get to Bullet, and she jiggled her. 'Are you sure I'm not intruding?' She bit her lip, and it became his new favourite thing about her. 'I just wanted to see you, really.'

'Frankenstein's monster, eh? Why do you keep asking if you're in the way?'

'I don't.'

'Don't you? No one's coming.' It clicked then. 'I don't have a girlfriend, if that's what you mean. It really is just me and Bullet.' Another connection formed in his mind, and it pissed him off. 'I don't ask anyone out for lunch, especially twice, and I wouldn't be doing it if I was involved.'

Her mouth opened. Closed. 'I didn't know it was a date.' He wasn't sure he bought that.

'Yeah, well it was. I'm not seeing anyone. Don't you want a drink?'

Ava was drinking from a bottle of milk on Hannah's lap, eyes half lidded again.

'No thanks, I need to go really. I just wanted . . . well, you checked on me. After the park. I figured we're square now.'

Go? Oh, hell no.

'Square? Don't like owing people, do you?'

Her lips pursed. 'I just find it easier to have full control.'

72

Brody laughed low in his chest. 'No such thing.'

Her look hardened, and he realised he really needed to take his meds. He was getting snarky. 'I disagree. It takes work, sure, but it's possible.' Her words petered out, and her face changed. She got a far-off look on her face. It wasn't the first time he'd seen it.

'Where did you go then?' he urged her to tell him. He leaned forward, but his ribs decided that he'd pushed it a bit too far. 'Ouch. Okay, that hurt.' He settled back down.

'Stop,' she half demanded. She'd shuffled, filling the space between them. Ava jolted a little, milk drunk, but was settled with a shush. 'Sit there, please. You're going to pass out at this rate.'

She turned the pram towards the doorway, putting Ava in and covering her with a blanket. She was quiet in seconds, Bullet moving to lie at the child's feet. Brody had given him the nod. He couldn't see the pair of them, but he could hear her soothing voice as Ava finally gave up the ghost and slept. Hannah leaned and dropped a kiss onto Bullet's lowered head. He licked her, and Brody's heart exploded in his chest. He almost looked down to see if his torso was still intact. He wasn't sure he could take many more surprises in a twenty-four-hour period.

'Where are your pain meds?' she asked, arms folded, standing in front of him. Close enough that if he reached out, he could pull her into his lap. It would likely kill him, but it would be bloody worth it to feel her on him. She was like a nervous little bird, and he wanted to smash whatever threats came her way. It was a quite visceral feeling in his gut, as he watched her trying to take care of him. Well, he just knew it. *You're fucked. This is it. You're going to have to learn to crack this woman's code, because you just have to have her in your life.* He'd known he was screwed the minute she'd thanked his dog in the park. She was dignified, independent. Kind. Moody. Complicated. Bloody hard work, he imagined. *All the best things are.*

'Brody?'

'Andrew.'

'Brody. Where are your pain meds?'

He motioned to the bag on the coffee table. She picked it up, hooking it under one arm and holding the other out to him.

'Come on, you need to get to bed. You can't sleep here. I'll take you.'

Colour me surprised.

74

Chapter 10

'She's still fast asleep. I let Bullet out for a bit. Do you need help to shower?'

A beautiful woman asking him if he needed help in the shower. In his lamplit bedroom. The pain meds she'd force-fed him must be kicking in.

'No shower.'

She wrinkled her nose at him. 'You need one.'

He laughed but regretted it. 'Ha-ha. Ouch. Fuck. Thanks.'

'I didn't mean that. The blood.'

He was still wearing the sweats he'd been given at the station. The force emblem on them made him look like an advert for a police fashion catalogue. The nurses had given him a quick wipe-down but the blood streaks were still visible in places.

'I can't shower with you helping. It would strip me of my manhood.' That got a smirk, so he kept going. Whenever she gave him an opening, he used it to learn a little more. 'How did you know about my ribs?'

He sat down to try to shuffle his socks off, but she knelt down and pulled one off softly. He sighed, but given that he couldn't reach that far, he didn't have a choice.

'I've seen injuries before.'

'As a librarian?'

'No. Do you want to get changed?' She motioned towards his dresser.

'No. Too painful. Where?'

'Around.' She went over to the bed, closing his curtains and pulling the duvet back. He was suddenly glad he'd had a clean around before work, changed the sheets. 'Come on. You need to rest.'

He stood, looking down at his bare feet. 'You took my socks off.' His eyes swam a little, and he shook his head.

'Observant for a copper, aren't you?'

'I prefer police dog handler.' She half pushed, half pulled him over to the bed. He couldn't tell – his feet were a little floaty at the moment. 'Where we going? Bullet?'

'He's outside. I'll bring him in in a bit.' He was sitting in bed now, and she was covering him over with the duvet. She didn't pull it up further than his stomach. She was gentle. His body was already contorting with pain with the effort of moving. She started fluffing the pillows behind him, and he sank into them slowly. 'You good?'

'Good.' He didn't want to lie down, not yet. He didn't want her to go. She pushed his head gently back onto the pillow. At the fifth time, she pushed a little harder.

'Oww. Come on.'

She'd poked one of his lesser bruises. One that wasn't raised like a bee sting. His skull felt like it had been tumbled in a dryer.

'Sorry.' She winced. 'That was a bit mean.'

He heard himself giggle. He must be high.

'Lie down.' She pressed. 'Do you need anything? Food?'

'A drink would be nice.' He licked at his arid, dry mouth. A minute later, a straw was being pushed towards his lips. Something sharp, tangy. It brought his mouth back to life.

'Lucozade. My friend swears by it, and she's a midwife. Cures all ills.'

He laughed, taking another deep pull. He tried to get his eyes to focus on hers, but his eyelids wouldn't co-operate.

'You're tired. I'll let you sleep, okay? I'll go see to Bullet.'

He didn't want to shock her, but his hand was around hers before he could stop it. She looked at their connected skin, but he didn't feel a flinch. 'Sorry. I just didn't want you to go.'

She sank back down to the bed. His hand landed on her lap, and she folded her own over it.

'I shouldn't be here.'

'Why?'

'I just came to see . . . I knew . . . I thought you might have been alone. I didn't want you to suffer.'

'I'm a big boy.'

She looked down at their hands, raising them slowly. She searched his face. 'Does that hurt?'

He shook his head. She turned their hands till their palms fitted. Hers was dwarfed in his. He suddenly hated his big, burly meat-hook hands.

'You're so soft, and dainty.' *That was the drugs talking again. Shut up, Brody.*

She smiled, but he could see it had failed to penetrate the Alcatraz of her feelings. 'You'd be surprised.'

'You always surprise me.' An honest admission.

He pushed his palm down on hers slowly, allowing him the luxury of flexing his fingers around hers. 'So soft.' He pulled his hand to his mouth, taking her hand along with it. She watched as he gently touched his lips to the back of her hand. When he pulled away, he frowned at the line of blood. She looked at her hand without reaction.

'You have a split lip. I'll get some water.' She moved her hand away, and Brody's world muted. She was gone out of the room before he could speak again. He heard the back door open, and then exhaustion took over.

Chapter 11

Ava snuffled when Hannah checked on her. She'd put her on the double bed in the spare room, surrounding her with a pillow barricade. Bullet was in the kitchen. She could hear him padding around every so often, his nails click-clacking as he made his little patrols. She'd never known an animal like him. She'd always wanted a dog. Company would have been nice. A protector wouldn't have gone amiss either.

Heading back into Brody's room, some fruit and another bottle of water in hand, she found him asleep. He was propped up on the pillows, which were grey but marred with blood smears from his head. He looked like he'd taken a real beating, but he hadn't complained once. Ribs were the worst, in her experience. Victor had broken three of hers once. Breathing was like sucking knives. The dislocated shoulder had been pretty bad. Putting it back in herself was far worse. She'd passed out from the pain. She got a telling-off for that too. Dinner hadn't been on the table. *Get out of my head, Victor.*

She had to consider her life choices again. Why the holy hell was she even here? She knew why, of course. Brody's look. His gait. He'd been hurt, and for no reason. He'd been trying to do good, to be good, and what did he get? An empty house and a kicking. She felt his pain. She had wondered whether he really was single. She was surprised to find he was. And disappointed. He was breaking every theory and tried and tested hypothesis she had on men. Not that she'd had plenty of research material over the years – just one man. Brody was breaking the mould. Which begged the question, why the holy hell was she here? She knew she wasn't going to leave till he could manage, but when would that be? And what then?

'God, you're so annoying. Shut up.' Gritted teeth didn't stop her words from flying from her mouth. The silence. It always made her think. Dredge up the past.

'Hannah?'

'Brody?'

'Yeah. I think so.' His eyes saw right through her. 'What's wrong?'

'Nothing.' She touched the pillow ruefully. 'I wanted to change the sheets, but I didn't want to wake you. You slept though me patching you up.'

He touched at his head, his brows raising when he felt dressings.

'Did I?' His smile nearly floored her. His split lip looked painful, his smile lopsided. 'Thank you.'

She resisted the urge to brush a piece of hair back from his face. 'We're square now. Debt paid.'

His jaw tensed. 'That again? Well, technically, we're not square. You still owe me one.'

Her eyes narrowed so much she could barely see him. 'What one?'

'For the job. I told you about the advert.'

'That helped your friends.'

'Granted. Still one.'

'No chance.'

He attempted to stick his lip out, but pain shot across his features.

'Don't pout. You barely have enough blood left in your body as it is.'

He laughed hard then and howled in pain. 'Jesus! Fuck!' he shouted, and she rushed to his side. Ava screeched, jolted awake in the next room. Bullet barked from downstairs. Nails click-clacking.

'It's okay. It's okay.' She placed her hand gently on his chest, over his heart and touched her side to his. The closest she dare get without hurting him. She pushed her cheek against his, whispering into his ear. He pushed his cheek closer, and she felt the bandage rub against her skin. 'Stop. Please. Just rest.'

'Okay, okay.' She felt his arm come around her, and she nestled in a fraction further. 'I'm good.' His hand slowly rubbed her back, and she could feel her breaths quicken. He'd hear it. Ava and Bullet fell quiet, and it was just the two of them again. She wanted to pull away. She didn't. He felt like he needed it. It felt good to her too.

'Don't you get angry?' she asked him. She kept her cheek still against his. 'With the violence? How do you keep it from taking you?'

His hand didn't stop, but she felt him shift a little. She didn't move her head. She felt his lips brush her cheek. *Did I? So fast, so light.*

'I've seen what anger does. I saw it in my family, growing up. On the job. Anger is not something I let in easily. It wrecks people.' He chuckled softly, and she finally pulled away. He was smiling at her, his head lolling on the pillow. He was a wounded man, and vulnerable. It was odd, but she could really look at him now. He was less imposing. Without the height and the uniform. With his lazy eyes hazed on pain meds, he was sedated. She had thought it would feel like being in the proximity of an anaesthetised lion. It had flashed in her mind when she'd seen him on the doorstep. He was like a lion with a thorn in his paw. It made him less scary, but she noticed it didn't change him. He was still Brody. Andrew. She liked his first name better.

'Are we playing the question game again?'

She pretended not to know what he meant but failed. 'Aren't we always?'

Another lazy smile. 'Will you go to lunch with me?'

'Still a no. Do you want to eat, or sleep?'

'Neither. Why not?'

'I don't want to date. I have a job and a kid . . .'

His jaw dropped in mock horror. 'You have a kid? No kidding.' His face turned serious. 'I love kids. Kids like me. Bullet loves kids. And I have a job.'

'Yeah, and what a job it is.' She pointed at his injuries, and his hand tightened on her back.

'I take down bad guys. Sometimes the bad guys hit back. That's all. Today was bad, but it's not like that all the time. I'll be back to work in two days.'

Her hands were on his sweatshirt. She lifted it slowly, her eyes pointed at his ribs like daggers.

'Oh yeah?' He pursed his lips at her, before looking down at his torso. His face remained impassive. 'Four, tops.' He pulled it back down. 'Is that it? The job?'

'No, it's everything. I think it's best we just leave it at square.'

'We're not at square, remember? We're at one. Have lunch with me.'

'No. Next question.'

'Have dinner with me.'

'No. Don't you want to go back to sleep?'

'No. Breakfast then.' She felt like yanking one of those plumped pillows away from his stubborn head. She had already gotten too close.

'I don't eat breakfast half the time. You can have more meds in an hour. Will you sleep then?'

'No. Cinema then?'

'Andrew.'

'I like it when you call me that.'

'It's your name. Do you want food? Is that it?'

'No.' He popped off a grape and shoved it into his mouth. 'Why won't you really go out with me?'

81

'Because I don't date – I told you.'

'Ava's dad.'

'None of your business.'

'He the reason you don't date?'

'Definitely. Are we done now?'

'One more, and you still owe me.'

'Okay, but then you sleep.'

'Do you fancy me?'

'Andrew . . .' She looked towards the door. 'I should get to sleep myself.'

'I'll let you go. Just answer me. Please.' His hand was on hers, hers on his beating heart. She could feel how fast it was racing.

'What's the point? I'm not going to date you.'

'I want to know. That's the point.'

'How would you feel if I asked you that?' She played for time. She should have just told him no straight away but seeing him there – so bloody cute – she couldn't do it.

'I'd tell you I fancy you, yes. I've asked you out enough times to prove that. That's another question you owe me.' His eyes flashed in time with his toothy grin. 'Do you fancy me?'

'Yes,' she admitted, biting her lip. He groaned, and she watched his eyes darken. Smoulder for some reason. 'But there's no chance.'

'Fine. Last question and then I'll sleep.'

'Promise?'

'That another question?' His brow raised in amusement. Daring her.

'No, hell no. Just ask the question.'

He smiled, triumphant. 'Will you let me kiss you?'

Chapter 12

When he'd asked the question, groggy from the medication, she'd thought he was joking. His face had told her he wasn't, and his crooked finger settled the matter.

'You'll have to come to me. I'm not sure I can get my head off the pillow.' His finger beckoned her. She tilted her head like a confused dog.

'You're high.'

'Maybe, yeah. Is that my answer?' He lowered his hand, closing his eyes and sighing heavily. She watched as his body slowly relaxed. He'd been fighting sleep the whole time. She straightened the covers as she stood up. She decided to leave the lamp on in case he needed it in the night. His face looked better now, relaxed in sleep and cleaned up the best she could. He wasn't exactly an easy patient. He was stubborn. Used to looking after himself. Nothing wrong with that.

Traces of dried blood still lingered, and some of his locks of hair looked as if they'd been dipped in it. Their ends were black, hard. She wondered what had happened. She knew it was nothing good, but he hadn't spoken of it. She found herself wanting to know. Bullet wasn't hurt, but she had noticed an edge to him. He wanted to be near Brody. She understood the dog even better than she thought.

She watched Brody sleep, leaning down slowly. Her lips were as gentle as she could make them, not wanting to hurt him further. Or wake him up. That would lead to more questions. She could answer this one, but only when he was out cold. Yeah, she was still a chicken. Big surprise. When her skin touched his, she felt the heat from his lips. The stubble that tickled at her mouth as she drew back and pushed her lips against his once more. When she pulled back, she thought she saw his eyelids flicker. His eyes never opened as she left the room on fast, light feet.

Wow. Oh God.

Shit. Shit. And wow again. She touched her fingertips to her lips as she lay next to Ava. A wall away from the man who was like the mastermind of winkling things out of her. Things other than information. Kisses. Fair enough, he didn't know they'd kissed, but still. She knew it had happened, and the secret thought kept her warm in her bed. She'd kissed a man. That wasn't on her new life bucket list, but it was a great big tick all the same. A kiss that she could linger over in the future, one without fear or worry or recriminations. It felt like the time she'd skinny-dipped in the sea, all on her own. Before Victor, before everything. She'd never felt so free, so out there and alone. Living her life. She tucked the memory of that kiss right along with it in the box in her mind.

Ava would be up soon. Hannah had the day off from work the next day, but she already knew what she would do. If no one else came to look after Brody, she'd stay and help. See him through this, then retreat back to her own life. Taking that memory with her. She'd still turned him down for the lunch; she'd told him it wasn't going to happen. Hell. If she was lucky, really lucky, he wouldn't remember his kiss question at all. The whole thing, being here, it was a lapse in judgement. She fell asleep soon after that thought. She dreamed of the wolf again, but this time it was in the distance. Sitting close by her, as

Bullet watched from a vantage point, his eyes as black as the night spread around them. The two animals watched each other, while she watched them both.

'Wha – arrggh!'

An unfamiliar noise had startled Brody's eardrums, and his jolt had sent hot knives stabbing through him. He felt like he'd been skewered.

'Brody?' He heard a couple of bumps and bangs from the next room, and Hannah bounded in. She was wearing the same clothes, Ava in her arms looking like she'd just woken up too. 'You okay?'

'You stayed?' He thought he'd dreamt it. *Ava. That was the noise.* He wasn't used to a baby in the house. 'You okay?'

She raised her brow. *Sexy.* 'I asked the question first.'

His laugh hurt, but it was worth it to hear her laugh right back. 'Fair enough. You still owe me one though.'

She blushed, hard. So that wasn't a dream either. 'The kiss question?'

He looked at Ava then and felt guilty. He was lying here propositioning her mother. She moved her daughter onto the other hip, coming close enough to touch his forehead. She frowned, pulling away and sitting on the bed next to him. Ava tried to reach out her cute little hands to him, but Hannah sat further back.

'No, darling, Brody's a bit poorly. Gentle. You don't have a temperature.'

'Good. You didn't have to stay. I'm sorry I put you out.'

'It's okay. Do you have anyone coming today?'

Brody knew John would check in, maybe some of the fellas from the station if they were off shift. They were his family. 'Nope.' He didn't want to scare her off. He knew she wasn't the uniform's biggest fan. The mugging was still fresh. He'd get John to put them off if he had to. 'You don't have to stay though. You have enough on.' He reached out his least-busted-up hand, waggling his fingers till Ava reached out and grabbed them. He pulled a funny face at her, and she giggled at him. Hannah looked a little worried now. Shit.

'I'll stay to make us square. I'll get some bits from home. Stay tonight.'

He just nodded along dumbly. He liked the sound of everything she'd just said.

'Thank you.'

'Square, right?' She wasn't going to let this go.

'Square,' he agreed. He had an extra night with her. That was more than he'd hoped for. He still pushed it though. 'But the question game stands. I like it.'

This time her smile was free, and bloody joyful to behold.

'You are a nightmare. Okay.'

'Okay?' he checked. 'My last question still stands.'

'Fine. My answer is yes, I'm fine.'

'What?'

Her lips twitched, and she gave in to her sly grin. Her whole face lit up with her devilishness. He wondered what the hell had happened to this woman to make her hide herself. Even her own emotions and feelings. Her smiles. Her laughter. Why the fuck was this woman not laughing her head off every single day, lighting the dreary village they called home right up, like Vegas?

It was getting harder and harder not to ask around about her. John had told him about the cash situation too. Why would a woman not have access to a bank account? It rang all kinds of bells in his head, but he couldn't see the full picture yet. He was too blinded by . . . her. She was still smirking at him.

'"Yes I'm fine" is not the answer when a man asks if he can kiss you.'

'Your last question was whether I was okay. I answered. I'm fine.' That smile again. He wanted to photograph it, to capture the shit out of its essence. He could do nothing but shake his head. He was poorly, and she was teasing the hell out of him. Even Ava, who was now being tickled by her mother, looked amused at the situation.

Hannah dropped a raspberry on her daughter's belly, straightening her on her lap. 'I'll plead no comment on the other question. I can't answer yes or no, really.' Her lips were twitching with mirth now, and he felt like she was in on something he didn't get. It was par for the course with her. It made him work all the harder for every morsel. 'Do you want some breakfast? I booked Ava in with the girls, so I was going to drop her off, get some bits from mine.'

The moment was gone, and with her daughter in her arms it didn't feel like the place either. He nodded along, putting an easy smile on his face to show he wasn't bothered. He knew he wasn't going to let it drop, not after that answer. But these things could wait. His pain meds had well and truly worn off, and he was feeling just a little uncomfortable. 'If you're sure. I have some cash in my wallet.' She'd mentioned cooking something for them, and he wasn't about to let her pay. 'Can I have my tablets?'

She went straight for them, but when he pointed to his wallet on the dresser, it was still there when the front door closed. Bullet had come bounding in minutes before, fed and watered and very happy to see his handler.

'Bullet man, you're going to crack the ribs I still have intact!' He pushed the animal away gently, stroking the heck out of him at the same time. He'd missed him too. When it had all gone down, he'd worried about Bullet the whole time. He could hear him working, scrambling and snarling. He'd kept waiting for a whimper, but none had come from his throat, even though he'd taken down one of theirs. Not a scratch on his fur. That was Bullet. The same dog that was now snuggled across his legs, as if he was on patrol and this was his mark. He couldn't get up if he tried. He needed to try to shower before Hannah got back, but he knew it wouldn't be pretty. He needed a minute.

Ruffling his dog behind the ears, he listened to the silence. 'Quiet, isn't it. Weird.' Bullet whined in response. 'Yeah.' Another ear ruffle. 'I think we're about ready for expanding the pack.'

* * *

'Morning, darling, come in. Have you seen the little outfit, Rubes?'

Ava was looking pretty cute this morning. Hannah had packed her best spare outfit in the changing bag. In case she'd needed it at Andrew's. *Brody's. Brody's. He's Brody, not Andrew. That's not his name. You of all people should remember that little nugget. Calling him Andrew will get you noticed round here. Half of the female population already have Brody on their permanent radar.* And he was a big bloody target. She remembered him propped up against the pillows, the injured beast of a man half asleep. Her lips, touching his. She snapped back to reality. Which took a minute, given her rather eclectic surroundings.

'Thanks, sale in that boutique in the village you mentioned.' Ava was in a really cute woollen dress, soft and lightweight, pink wool that matched her cream tights and kicky little legs. 'What is it today?' She took in Martine's outfit. 'Miss Trunchbull?'

Martine, who had been standing there waiting excitedly for Hannah to guess what her outfit was about, deflated like a balloon. Ruby cackled like a witch as she came to meet them in the hallway.

'I told you that's what you looked like!! Ha! Have that! Hiya, love.' She reached for Ava, who practically jumped into her arms. Ruby was wearing a wetsuit, a snorkel on her head. Ava didn't even bat an eyelid. She was definitely settled with these two. 'She's a shot putter. We're having a mini Olympics today with the kids. We thought we'd dress up. What you up to today, with your day off?'

Half an hour later, Hannah was only just walking to the supermarket from Ruby and Martine's. She hadn't meant to stay so long, but she'd ended up telling them about looking after Brody. She never mentioned the kiss, or their little questioning game. The game that was terrifying. Then annoying. Now, it was almost sensual. She was blurring the lines here, but then again, it had an end. One more night and then they would be square, she'd told him by way of reason. The fact that she'd slept better with Bullet and him in the next room was a bonus, sure, but it was just to help him recover more. Wasn't it? Well, it had to be. One more day and she'd be back in her little house. She needed to concentrate on saving the money for her next rental. A more permanent one. Perhaps in the village even. She liked it here. She needed to be out of the house Kate had organised for her in mere months. She had the money, the furniture. She just needed a couple of months' rent to put down, to give her a cushion. The next place wouldn't be as cheap as her current home.

Good. Thinking about money brought her back around to her reality. She wasn't in some cute little love story. She was making a life for her daughter, and she wasn't there yet. The checklist wasn't complete. She hadn't gotten far enough away yet. From her past. From the past her. She could still feel her sometimes. She shielded herself against the fear of her old life with the memory of the kiss. She'd done that. All on her own. The old trapped her would be bloody cheering. She was just sad that she couldn't see this through a little further. She liked Brody, but she was playing with fire. He was on the force. She was in hiding. It would never work. She was playing the question game, but it wouldn't be fun anymore if he knew the truth. It would hurt him. She was coming to realise that he might actually be a truly good man. The irony of that had her mooching around the supermarket, choosing to focus on what she could do. Not what she couldn't.

When she'd finished telling Ruby and Martine about the night (sans the kissing and the questioning) they'd been aghast that she'd stayed the night at Brody's. Ruby had had a weird look in her eye, and Martine was exuberant. She jumped on the spot, clapping her hands at one point at the gossip.

'Oh my God, I need to go wrangle the kids,' said Martine. There was a crash from the other room, and a toddler laughing. Ava was in her arms playing with her sweatband. 'Oh God, what was that? Ruby, I want to know what I miss. This is so good!'

Hannah had managed to get out of the door then, taking the opportunity to remind them of the fact she needed to go feed the man they were painting an imaginary life for her with. She had told them though; it was her own fault. The people in this village were winkling little bits out of her too easily. She knew to keep her mouth shut, but she'd only related the facts. It wasn't as exciting as they seemed to think it was. *Was it?*

He was hurt. She'd gone to help, because he'd helped her a couple of times. Well, a lot of times. Saying it like that, it sounded simple. It was simple to her too but stripping it down like that didn't quite capture the whole of the story. How looking after the hulk of a man, so prone flat out in bed, so gentle had confused her. He *was* gentle. She believed that now. She saw the way he interacted with everyone around him. He was well liked, polite, respected. Victor was all of those things too, as well as a monster and a liar. But Hannah didn't see any of that in Brody, no matter how hard she looked for red flags.

She was mesmerised by the man. It was going to hurt a little to let him go. Maybe she could look further afield for the next house. Away from the park, but still close to work. But the point was moot. She would see Brody anyway at work. Around the village. She was going to have to deal with it later. She'd turned him down enough times now; he'd soon move on. She realised that she might see that too. After all, he wasn't going to just keep asking her out. He'd move on. Find someone who could date him. Someone who could see how gentle and kind he was. She walked a little faster to him, shopping bags hanging from her hands.

Chapter 13

Bullet woofed, jumping from the bed. He went to the bottom of the stairs to greet Hannah, who sounded like she was carrying something heavy.

'Good boy, Bullet,' she shushed him and her voice quietened. Brody could hear her putting things on the worktops. The back door opened, and Bullet's paws skittered out on the patio. Brody could hear him through the open window. The TV was on, for something to distract him from the silence. Some home renovation show had been playing. One where the presenter painted everything Day-Glo. It made his head sore to watch after a while, so now it was on reruns of *CSI*.

He listened to her, moving around the kitchen. Opening cupboards, humming a tune he didn't recognise that made him smile. It was nice to hear some sounds in the house. She was so tough, so stubborn, but yet she'd come to nurse him. Maybe he did have a chance of that date after all. Perhaps he was growing on her. He was still smiling when she entered the room, tray in hand.

'You're awake. Good.' She pushed the door open wider with her feet, an easy movement that she didn't even notice. He did though. She was getting more comfortable around him. She didn't flinch as much when he was near. He wondered if it was the fact he was supine, like a battered bird. He wasn't a fool. He knew women baulked at the sight of him sometimes. He was a big man, and the uniform only grew his stature. He knew that she'd taken in his size. He'd seen her watch him when he spoke to people, as if trying to work him out. He wanted to date the woman, not scare her. The way she'd first looked at him that day in the park, he'd felt almost like he'd been the one committing the crime. She'd looked angry with him, distrustful. She hadn't looked at him with any relish or relief when they'd locked eyes for the first time.

It had bugged him ever since. Her actions that day. How cold she was around him. Even now, she was paying him no attention, not looking his way. Normally, mugging victims were thrilled to see him. It meant safety. That the police were there to resolve the situation. End the danger. She had looked at him that day like he was the enemy. He'd never forget that look. He searched for it constantly in her face. Right now, she was placing the tray on his lap, fluffing his cushions. Looking everywhere but at the man in the bed.

'I just made something simple, for now.'

She'd grilled him a breakfast that made his whole body pang with food lust.

'Jesus.' It filled the plate, with rounds of buttered toast as well. Next to that on the tray were a bunch of pills, and what looked like sludge-green puke in a glass.

'What's that?'

'John stopped me on the way back. He's been making smoothies for the café.' She picked up the glass. 'Want to try it?'

He looked from her to the vomit drink, and when his eyes caught hers again in their usual dance, he knew she was messing with him.

'Not really. Where did he scrape it from?'

'I dunno.' She tilted the glass, and the contents didn't move. 'He sent a few bottles over, different flavours.' She definitely smirked then. 'He said to tell you he made it special. It's very healing apparently. He used the words "man juice" at one point, but then he kinda lost me. Something about pussying up?'

He was glad she didn't decipher that one. John and he had their own shorthand. They didn't do soft talk, but that was John's way of telling him to get better. The smoothies were his way of helping.

'Right.' Brody laughed when she huffed at him. 'Cop talk.'

'Come on! Don't go all monosyllabic on me again. What did he mean by pussying up?' She pushed the glass into his hand, and he eyed it warily. It smelled like dog farts, and that was saying something given who he was used to living with.

'He was telling me what to do, as per. I can't drink this. I'd rather get beaten up again.'

Hannah rolled her eyes, taking the drink from him and pushing the tray of food closer.

'Where's Ava?'

'Childminders', remember? I'm on my day off?'

'Ah okay.' He had forgotten.

'Did you manage to sleep? You look rough.'

'Thanks.' He couldn't help but chuckle as he lifted his first forkful. Once the food hit his taste buds, he forgot about everything but how hungry he was. 'Oh God, that's good.' The woman could cook too. It was nice to be taken care of, he thought, in a quiet voice in his broad, bruised body. 'Thanks for looking after me. I do appreciate it, squares aside.'

She smiled, nodding to the glass. 'I'll just feed this to the garden. I think it might save your rose bush.'

Chapter 14

He looked awful, but his appetite was back in full flow. After breakfast, he'd used the bathroom. He'd obviously given up on shaving, and his stubble cast dark shadows across his purpling face. He hadn't let Hannah help, but by the time he was in a clean pair of tracksuit bottoms, the fight had clearly left him. She found him lying on his bed, half under the covers. His chest was bare, and she could see the colours of his pain like a rainbow stitched with white dressing clouds.

'You could have asked for help,' she muttered, bringing the ham sandwiches and cups of tea she carried to the bed. She'd made herself one too. Two little lunches, sitting on a tray. K-i-s-s-i—

'I'd have probably flattened you. I'm a bit unsteady on my feet.' He eyed her lazily. The blackness around his eyes made his eye colour look all the brighter. The green flecks looked like tiny fields in the landscape of his irises. 'Besides, you seeing me like this is bad enough.'

She didn't ask why. 'I don't mind. I've seen worse.'

The look he levelled at her had her hiding behind her own placid expression.

'You'll have to tell me sometime.'

'Probably not. What happened? On the job I mean?'

94

She motioned to his body. He patted the covers next to him, motioning for Bullet to get down. She put the tray down on the bed, and they both started to eat.

'I can't tell you the specifics, but we're almost at the end of something at work. It's taken a hell of a long time to get here.' He sighed heavily, slowly, as if he was sneaking the air past his shattered ribs like a secret. 'We got jumped. Tip-offs happen. They get erratic when they realise we're not going to stop. This was a message.'

She finished her mouthful, and then took a sip of tea.

'And are you going to listen?'

He was already shaking his head, a wry smile on his face. Bullet huffed once, deep in his throat. A doggy hoo-raa.

'Andrew,' she began, and his hand reached for hers. The one gripping the tea shook. She'd nearly tipped the whole thing over him. His hand stilled when she flinched. It was a reflex that time. She hated her body for constantly being fight or flight. She didn't move her hand, just kept drinking her tea. After a long moment, he slowly ran his thumb along the inside of her wrist, his fingers wrapped around hers.

'I love it when you say my name. Everyone else calls me Brody.'

'That's not what I asked.'

He sighed again. 'It's my job. This was a one-off. They got a lick in, that's all.'

'It's more than a lick. People like that don't stop.'

'I know that. What's this about? You worried about me?' He was smiling, but she knew he was searching her for an answer yet again.

'No, of course not. I just . . . nothing.'

'Tell me. I know something's going on with you.'

He wasn't accusing her or pushing her. She could feel the frustration in him though.

'Hannah?' He said it so softly, she could easily ignore it if she wanted to. She wanted to tell him she did worry about him.

She knew how it felt to be hurt, in pain. Angry. Frustrated. It was different, she knew, but the pain was the same. She worried about him, out there with Bullet every day. She didn't like it. She had enough to worry about. But she hadn't been able to stop herself from coming here. It wasn't about favours or being square. She wanted to be there, because she didn't want him to suffer on his own. She found the thought of it upsetting.

'Hannah, are you in trouble? You know that you can tell me anything, right? You can trust me.'

She nodded mutely. 'I know. I'm fine.'

'Liar,' he poked grumpily. He settled back down into the pillows, pushing his mug onto his bedside table. The sandwiches were long gone now. She busied herself with the plates. She had ignored his dig, but he was right. She was a liar. 'You don't have to tell me. I just wish that you would. I think we can agree we are at least friends now.'

He sounded so sad, it stilled her exit. She emptied her hands and went back over to the bed. He reached for her arm and pulled her to sit down again.

She sighed, enjoying the feeling of his hand in hers. Another minute, and she'd leave his bedside. She'd straighten up his house. One more day and she'd be back home, back in her bubble.

'Hannah, I don't know what's going on. It's driving me insane. I think you like me, and I *know* I like you. I don't do this, Han, not ever. I really want you to trust me, but I can see you're just not there. I don't want to push something that's never going to happen.' He looked boyish again. 'Can you tell me anything? Put me out of my misery?'

She thought for a moment. If she told him, told him the truth, it would end anyway. His job, his current state. He'd been hurt by being a good man. How could she tell him she was in hiding from a man who was evil? Someone Brody would arrest on sight? Her bruises were fading, but she still bore the scars. Literal and in her head.

She didn't know what he'd say if she told him, but she knew she couldn't bear it either. She didn't want him to see her that way. As a victim. Like the day they met. This couldn't be, so there was no point telling him. It was moot. Like her marriage certificate. She took a moment to take in his features up close, while she could. Even with his bruises, and lumps and cuts, he was still so beautiful. He was a big bear of a man, and she was fast realising that he was as soft as a teddy bear underneath. Ava controlled him entirely whenever she was in his orbit. He was a good man. They didn't come out of the factory this way – Hannah knew that. Another couple of minutes would give her more comfort than leaving to protect herself.

She slowly put her hand up to cup his cheek, careful to avoid the worst of his wounds. Leaning in, so slowly that she couldn't bear the distance a minute longer, she kissed him.

'Hannah,' he breathed. 'Tell me . . .' He'd pulled away, but she could see it had taken the rest of his strength. She pushed forward, sealing his mouth with hers and suffocating the words. He pulled away again, biting at her bottom lip with a growl.

'Hannah, this is not what I meant. Tell—'

'You asked me to let you kiss me. I can answer that.'

He pulled back to take in her face. His expression was changing from lustful surprise to utter shock. Pain, even. He looked so conflicted.

'I can't be with you, Andrew.' His eyes darkened, and she corrected herself. 'Brody.'

He flinched, the tiniest movement. 'Back to Brody, eh?'

She gave him a sorry-looking smile, and he pulled her in to his chest. She protested about his ribs, but he ignored her. 'I'll live.' She found herself lying half on his side, half on his chest. His hand was on her back, the other in her hair, stroking her face. They lay there for the longest time, neither of them saying anything. 'Are you leaving?'

She shook her head. 'Ava and I will stay tonight, go home tomorrow after work. You should be mobile enough by then.'

'That's not what I meant.'

'I know. I don't know that answer.'

He ran his fingertip from her earlobe to the tip of her chin. It felt so erotically charged that Hannah forgot to breathe. This man only had to point his hands in her direction and she melted.

'Did you kiss me just because of the game, or because you wanted to?'

'Yes,' she giggled. He groaned.

'More specific?' She heard the exasperation in his voice and raised her gaze to meet his eyes.

'I kissed you because I wanted to. Both a yes.'

That got a smile, his lip curling. She wanted to take it between her teeth. He noticed her watching him.

'If I don't ask any deeper questions, would you hang out with me some more?'

Hmm. Interesting. No, Hannah. Nurse him better, and then leave.

'How long for?' she found herself asking.

'A week?'

A week was a long time. That would be enough. She'd have gotten rid of him by then. He'd have tired of trying, and then it would be easier. On them both. Although, she needed to stop kissing him. That was two more than she'd planned. He knew she'd kissed him this time. No denying it. It was out there.

'What do you want in return?'

'Well, a lunch date for a start.'

'I already said no.'

'Ah, but now I owe you food. If we're going to continue the tit-for-tat thing we have going, then I am technically in your debt for the food. Let me take you to lunch, and then we're square.'

Shit, he was using her own words back at her. She was used to that, but not because the man in question wanted anything honourable or good.

'That it?'

His mouth twitched. 'For now, unless you want to kiss me again.'

Her bum was off the duvet before he could even raise a pain-streaked laugh.

'Nope, that's fine! I'll let you sleep.' As she closed the door, she didn't know whether to put her fist through the wood or air punch. Another night. That was it. Now it was a lunch date. She could cope with that, right? It wasn't a date either. Just lunch to say thanks for her Florence Nightingale skills. She'd enjoy the moment, and then do what she should have been doing a lot longer in life. She was going to get the hell out of the way of his man, before she got hurt again. She had a feeling that this pain would be the end of her if she let it.

After heading down his stairs, Bullet at her side like a sentry, she busied herself with making some batch meals for his freezer. She'd get it all shipshape, see him through the night and then go back home. This time next week, it would all be a distant memory.

Chapter 15

'Well, this isn't exactly what I imagined when you said lunch.'

There were no restaurants here. He'd driven around the back of the police station, heading down a side road towards a large outbuilding and kennels. They had parked up in front of a wire fence, and she could see people wearing police crests on their T-shirts walking around. Her mouth went a little dry.

'Oh?' Brody frowned, and Hannah couldn't help but think how cute he looked. The little lines on his forehead softened him somehow. He looked boyish. 'What did you imagine?' He put his hand on the gearstick, checking the rear-view mirror of his car. His very neat and sweet-smelling car. It no longer smelled of dog. 'I'll back the car up. We can eat in town if you prefer? Italian, maybe?'

His words came out in a rush. It seemed out of character from what she'd seen of him so far. He was still recovering, she could see. His movements were just that fraction slower. It had been a couple of weeks since their sleepovers. With Brody recovering, and Hannah busy at the bookshop café, she'd managed to stall it a little. She knew it was stupid, but Brody didn't push once. They spoke on the phone. Sometimes he sent her funny photos of Bullet. Some nights she'd take round some food. He'd ripped through her freezer meals with gusto. It was nice to cook for such an appreciative audience.

She never stayed, never got as close. Never sat on the bed again. She didn't let herself. It was absolutely nothing to do with putting off the end of them hanging out – she could pretend even if she knew better. The minute Brody was back on his feet, he was on the phone. He wanted that lunch date, and as he said, a deal was a deal. They needed to be square.

It was nearly April, and the weather was brighter, warmer. She always liked spring. Summer was even better. She wondered what season Brody loved.

She'd headed back to work and Ava, and routine once she'd left his bedside. She had thought she wouldn't hear from him, till the lunch. He'd been recovering at home, but she always felt him in her life, telling her about his day. Sending her text messages moaning about daytime TV. She found that she kept her phone on more often. He was funny. A bit less serious than he was in person. He didn't ask her questions, other than about her day, how Ava was doing. They had bonded more, which she knew would only make it harder after today. She should change her number maybe? No, that was petty. She'd be aloof, cordial.

Everything she wasn't feeling in this car. She'd not stopped thinking about those kisses. She was drawn to him. He'd managed to get her here. Willingly. Not only willingly, but almost happily. *Go figure.*

She was sitting in his car, and it wasn't freaking her out. Which freaked her out in itself. She was getting in deep. She noticed he was tapping the steering wheel.

'Are you nervous about something?'

His hand stilled on the wheel. 'A little. Sorry. Something John said earlier. Usual pep talk about life. Don't mind me. We don't have to stay though. We can get lunch properly. I'll give these sandwiches I've made to the lads.'

'No, we're here now. This is good.'

She took the brown paper bag full of food he'd picked up on the way and reached for the car door. He reached out to touch her hand, and she looked back at him.

'Sorry, I didn't mean to startle you.'

'You didn't. Everything okay?' she asked.

'Yeah I suppose.' His jaw clenched. 'I wanted to ask if you'd consider making a new deal.'

'This is the deal. Lunch and we're square.' She said it with far less conviction than she felt. Which was naff all in the first place.

'I know, but I think I can convince you otherwise.'

'Really?'

He reached for her again. She let him. 'Really. I think you like me too. Just a bit.'

His hand was shaking in hers. The vulnerable aura about him gave him that boyish face once again, and she couldn't take her eyes off his. She was feeling emotions she knew well but hadn't experienced in a long while. She wanted to . . . to . . .

Brody started talking, and she moved.

'I want to da—'

She didn't hear the rest of his sentence, because she'd silenced it. She pushed her lips against his and felt his whole body freeze. She was about to pull away when he reached for her and deepened what she'd started. She opened her mouth, just a little, and felt his tongue touch hers. It felt so . . . different. Feverish. Not like the other kisses. Any of the other kisses she'd had. She kept waiting for the panic to hit her, the urge to throw open the car door and run away, but it never came. His hand was on her face, the other one still on his lap as they kissed. He was so soft, so gentle. It made her stomach flip. She reached up, letting go of the bag in her hand to run her fingers through his thick dark hair.

She had just entwined her fingers into his locks when she felt him pull away. He sat back in his seat a little, his hand meeting the other on his lap. She straightened herself up and scrambled for some composure before she looked back at him. He had a smile on his face that made her burst into lust once more.

Jesus, what is it with me when I'm around him? I'm so . . . me. Hello, me. Where have you been? You missed a lot. Come out. Help me make sense of this. You're the ruddy strong one.

'I'm really sorry, but I didn't want the lads to see. I like to keep my privacy, and yours.' He laughed a little. 'As much as we can around here. That was . . . I thought you said it wasn't a date?'

'I did say that. I don't know what that was. I'm sorry.'

His eyes were on hers, his head shaking. 'I'm not. I was just going to say it was amazing. Not a date.' He nodded his head, the little smile still on his face. 'Fair enough. Shall we go in?'

She grinned at him, reassured that she hadn't just jumped into something without it meaning something to him too. Even though the whole thing shouldn't have happened. She didn't quite know where it had come from. Three times at the last count. 'Ready.'

He frowned, just a little, and flicked his gaze towards the police dog training office. Leaning closer, he kissed her again. He pulled away after, dropping a slow sweet peck on her lips before looking at her with a big daft grin across his face.

'Look at you.' She laughed, blushing and not even caring. 'I like your smile like that.'

He smiled again, giving her a wink that she felt through her entire body. Her hormones were all over the place. 'I don't smile like this. I don't even talk like this. This is the best non-date I've ever had. I'm glad you came to town, Hannah.'

Her smile had been filling up the car till he'd said that. Jesus, it had filled up the whole world. And that kiss. Wow. It was like she'd pulled the image from his own head and acted on it. Even now, with his instincts trying to tell him something was up, his bloody emotions were overpowering every single nerve ending. They'd left the car after that, close enough to touch the whole time they walked to the benches that overlooked the fence to the training field. He had one more shot at this. She'd kissed him. That had to be good, right?

He'd taken the bag of food from her, but his free hand itched to hold hers. He hadn't missed the look on her face when he'd mentioned her coming to town. Like she'd been woken from a pleasant dream, not liking the reality. *She doesn't like the questions,* he remembered with a thud. Anything hinting remotely at why she ended up here. In his village. In his life. He kept pushing her, but it was hard to see just how brittle things were. Sometimes he got something; sometimes she took a step back from him in her head. It was a fine line to tread, but he walked it anyway. He needed to really know her, the real her. He hated the barriers she kept throwing up between them. He knew that they trapped her behind them, not quite close enough for him to pull her through them. Hell, he wanted to break them down with his bare fists.

They sat down on the same side of the bench, looking out towards the training field where the young police dogs were all larking about in the grass enclosure, burning off their energy with their human partners. They were halfway through the first sandwich each when she spoke again.

'Did you go through this with Bullet?' She nodded towards the dogs, watching as one Collie ran through a tunnel to meet his pals on the other side.

'Bullet was a little different in how he came to the program, but yeah, basically.'

She gave him a look that had him laughing out loud.

'What!'

'That's it?'

'Basically, yeah.' He could feel himself frown, but somehow that seemed to make her smile even more. 'What does that look mean?'

'It means that you don't say much.'

'Never have. In fact, I think we've had more chats than I've ever had with a woman.'

'I don't believe that.'

'It's true – I don't lie. Well, sometimes you have to on the job, but not in real life. I hate liars.'

She smiled tightly, which made his insides turn to jelly. This woman was something else, and he couldn't quite put his finger on it yet. He was intrigued though, he really was. He was also trying his damn best not to think about what John had said to him. About her under-the-table wages. The fact that she'd been upset at the thought of someone hurt. Him hurt. Either way, her skittish reactions at times when he was around always put him into high alert. It had just confirmed what he already felt in his gut, and he didn't want to find out the rest. Not till he had to.

Get two coppers together, they'll always have some kind of hunch about people. It was their training. It didn't mean they were right every time. Lola hadn't said anything, and that woman was as sharp as a tack. He and John always joked that she would have made a good detective. Lola would have said something.

Hannah had a past. He knew that much. It was the present he was concerned about now. He didn't want to let this opportunity slip through his fingers.

'I can believe that.' Her words brought him back to her, and he concentrated on being in the moment. 'Tell me about Bullet. Come on. I know how you met, but that's it.'

His heart double-thumped in his chest at her words. She trusted him not to lie. It wasn't something that Brody had really ever given much thought on before in his life. He was just Brody. Andrew. She liked to use his first name. When she let her guard down enough. He liked it even more that no one else did. He was an enigma to her, like she was to him. Even though he'd always thought himself a pretty open book. Quiet, ever watchful, he saw what lies and duplicity caused people every day in his job. In his life. He had no real family, but the people he chose to surround himself with were special to him. Handpicked by himself and trusted beyond doubt.

'John used to be my partner on the force. When he and Lola started trying for a baby, things just got busy. We were doing all hours, Lola's business had to expand overnight, then they found out they were expecting. We had some really hard times on the job. I knew John was done, but I don't like having someone watching my back that I don't know as well as I did him. We've been through a lot. It took a lot out of us both. I don't trust people easily.'

'I can understand that. Trust is a lot to give to a person freely.'

'I agree,' he said, taking her eyes in once more. The more he looked at Hannah, the less he saw the panicked mother of that first day, but the one who was brave enough to wrestle a scumbag for her daughter's safety. She had a fire in her, he could see it even though it was carefully muted within. She was guarded. Even now. After THAT kiss. He longed for her fires to lick at him, meet his own. 'I met Bullet in a different way to the other canine officers. He actually helped me take down a suspect, and that was just how we met. I took him home, badgered my boss to give us both a shot, and here we are. He had to be trained a lot.' He laughed as if reliving the experience. 'He was a bit of a handful, but his instincts were there. Now, he's the best dog on the force. I trust him with my life.'

'So he lives with you, not here?'

'Yeah, he's my dog. He didn't take to kennelling. He's had all the training, and the kennel outside my house is from the force.' He grinned a little cheekily. 'He does come for the odd sofa cuddle though on a night.'

'Oh really!' Hannah laughed. 'Bark worse than his bite, eh? I knew he was a big softie really.'

'We both are I think.'

It came out dirtier-sounding than he meant it to, but she just smiled back.

'Can I ask you a question?'

Hannah was chewing when he asked, and he waited for her to finish. To give her time.

'Depends on the question. I thought we were done with these, Detective.'

She didn't say yes, and she was looking pretty much anywhere but at him. He needed to know though, the officer in him was not letting him enjoy the moment. He'd just met the girl, and he couldn't stop worrying about the puzzle she presented.

'Why did you decide to move here, to Leadsham? I don't mean the whys, I mean why here?'

This was it. She'd known it was going to happen. A single woman couldn't just rock up somewhere like this with a baby in tow and not expect questions. The fact that he was a police officer made it all the worse, but she didn't want to lie to him. She wished that Kate was here, to give her advice. She didn't even know about her spending time with Brody, let alone the fact that Hannah had just kissed the man. For the fourth time. She wasn't sure that Kate would be very happy, and given how she'd helped her, it felt wrong to worry her further.

'I needed a fresh start, to be honest. I wanted somewhere I could breathe. Cities choke the life out of me. I didn't want Ava to miss out on a better life.'

Brody's face was neutral, his piercing eyes once more focused on hers. *God, why did you kiss him? It's not going to work out. What did you think, you could just rock up like some romance novel heroine, all broken and depleted, waiting for another man to scoop you up? This wasn't the plan.* She took a deep breath and decided to just tell the truth. Something about him made her *want* to tell the truth.

'I left a bad situation. I needed to get away. Be on my own.'

She turned to watch the dogs, trying to form her words through the flashes of the past assaulting her brain. Hard slaps. The time she'd broken the coffee table with her back. Her fault, of course. Her stupid back did it. Didn't she know it was walnut? That stuff wasn't cheap to replace. The times she'd had her keys taken away. Money taken from her purse when she slept.

That wasn't it either. It wasn't the hitting every day. It was walking on eggshells for every little thing. Wondering what he would think about what she chose to wear, or dress their daughter in.

All the other tiny little seemingly insignificant things. Not putting a lid back on tight. Not ironing his shirts right. Even the little things that started as tiny pebbles rolling down a hill had an effect. All the little moments that rolled together to form a boulder. A boulder that she knew she was still running from. She just had to stay ahead. She didn't have time to take on a passenger, as handsome and wholesome as he was. She wouldn't bring this into his life.

'Ava's father?'

She nodded, not liking the sound of those two words together.

'Does he see her?'

Hannah shook her head, and a small tear rolled down her cheek. She brushed it away, but then another came, and she let it fall. She turned to face him, and he rubbed the salty trail away with his thumb.

'Sorry, it's not my business.'

'Well, I kissed you, so I guess I owe you that.'

'I kissed you back, and you don't owe me a thing.' He sighed deeply, and his hand covered hers, only for a moment. 'I just wanted to see what the situation was, I guess. I don't want to pry.'

Hannah thought of the hospital room she'd given birth in. How she and Kate had cried together after, when he'd finally left to sleep in the waiting room. Broken about the situation but knowing that nothing was going to be resolved if she stayed. How many months she'd been squirreling away meagre possessions, and money. Readying for her escape.

'You're not, honestly. And I don't want you to think I'm some man-eater either.'

Brody's soft, low laugh rumbled right through the wooden bench, and she giggled along with him.

'You know what I mean! I just had a baby. I didn't want you to think . . .'

'I thought that you were the prettiest mugging victim I'd ever seen.' His smile turned from being goofy to pure sex in the space of a nanosecond, and Hannah felt her whole body go hot. *Damn you, hormones.* 'I kissed you back, Hannah. I come to the bookshop to see John too, but really . . .' He rubbed the back of his neck with his hand, and the boyish look was there again. She pushed her lips to his, and he folded his arms around her, pulling her closer to him on the bench. They kissed like a courting couple; soft and tender, but his arms around her felt amazing. He was so gentle, so caring, so quietly dependable. He wasn't like any man she'd ever met before, and she just couldn't stop kissing him. They came up for air eventually, dissolving into giggles like a couple of school kids behind the bike sheds. Brody's head snapped to the field when he heard a wolf whistle, and two of his colleagues were standing there open-mouthed looking at the pair of them.

'Bastards,' he said under his breath. 'Sorry.' He tightened his arms around her, pulling her closer still. 'They're good lads – they won't tell people.' One of them was pulling faces at him over the fence, and Hannah laughed when Brody grumpily flipped him off. 'We'd better get you back to work anyway.'

They packed up the sandwiches and headed back to the car. Brody's arms released her, but he slipped her hand into his and held it all the way to the car. He opened her car door again without thinking, waiting till she had slipped inside before taking his seat. It was only a short drive back to the bookshop café, and Hannah's disappointment flooded through her.

Once they'd pulled up outside the shop, on the corner of the next street, he killed the engine and turned to her.

'Thanks for coming to lunch.'

'Thanks for inviting me. Well, bribing is probably a better word.'

They could both feel the tension in the car, the newness of it all bouncing around them. She was giddy to be holding his hand, and as much as she wanted to scream at herself that this was dangerous, and stupid, and the last time, she couldn't. She just couldn't quieten her heart enough to fully listen to her brain.

'Are you staying here? In Leadsham, I mean?'

Hannah looked at her new workplace and thought of how to answer when she wasn't sure herself.

'I want to, yes. It's nice here.'

Brody's daft grin told her that this is what he wanted to hear, and she wanted to stay, but she didn't say what she really wanted to say. That he couldn't rely on that. Things changed. She knew that well enough. She would stay if she could. Any guarantee beyond that she couldn't even give herself. She'd run once before, and it hadn't lasted. This time, it would be far worse if Victor found her again.

'So, if I asked you out on a proper date? No hassle, of course. I'd just like to spend some more time with you. Proper time. Two people, out together. Fancy clothes. Talking.' She felt him hold his breath. 'I'm pretty sure I'm not alone feeling like this. Right?' He looked like an inquisitive puppy; head tilted. She caved after that.

'I know, and I feel the same. Slowly, and I mean slowly. I would say yes, but I don't have a sitter on an evening. And talking? You sure?'

'To get you out with me? I'll recite from the bloody menu. A sitter's not a problem. Lola and John would have her if that was okay with you. They often watch Bullet for me.'

'Are you comparing my daughter to your hound?'

Brody laughed again. 'No, Bullet is pretty cute, but Ava is a sweetheart. I just meant that you have the help, if you need it.'

'They gave me a job; I can't ask more of them than that. I barely know them.'

Brody brushed her off with a shake of his head. 'It's not like that; they needed the help.'

'And you sent me.'

'I thought it would be a good fit. Lola is obsessed with books; John's not a big reader. I was always telling him to give it a go, but sports biographies are about his limit.'

'You read a lot?'

'Yeah. Bullet loves a good cookbook, but he just looks at the pictures really. I read when I can. It calms me down after the job. Saves me from binging too much TV.'

'You've always lived alone then, just you and Bullet? Nobody else?'

Brody looked at her, a frown clouding his handsome features.

'Er no, I'm not normally one for dating. The job kept me busy enough. I don't go around kissing every mugging victim I meet you know.'

'I'm so sorry. I didn't mean it that way. I . . .'

'You don't need to explain yourself; it was a valid question. If I could ask one back, I'd guess I'd be interested in what your plans were.'

Hannah felt a ripple of nausea. She wanted to be truthful. She always found herself wanting to be truthful around him. Shame old habits tended to die hard. She tried anyway.

'Bit close to the rules, these questions,' she chided him, but his eyes brooked no refusal. 'My past is over. For good. I'm trying to just keep moving forward.'

Kate would have been proud at her words. She couldn't wait to tell her one day.

Chapter 16

'Hello again, dear. Did my book come in yet?'

Hannah reached under the counter and handed over the package.

'This morning. The next one in the series is out in October. Do you want us to order it for you?'

Mr Jeffries, or Albie to most, pointed his finger in Hannah's direction and turned to John, who was busy picking orders from the shelves.

'What did you do without her? She's a real treasure.'

John chuckled, picking a hardback from the shelf in front of him and putting it into his order basket.

'Don't I know it. She's great.'

He went back to the office where Lola was busy on the computer, and Hannah rolled her eyes good-naturedly at Albie.

'You'll make me blush.'

Albie waved her off with a flap of his hand. 'Aww, none of that. I tell it like I see it. Settling in just nicely, I think.'

She walked Albie out, noticing that the second-hand table at the front of the shop had been rifled through, and needed a bit of organising. She was just rearranging the books when she spotted the two childminders, Ruby and Martine. They were walking towards the bookshop, a pram each and a toddler on reins walking along at either side.

'Hi! Oh hi, Ava!'

Ava was beaming away in her pram, looking comfy in her little cute new-to-her summer outfit. When Hannah had had her first week's pay, she'd hit the charity shops and kitted herself and Ava out for the next few weeks. She'd even picked up a really nice dress, one that fitted her post-baby body well. It looked so pretty, she'd tried it on when she got home and stared at herself in the mirror for a long time. Her body was getting back to normal slowly. She'd been lucky when pregnant – she hadn't gained much weight, and her bump had been small and compact. She didn't even show till she was quite far on, which she knew was part of the reason she was able to be stood here today. Pregnancy had caused such anger in her last home. It seemed the bigger she got, the more moody he grew. Talking about not being her priority anymore.

I knew who was the priority. I would never have been allowed to forget that fact. It ruled my existence, before escaping here.

She felt like a very different woman now, and when she'd seen how she'd looked in the second-hand dress, she'd felt so pleased. She was finding herself all over again, and it felt amazing to be able to breathe for once. To think for herself, and not worry about the condemnation of others. Or the retribution.

'She's been as good as gold. We thought we'd bring her to Lola for you so you don't have to come over and pick her up, give you a bit of time to yourself.' Martine was in a good mood, even for her.

'Are you excited? Oof! That hurt!' Martine had jabbed her elbow into Ruby's side.

The two women gave each other a look, and Hannah blushed.

'Does everyone know about my date?'

The resulting round of awkward laughter told Hannah that yes, they all bloody knew. Leadsham truly was one of those old-fashioned places, where people genuinely cared. And were ready to stick their oar in at the mere sniff of anything exciting.

'Sorry, but yeah.' Ruby, as blunt speaking as ever. 'Not much passes for entertainment here really. *Are* you excited?'

'Don't question her like that! Remember when we got together?'

Ruby's face dropped. 'Oh God yeah, I remember. I thought we were going to make the parish newsletter to be honest. The bakery even named a rainbow iced bun after us.'

'The rainbow bun! Oh my God yes!'

Hannah looked aghast at the pair of them as Martine exploded at the memory. 'They were tasty though. The whole village put a few pounds on that week!'

Hannah's bemused face stopped them from babbling any further, and they ushered her into the shop with their posse of toddlers and prams. They kept up the chatter the whole time, telling her about Ava's day, what they and the kids had been up to. Before she knew it, she was leaving the bookshop, heading for home. Ava had settled into Lola's arms the second she'd been placed in them, and watching her and John coo over her, marvelling at every little yawn and fart and gurgle she produced, Hannah's heart swelled. Even when she swiped a basket of potpourri off the shelf, Lola had laughed and John had just swept it up and started dancing around with Ava in his arms.

She'd been worrying about being alone here, and her daughter growing up to feel the same way. Looking at the people who already cared so much for them both was such an alien feeling, but it felt so right. As she turned the key in the lock of her new home, she couldn't help but feel a real frisson of excitement. Tonight, after a week of anticipation since that bench kiss, she was going out on a date with Brody, and she skipped up the stairs to get ready to meet him.

*   *   *

It was strange being alone in the house. Ava had never slept anywhere without her before. She knew John and Lola were excited to have a baby for the night, and it did feel good to have a little break. It was strange, quiet. A little too quiet, though in every room there was evidence of Ava. A sippy cup in the sink, a bib in the laundry basket by the bed. The house always felt a little empty, and the wooden floors and the lack of furniture meant the echoes were often a little louder. It wasn't uncomfortable though, like her old house felt. There was no dread there, no panic about things being out of place, or a little messy if the afternoon had gotten away from her. It didn't matter here whether she washed her coffee cup up straightaway. A little mess didn't terrify her now; she even left things sometimes. The dishes in the sink from her supper. Sitting there while she went to bed. A little act of rebellion that had her smiling the next morning.

Whenever Hannah looked around her at the neat tiny little home, the one she had just for now, she felt a burst of pride in her chest. It was a little shitty, sure. The bills didn't stop coming, and Ava was growing, but she was here. She was doing it, and tonight, she was a woman going on her first real date in forever.

Brody was right on time, ringing the doorbell with flowers in his hands. He held open the car door for her, and she slipped into the cool leather seat.

'You warm enough?' he asked, taking her hand in his as he pulled out onto the road. She nodded, but he turned off the air conditioning anyway. 'Bullet likes it cold; he moans when I have the heat on.'

'I bet. Passenger-seat drivers are the worst.'

They both spoke at once.

'So, where are we going?'

'Have a good week?'

'Nosy, aren't you?' he quipped. 'It was supposed to be a surprise.'

'Yep. I hate surprises.'

'You don't hate surprises. No one does.'

'I do. I like to know what's going on at all times.'

'I'd like an answer to my question.'

She looked across at him, and he was smirking. They were heading down the streets, away from Leadsham onto one of the country roads. Brody turned the radio on low.

'I went to work, fed the ducks a million times with Ava. Read some books for reviews in the shop. Nothing earth-shattering, but good. Ava's been the busy one. Ruby and Martine never stop. Do you know they dress up regularly? It's scary at drop-off sometimes. Martine was dressed as a carrot the other morning. She looked like a fluorescent phallus. I didn't know where to look!'

He laughed. His face always lit up when she talked about her day, or Ava. Sent laughing emojis over text. It shocked her every time how much people loved her here. She wasn't tainted to them, neither of them was. It was different with Brody though. She couldn't help seeing his face light up and wonder why Victor's had never really had that same glow.

'It's good they keep her busy, bet she'll sleep well for John and Lola.'

'Yeah.' She laughed. 'I bet John will be relieved. He looked a bit scared.'

'He'll be fine. I've seen him do some pretty hard stuff. Ava won't take him out. Not in one night anyway. She's too sweet.'

'She's not so sweet at three in the morning, let me tell you.' She looked around her, as he signalled to turn down a dirt track. It didn't look like it was leading anywhere. 'Okay, so is this where Leatherface lives or what?'

'What?' Brody's eyes were wide. 'No, it's where we're going. You don't want to go?' He put his foot on the brake and the car came to a stop. 'The lights start just over the ridge of that hill. It looks better then.'

She gripped his hand a bit tighter. 'I was joking – it just looks like nothing's round here.'

Brody chuckled. 'Ah well, Leadsham has some pretty inventive people.'

He reached the top of the hill and took the next left. Halfway down that dirt track, the lights started. They were wound around the tree line, lighting the way to a large barn, with a car park to the left. Up to the right, she saw the farmhouse, the outbuildings around it.

'It's a restaurant?' The whole place was wood, painted and polished. Lit from the inside like the belly of a glow worm. It was almost ethereal in colour. 'It's gorgeous.'

'I knew you'd like it. It's locals only really, not many fancy the drive, or venturing out here in the dark. Means a designated driver I guess.'

'Lucky me, eh?'

'Lucky me you mean. I can get you rat-arsed on wine and have my way.'

She was just about to say something a little dirty back, but she saw his face change as he heard his own words. 'Sorry, I didn't mean to say that.'

'That's a shame.' He looked at her, and she leaned in. 'Sounded like fun.'

He blushed, and she knew she was being daring, but she was enjoying herself. She loved seeing how he reacted to her. She didn't have to second-guess every word she said, every action she took. Was she pushing him, to test him? She shoved the thought viciously out of her head.

His breath was on her ear, and the teasing tables were turned.

'I'll remember that.' He pulled effortlessly into a space.

He was at her door before she'd put her hand around the door handle, and they walked close together across the shale-strewn parking area. He put his hand on the small of her back, and she could feel the heat of him through her dress.

'It's kind of out of the way here. It's a nice place.'

The wooden surface of the building extended out in a huge decking area, a dance-floor-sized space at one end. There was

117

music playing, and she could see speakers tucked away on the walls around them. They took a table in the corner, away from most of the other tables. It was a nice night, a little cold. Crisp, but clear, and the majority of people were happily ensconced on the tables outside, under the many outdoor heaters. There was an Easter theme in places, decorated baskets of painted eggs scattered around.

They had a booth, and Brody led her in with his hand still on her, and when he sat down, there was no space between them. He put his arm around her and reached for her hand again.

'Brody flinched, pulling her hand away from his. He frowned and released it. A waitress came over, brandishing menus and a smile. One that widened when she took in Andrew Brody.

'Good evening, here are the menus for this evening. Can I take an order for drinks?' She was firmly focused on Brody, but he didn't even notice. He turned to Hannah, who was sitting in the crook of his rather muscular arm.

'What would you like? I'll have an iced water please. Driving.'

'A white wine would be nice,' she said to the waitress, who from the look on her face was sizing her up.

'Perfect,' she said, smiling inanely again and leaving them to have a look at the menu. She didn't make a squeak until the waitress returned half a minute later with the drinks.

'What's wrong?' Brody asked her the minute they were alone again. He sat back in his seat but didn't move away. He ran his hand through his hair, leaving it stuck up at funny angles. He didn't seem to care. 'Have you changed your mind?'

'No, of course not. It's lovely here. I just . . . we're in public.'

'On a date.'

'Yes. Exactly.'

He frowned. 'This is what dating people do.'

'And the dog park?' She swallowed hard. 'You kissed me there, in front of your colleagues.'

'Am I missing something? I seem to remember you started it that time.'

'That was . . . a moment of madness.'

'That my friends saw. If that was madness, why are we here?'
She felt like she was being questioned.

'I'm single, Hannah. I have been for a very long time. Believe
me, I have no problem with people knowing that I am out with
you for the evening.' His eyes were darker now, burning into her.
His jaw was flexed, and she felt bloody awful. She was torturing
the poor bloke. 'Do you?'

'It's not you, it's just . . .' She struggled for something to say
to him, but she had no answer that wasn't a bare-faced lie. The
waitress came back over, but Brody glared at her till she left.

'Go on,' he said, picking up his glass. 'Tell me what's wrong.'

She took a large sip of the wine. 'I've just not dated for a while.
It's not something I'd even thought of again, especially with Ava.'
They locked eyes. 'I didn't see you coming, and I'm just not used
to this.' Not without it being fake. Without being nipped under
the table. Brody was breaking the patterns she was used to in a
relationship, and it was terrifying. He was too good to be true. That
scared her to the core. She had enough to deal with. Staying away
from him wasn't working, obviously. She wished she could work it
all out. It all seemed like a dead end. Too dangerous. He was too
good to pull into this. Something else Victor Nuffield had spoiled.

Brody reached for her hand under the table, and she realised
she'd been clenching her fists. She didn't release them at first. Her
mind told her to, but it took a minute for her muscle memory to
realise he wasn't about to appear in the room. Calling her mental,
unfit. Other things. Lies and slurs.

'Okay.' He patted her hand, stroking down each finger, slowly
soothing. She uncurled her grip. One finger at a time. 'I'm only
asking you to spend time with me. No pressure, no expectations.
Just us. If you don't fancy me, you just have to tell me. I'm a big boy.'

She laughed, and her hands relaxed. She slipped them into his.

'No, it's not that honestly. It's just been a while, and with
Ava, I just kind of figured I wouldn't.' She smiled then, thinking

of their interactions. 'I guess you broke my rule.' The rule that should never have been broken. With the worst man *to* break it with. A man of the law. A good man, who would probably take Victor on. She didn't want any of that to happen.

'Your rule? What's that?'

'No men,' she said confidently. His brow arched. 'I failed, obviously. Fairly quickly too.'

'Are you sure about that?' His look of concern was muted now, but she could see he was still curious. 'The first time we met, you couldn't get away quick enough.'

'The mugging, remember.'

He slapped his forehead with the palm of his free hand, pulling a goofball expression that made her laugh again. The waitress looked in their direction, but Brody shook his head at her.

'You know what I mean.' She knew what he meant – he wanted to ask her questions. He always wanted her to ask her questions. It was as though he couldn't know enough. She felt seen under his gaze, like she was lit up from the inside. Just like this barn.

'I really love this place. It's beautiful.'

'It's not the only thing.' He lowered his gaze, and she felt cheated. 'Sorry, was that crossing a line too? I need to know the rules on this.'

'Rules?' she echoed. 'Do we have to do that now?'

'Well, yeah. I say quickfire round.' He looked irritated as the waitress made her way over again. 'After we order.'

He'd ordered the steak, and she the salmon. Potatoes and fresh vegetables for the table, with crusty bread, butter made on the farm like pretty much everything else on their plates. She'd refilled her glass and prepared for the onslaught.

Brody crunched on a piece of ice from his glass, and Hannah couldn't stop staring at his lips. He looked even hotter under the warm glow of the lighting, and the romantic, low-key feeling of the place was making her relax. This was a date, and she did want to enjoy it. It was the last one, but she'd told herself that before.

If Victor found her, with a policeman boyfriend, he would be so angry. He could hurt Brody. Out her to everyone. Lola was pregnant; she didn't want to land any more on her plate.

She didn't want to drag anyone else into this. Kate was already worrying about her. They spoke regularly but it wasn't the same. She missed her friend, was sick of not being able to visit her. See her. Spend time with her and not talk about Victor. Lying to people. Not answering questions. Even Brody would tire of it, even if Victor never found her. She would never do that. Someone like him deserved a woman who was free.

He turned to her the minute the waitress had left.

'Ready?'

'Really?'

'Really.'

'I don't have to answer, right?'

'Right.'

'Same for you?'

'Nothing to hide.'

She gulped at that. He leaned forward, and for a second she thought that he was going to kiss her. She put her hand out in reflex onto his chest, to stop him. But when her fingers touched the fabric of his shirt, she curled them tight, taking the material in her hands and pulling him to her. At the same time, he pulled something out of his back pocket, and pulled back to sit up. A button from his shirt pinged off, and they heard it hit something metallic in the distance. The waitress whipped her head in the direction of the noise but shrugged it off.

'I was getting this.' He showed her the coin in his hand. 'Heads or tails?' He sounded breathy. Surprised.

So am I, but damn.

Hannah's lips were parted, her face flushed with the thought of his lips on hers. She felt her face explode with colour, and his expression changed into stark recognition. His head moved, just forward a half-inch, and she released her grip.

'Sorry.' She smoothed the material out, seeing the flesh of his chest through the gap in the material. She'd pulled off a button right in the middle of his shirt.

He righted himself, looking as shaken as she felt. She scanned the room, but everyone else was immersed in their own evenings. The music had gone up a little as the night went on, and the other customers were oblivious to the charged booth in the corner.

'So, we obviously like each other,' he said smoothly.

'That's not a question.'

He raised a brow. 'Do you like me?'

'Yes,' she answered. She blushed again and shook her head. Her body always seemed to betray her around him.

'No?' he teased. 'You don't like feeling embarrassed, do you?'

'No. And that's two questions for me.'

He groaned, sipping on his ice water and crunching at the ice. She laughed and he dropped his scowl.

'Why did you ask me out?' She dropped the question she still didn't quite understand.

'Because I like you.'

'You already said that. Different answer.'

'Pushy!' He rolled his eyes. 'Okay, I *really* like you.' He looked her in the eye and leaned further in till their noses were almost touching. 'Because when I get this close to you, it feels right. Like this is where I need to be.'

'Better.'

'Thank you, Columbo. Next question.'

'I . . . er . . . I don't have a follow-up.'

Brody grinned. 'This was supposed to be a quick-fire round! You pike out now? Come on! Truth or dare.'

He waggled his eyebrows at her, and she pursed her lips to keep in her laughter. 'You are such a dork. You think you're funny don't you. A funny daredevil.'

'I'll have you know—' he dropped his voice '—not only am I a daredevil, I also wield a rather huge weapon when I work.'

Hannah laughed when it clicked. 'Eugh, your dog!' She batted at him as she choked with laughter. 'Who says that!'

He looked offended for a second, and she stopped laughing. 'Oh God, sorry.'

He laughed. 'You said I was funny. Obviously, you were right. I get another question, yeah?'

'No! That game sucks.' It was her turn to scowl.

'Go on, one more. That can be your dare.'

She rolled her eyes, but she was thoroughly enjoying herself, so she played along.

'One more, before our dinner comes.'

Brody smiled, and she realised that he'd been waiting for her to say that. He looked around, dipping his head back to hers. Whatever his question was, it was asked and answered with the touch of their lips.

Chapter 17

God, he's a sight for sore eyes. Brody was standing in her doorway, jeans and a shirt on, looking every inch the man she'd recently had a wonderful date with. She really wished she'd checked her appearance before she'd opened the door. It had been one of those hourless days. A never-ending stretch of time that didn't translate to the clock. She'd microwaved the same coffee four times. The clock hadn't moved an inch in hours, she was sure of it. *Damn, I'm tired.*

She hadn't even checked who was there at the door before opening it, and the thought unnerved her. She needed to get some sleep. Being this tired made her sloppy. But Brody was lit up by the setting sun, looking even hotter than normal. She smiled inwardly at herself. She was thinking about another man in *that* way again, and that was sleep-deprived with a toddler who had been projecting from both ends. She was making progress. It was unnerving that it was all down to the man in front of her, bringing the real her out again, but she knew if she had learnt anything, it was to trust her gut.

'I just wanted to check how you were doing. John said Ava wasn't well. I've not heard from you.' She'd barely been able to keep her eyes open, never mind check her phone.

'We're fine now, thank you. Ava picked up a bug from the childminders'. She's been a bit off, but I think she's on the mend.' Thank God. She'd taken the bus with her to the GP. He'd declared it a viral infection. Prescribed fluids, rehydration salts and rest. Calpol for the temperature. Bland food when she was a bit better. It had settled her mind so much. Things like this were going to come up. Kids got sick. She pushed the thought away. She was smart enough to realise that it was just a nasty bug, but she was also a mother and she worried. Even when it was just normal life. Part of life. Ava was mixing with other kids. She'd been having fun just the day before at the Easter egg hunt Martine and Ruby had put on for the kids. Ava and the other children had loved it. Just a shame she'd picked up more than a couple of chocolate eggs.

'I'm just glad I had a day off from the bookshop. I didn't want to stress Lola out.'

Ava was silent, her snuffling little snores just audible on the baby monitor. Poor little mite had finally worn herself out and she was sleeping in her cot, her fever having broken. Hopefully the meds would let her get the sleep she needed. Given the time, she'd be up in the night. Hannah was already dreading it. No wonder they used sleep deprivation as a torture device. She would have pretty much agreed to anything, just for a chance to lay her head down in blissful sleep. Just an hour, and she was sure she'd be a new woman. *Ha. I told you. Not without me. Without me, you fail. Every. Single. Time.* Her helplessness had combined with her fatigue and let his words slip through, she'd noticed. He was wrong though. The doctor said Ava was thriving otherwise. He'd even given her a sticker. *Bollocks to you, Victor. I'm doing okay.*

'You look tired.' Brody offered it up as a statement, and Hannah laughed. Looking down at herself, she saw yesterday's sweatpants and a stained top, knew her hair was in a very messy bun where she'd tied it up half exhausted that morning. 'Beautiful too. I just got off work, so I thought I'd come check on you.'

'Thank you.' She was still processing the beautiful comment, while her stomach recovered from the flip his words had provoked. 'You're so sweet. Sorry if I worried you by being quiet. I've just been trying to keep Ava cool. She's not a good patient.'

'You don't have to answer to me. I just wanted to check on you both. I should go. Let you get to sleep.' Her heart sank. It was nice to see him there. Was it because it was him though? Or was she just overtired, afraid of the shadows? When their eyes met, she knew what it was.

She looked past him at the door, and he noticed, moving back to leave. He came to a grinding halt when she reached out and brushed her hand over his. 'Don't leave. I wasn't looking at the door for that.' *I was double-checking for a shadow that isn't there. I don't want you curled in the fog too.* He turned to look at her, planting his feet right in front of hers now. Looking down at her, he slowly moved his hand to hold hers, stroking her thumb with his. Just once. She looked down at their joined hands, and slowly back up to him. The force of feelings that cascaded over her when their eyes met almost took her breath away.

'Come in for a while?' she asked him softly. He nodded, just once, and she closed the door behind them both.

'I have wine, if you like? Or coffee?'

'Wine would be nice. I would have to leave my car here though, so better not.'

Hannah considered this, but he wasn't in his police car, blue lights blazing and sirens blaring. A car outside her house would make it look less empty. She knew it was more than her heart talking when she replied.

'You can leave it here.' Another thought struck her. 'Although, there might be questions in this place. I've noticed Leadsham is a little close-knit. Wagging tongues and all that.'

'I'm pretty sure those tongues have been wagging a while.' He sounded amused by this.

He was only a couple of small steps away from her, but she still saw him glancing down at her body. She knew she looked ratty, but the expression on his face was far from disgust. He noticed her looking and cleared his throat, averting his gaze. *Ever the silent gent.*

'Let them talk,' he said, throwing her an easy smile that made her stomach flip. She led him through to the lounge, checking the baby monitor screen sitting on the coffee table. He took a seat in front of it, leaning forward to look closer.

'She's adorable. Fast asleep I see.'

Hannah remembered the night before, and the sheer exhaustion she'd endured. 'She looks like an angel, but she was a little bugger last night. I tried everything from pleading with her to playing whale songs at full blast. The parenting books I read are all useless with stuff like this. I want to throttle each and every author.'

He said nothing for a second, and then burst into laughter. She looked at him bemused.

'Sorry. Too much? I am a tad tired.'

'No, not that. I like your . . . fire. You speak your mind.'

She was about to correct him, to demur, but she stopped herself. Having looked away, she looked back to realise that he'd seen the changing expressions on her face before the shields had clanged back tight.

'I'll get the wine.'

She practically ran to the kitchen, gripping the worktop to catch her breath. *Idiot. You can't flip out over every comment. He is not HIM.* She had always spoken her mind before HIM. Trying to do it after was not so easy. She had the spark; she knew it had got her this far. It just kept bloody shorting out, often at the worst possible moments. She panicked after, as if her body was waiting for the punishment. *He's not here. Be you. Live!* There had been many moments with the man standing before her. Too many to ignore. Too many to want to ignore.

She grabbed the wine bottle out of the fridge, and kicking it shut with her foot, she reached for two wine glasses and turned to face the music. He was standing, filling the doorway. She hadn't heard his feet hit the lino.

'What did I say?' His voice was gentle. Just like always. 'I saw your face, Hannah. You practically ran from the conversation. Tell me?'

He didn't move an inch. She came to him.

'Nothing.' She made a move to leave, and he stepped aside immediately.

'I should go.'

'What?' She'd only just put the contents of her arms down on the coffee table, and he was leaving. 'You don't have to go. I don't want you to.'

He studied her face for so long she wanted to look away, but he nodded once. He took the same seat on the sofa, and Hannah sat next to him. It was only a two-seater affair, and he took up most of it.

'Ava over the worst?' He nodded towards the baby monitor, and the tension in the air popped. He poured the wine out without being asked, and she told him about Ava's virus, the GP visit.

'Poor Ava. It's par for the course I think when they mix with other kids. I have caught the odd bug visiting schools with Bullet.'

'Yeah, so I've heard from the other mothers. She has led a bit of a sheltered life up to now. Where is Bullet tonight?'

'He's tucked up at home, watching the box.'

She laughed, taking the first sip of wine and letting it sink into her tired bones. 'Oh that's good.'

'Looked like you needed it.'

'Yeah, it's been a while since I indulged. Thanks for coming to check on me.'

'Any time. You eaten?'

Hannah blinked at him, bleary-eyed, and he reached for his phone.

'If you have to think about it, the answer's no. I'm famished. Chinese?'

Brody rose to answer the door when the takeaway arrived, and she didn't move to stop him. He went straight into the kitchen, and she could hear him opening cupboards.

'I can do that,' she called.

'I've got it. You. Sit.'

She did as she was told. She was cradling her second glass of wine, the movie DVD they had picked on pause. It was some comedy romance, something light, slapstick. She hadn't been paying much attention. The heat from his body, sitting so close to her, was making her feel relaxed, sleepy even. They hadn't talked much, not that Brody was an excessive talker anyway. It wasn't awkward though, and the initial dancing around each other was getting less and less at each meeting. It was getting more charged though. Deeper. With each time, she learnt more about him, and found herself wanting to know more. The question game wasn't so annoying after all.

'You ready for this? I think I may have over-ordered.' He walked in with his arms full. There was a huge amount of food there for only two people, but Hannah's stomach rumbled at the sight. He set out several steaming dishes, spreading them out on the rest of the coffee table space, and returned to the kitchen for cutlery. The pair of them tucked in till they were full, pointing at cartons and urging the other to try a bit.

'Well, that was lush.' Hannah sat back, patting her food baby of a stomach. 'I'm stuffed.'

'You did some damage. I thought you were going to rip my finger off for the last prawn cracker.'

She narrowed her eyes at him, laughing. 'I regret nothing. Thank you. Really, this was great. I owe you a meal.'

'I'll hold you to that. Next Saturday? I'm on an early shift. I figured we could ask John to babysit, go a bit further afield?'

Hannah wanted to say yes, but she was getting deeper into this every time she saw him. There would be so many more things that would come between them, when she couldn't do anything. She was free, but still trapped in limbo.

She had Ava to think about, and everyone she cared for here. If she was seen by someone who knew her and Victor before, then that would make it harder. She had had a life, before Victor siphoned it off slowly. Leaving only him at the bottom of the empty shell. Here she could have a life again. And Ava loved it here. She was going to go to school and be a normal kid. Not have to worry about what would happen that night at home. Hannah wanted unicorns and fun and everything for that girl. She wanted to be the old her; start a proper, full life. But she couldn't have everything. That was the price of the freedom she had now. Hiding and living. Safe.

'I don't think I can. Andrew . . .'

'I like it when you call me Andrew. No one really does. It's Brody and Bullet normally, but hearing you say it, it's different. Listen.' He put down his plate, wiping himself down with the napkin and reaching for her. He stilled when his fingers almost met hers, and then he claimed her hand. 'There's a drive-through movie theatre about thirty miles from here. A farmer friend of mine runs it. It's not well advertised. It's basically a big screen and a huge field. I'll drive, in my car.' His jaw flexed when he saw her shaking her head.

The idea of a cosy drive-through night under the stars with Brody meant that it took her a good minute to catch up with the rest of his words. Now in her head, *he* was sitting behind them, watching the movie from the back seat and sneering. She shuddered, and Brody's hold tightened just a touch. 'Think about it. Let me know. If it's not your thing, we can pick something else to do. Is there a reason why you don't fancy it?'

'Why is it so important, to know everything all the time?'

'Well, it helps to know some things. Especially if I'm trying to date a woman I like. Dating is involved. That means going places. I just want to do something you like. Give me a hint.'

'You don't need to study me. I'm not one of your suspects.'

'For God's sake, Hannah, I never meant . . .'

'Look, can we just drop it? I can't go.'

'Sorry. Forget I – hang on . . .' He looked agitated, and Hannah steeled herself for his anger exploding. It didn't happen. 'I don't really know what I'm apologising for. I just want to take you out.' He ran his fingers through his thick locks. *He's hurt,* she realised with a pang. She was upsetting this wonderful, caring and gentle giant of a man. A man who she hadn't expected to meet. She hadn't expected to care either. She owed him some truths, she knew. It was always going to come to this, wasn't it?

'You haven't done anything wrong. I just want to stay here. In Leadsham. Going to the same places. I don't need an adventure, Andrew.' She motioned around her surroundings with her arms wide. 'I'm barely hanging on as it is.'

His frown was clear. He didn't agree. The knitting together of his dark brows told her that in no uncertain terms. She tried again. Her hands were knotted together, fingers gripping each other for comfort as she found the words she never wanted to speak. Least of all to him. He noticed her pulling away and wrapped his hand over her knotted fingers.

'It's more than that. Ava's father wasn't the nicest person.'

Another jaw flex from him, harder this time. He moved his thumb in small circles on her skin.

'I gathered that much.'

'I can't be seen out too many places, till things calm down at least. It's quiet here. I can live pretty normally.' It sounded pathetic really, and she knew that it would be hard to keep up the lies, the stupid reasons she couldn't go anywhere. With the man currently whispering such nice things in her ear.

Hannah. I'm here.

She kept her voice strong, but it wasn't without effort. 'It's complicated, that's all. Raw still.'

'Does he plan to see Ava?'

'No,' she replied a little too quickly, too forcefully. 'He doesn't see her. Not anymore.'

'Will you tell me his name?'

'No. I can't.'

He pressed his lips together before replying. 'Hannah, you don't have to worry about what people think. I know Leadsham is a little bit of a goldfish bowl, but the people here mean no harm. I don't think either of us want to walk away from this. Right?'

'I just don't want people to know my business.' She did before. Several, actually. She'd tried to tell many people. Asked people behind glass screens for help: housing services; the benefit office; the police, even. She'd walked right into the police station, pregnant and black-eyed. *Result? Diddly squat.* Just more paperwork for the police. It was his word against hers. Injuries didn't count apparently. They could have been done by anyone, herself even. She'd been online at the library, read stories that had started with hope and ended in hell. A child with no mother. A grave, premature in its inception and utterly avoidable. She didn't want her story to end like that. *No one does,* a voice inside her said with authority. *No one dreams of living like that. No one deserves that.*

'I just want to live my life, try to forget about the past.' *Kind of hard when the past won't be put away or ignored,* her inner voice mocked. *You can't do this alone. You can't do anything.* She shuddered at the words in her head. It was his voice she heard now, not her own. She shut him out of her head. *No thanks. Stay out, Victor.* 'I'm sorry, but that's all I can do. It's the life I live, but I don't want it to be yours too.'

His thumb stopped for a second, like a stutter on her skin. A shudder of a different kind hit her then. A much more unpleasant one. *How am I supposed to give him up?* The thought rattled around in her head. She'd been asking herself that question for some time. Brody resumed his slow, sensual circles again, and his deep voice filled the silence.

'Don't worry about me. I wasn't asking to quiz you, Han. I would never do that. I meant it, that I'm here, now. I don't plan on going anywhere either. I like you, Hannah. And Ava, of course. Whatever happened with Ava's father, that's not me. It's not us.' He broke his intent gaze to flick his eyes to the monitor, where Ava was still fast asleep, the flush on her cheeks less noticeable on the camera screen now. Hannah had not long checked on her, relieved to see she was doing much better, just exhausted from her rampaging the night before. His eyes were back on hers, and she was focused on him once more. The room shrank to that little couch.

'I don't want to complicate your life.' He took her other hand now, again pausing to ask permission once more. *Who was this man?* Hannah was starting to think he was sent from the heavens, but her gut told her to hold back, just a little. That voice was getting weaker though. Right now, it was little more than a whisper in the wind.

'I just want you to know that you are safe.' His low rumbling voice washed over her. 'With me, you will always be safe.' The emotion of his declaration of intent was like an electric shock to Hannah's system. She wasn't expecting him to say that, but she was bloody glad he had. 'Besides—' he raised a brow comically '—Bullet has seemingly adopted you two as one of his pack, so between us, we're good.'

She laughed then, the emotion finally spilling out of her. It didn't last long though, before she dissolved into tears. 'I don't want to cause you any trouble either, Andrew. It would be too hard. I need to stay off the radar.' His eyes were fixed on hers, and she saw recognition etched on his features. He knew what she meant now. Fully understood. She could see it on his face. He had to have had inklings, given his job. Now he knew. He'd have seen it all on the force.

I wish he'd been in my police station that day. When I arrived, desperate for help. Things might just have been different.

'Hard, schmard,' he retorted after a pause long enough to make her palms sweat as she waited. 'We don't have to go anywhere you don't want to. I would never put you at risk. I just want to spend time with you, that's all. No pressure. Just two people, getting to know each other. The job won't come into it either.'

'It will, if he finds me. I need my life here to work. I can't go backwards.' She took a breath. 'He could find me. I'd have to run. If that happens, Ava and I will be gone, and I won't be able to say goodbye. No going backwards.'

She looked away, considering the remnant of their night together. She'd told him as much as she wanted to, as much as she could. Kate's safety relied on her keeping her mouth shut too. She'd helped a patient; she'd plotted to help Hannah escape. Given her money. She had too much on the line, and Brody's job did affect this. He loved his job, his life with Bullet. Hannah didn't want to take the man in front of her down with her, but she didn't want to break her own heart either. She already felt far more than she should, and she needed to keep a clear head. She wanted to be honest and give him an out too. She just didn't know *why* he would want to get involved in all this, for a single mother scraping away a life. What did she have to offer him, really? She still had PTSD from her last relationship, and the debris of that was still scattered across her daily life. Causing obstacles, some insurmountable to her.

'It won't come to that. Don't leave. No goodbyes, okay? Promise me.'

He released one of her hands to offer a handshake, and she wiped her eyes. She didn't realise that she'd been crying quite so much.

'I think you need to think about it.'

'I have.'

'Properly.'

134

'I have.'

'You can't have. I only just told you.'

'You don't trust me now?'

He said it lightly, but she knew that he wanted a true answer to her question. She thought for a moment before answering. She already knew the answer, but it came from her gut. That took a second to get over. Progress, progress. *You do trust him, possibly more than you ever have a person other than Kate.*

'I trust you.'

'Then the answer is still the same.'

'Why?'

'Because I want to date you, and none of what you told me puts me off. In fact, I like you even more for it. You're stronger than you think, Hannah. I just want to make you smile, that's all.' He blushed a little then, and she grinned at him.

'You're pretty goofy when you want to be. Cute too.' She was teasing him now, but only to try to dampen down the urge to kiss his face off.

'You make me like this,' he groaned, reaching for his wine. It was empty. 'Oops, two glasses down.'

'One more?' she asked. She didn't want him to leave. He flicked his gaze to his watch and nodded. She poured them both a glass, and he held out his hand again.

'Before we drink this, we still need to shake on it.' The green flecks in his eyes were emerald tonight, she noticed. 'Hannah, promise me. No running, okay? You come to me. And not to say goodbye.' His jaw flexed with the conviction of his words. He was begging her with his eyes to agree. She wanted to, so much. Selfish. She was being selfish, but she would rather hate herself for that than lose him now. He was too important to her.

She gave him a look but put her hand into his. He shook it once but didn't let it go.

'I have a condition.'

'Underhanded,' she retorted.

'Necessary,' he countered. 'Ready?'

'Go on.'

'My condition is that you tell me what you can, when you need to. It doesn't have to involve the job – that is your call. I can just be Andrew, but I would like to know that the mother I'm dating – and her child – are happy. If you're not happy, I need to know. Deal?'

He was rubbing his forefinger along her wrist, which was very distracting. When she looked at him, she saw his brow arch devilishly. *It made him even hotter.* She put the wine glass almost to her lips, narrowing her eyes back at him.

'Deal.' She took a sip of the wine, not taking her eyes from his. He took a deep gulp himself. Moving her hand to hold his, she reached for the remote. The film was long over, but she flicked onto the image of another one they had talked about earlier. 'Fancy this? You don't have to stay till the end.'

He wrapped his arm around her, snuggling her in closer to him.

'I'll be here. Put it on.'

Chapter 18

'You finally came!'

A group of mums sitting on the floor turned their heads to look at Hannah as she walked through the doors of the community centre. Ava was in her arms, the changing bag hanging heavy on the other hip.

'Er . . . yeah.' Hannah walked over to a table at the back, where Martine and Ruby were busy making drinks in reusable lidded cups. As ever, the two of them were happy being busy. Kids all around them. Ruby tapped Martine on the arm.

'Sorry, she didn't mean to announce you to the room then. We're so glad you came though!'

Ava was in her arms, but having seen her friends from the childminders' there, she tried to make a break for it.

'Okay, little wiggler.' Hannah went to sit her down with the others on the playmat, settling her with a cushion behind her. She was far more mobile these days. She'd been walking for the last few days, and Hannah had recorded it for posterity on her phone. She'd sent it to Kate, but her exuberant text back wasn't the same as seeing her face. Going back to where Ruby and Martine were stood, she realised that she could share the joy with them.

She hadn't mentioned it to Brody. He was on shift a lot, and she hadn't seen him since the movie night. That night, she'd woken up on the couch, covered with a blanket. He'd locked up and posted the key through the door. She didn't feel like she could just ring him and tell him about Ava's walking. He'd only met her a handful of times, and she didn't want to vomit baby news at him. Whatever they were now, they were dating, and she wanted to take it slow. He wasn't some kind of daddy replacement for Ava either. She owed it to her to introduce her to people she really trusted and cared about. It occurred to her in that moment that she might not have made the worst strides in that direction. It was nice here at the toddler group; it felt normal. Life in all its simplicity before her.

'Did you have a nice weekend?'

Ruby handed her a cup of coffee, and she took it with a smile.

'Quiet thanks, I had the weekend off so I got on with some jobs, went to the park with Ava. She's walking now you know. Only a few steps, but still.'

'No way!' Martine half screamed in delight. 'Gutted we missed that, but so glad you saw it! You can't beat these milestones.'

'I got it on video, pure luck.' The two women looked at her expectantly.

'Show us then!'

Seconds later, they were all crowding around Hannah's phone, watching Ava on the screen.

'Oh my God, you're going to need some safety gates at yours now!'

Hannah groaned at the thought of the expense, but she didn't let it show. She was slowly running out of savings, even though she was only buying the bare minimum of what they needed. She still had furniture bits to save for, and Ava was going to need more clothes, more equipment . . .

'We've got some spares in the garage, if you need them. We keep a few sets around.'

'Oh no . . . I—'

138

Ruby silenced her with a look. 'Listen, we don't need them. You do. You can give them back when you're done. We pass them on to the next mum.'

Martine nodded her head as she rammed a chocolate cookie into her mouth. 'Mm, true.'

'We all tend to swap stuff about. I have a tonne of bagged baby clothes too, if you want a look.'

'Thanks, but I can go buy that stuff.' Hannah didn't want to feel like a charity case.

'Give over. Listen, when we came to town, we didn't have much. We were newly together, trying for a baby, new house, new jobs. It takes a village, and Leadsham is good at looking after its own. No point spending money when you don't have to, and if you want to donate Ava's baby stuff to make you feel better, we can pass it back on with the rest.'

They all fell silent as the video came to an end, Ava comically moving across Hannah's lounge, laughing. Just as it ended, a text message notification came up on the screen.

Hi, hope you and Ava are having fun at the group. Call you later.

He'd signed it off with a policeman and dog emoji, making her laugh.

'Is that Brody?'

Martine gave Ruby a look over Hannah's head and Hannah blushed furiously.

'Er . . . yes?'

'Nice! You're getting on well then!' Ruby clapped her hands with glee.

'I told you! Hey, Kenzie, let's not do that.' She headed off to wrangle a couple of the children, who were in the play kitchen fighting over a plastic frying pan. Kenzie had already hit the other one around the head with a fabric cauliflower, and things were escalating fast.

Martine put her arm around Hannah's shoulder and pulled her away to sit on one of the seats placed on the outer sides of the room. Once they were sat cradling their coffees, Martine turned to her.

'Sorry about Ruby. She's a bit much sometimes. We're all just a bit excited, I think. Brody is one of the eligible bachelors of Leadsham, and although we don't have a horse in the race, it has been nice seeing him so happy.'

'Do people know?'

Martine rolled her eyes. 'Of course, this is Leadsham. The villagers around here are a surprisingly romantic bunch.'

Hannah couldn't see the funny side of things. All she could think about was the attention.

'The more I see of Leadsham, the more I believe you.'

'You don't seem too happy about that. Everything okay?'

Hannah looked at Ava, who was busy now with Ruby in a singing game. Ava was sitting clapping her hands in time to the music with some of the other mums and tots.

'I just don't want things to get so complicated. I have Ava to think of.'

'Brody is great with kids though. I wouldn't worry, and as for the gossip, it will die down.'

Hannah smiled at her friend, but it didn't come across as more than an awkward grimace.

'Sorry, I didn't mean to upset you.'

'No, you haven't upset me, it's fine.' Hannah tried to reassure her new friend. 'It's just a while since I've been in this situation.'

'Dating a hot policeman who clearly likes you? I can imagine the hardship.' The two women burst into laughter when their eyes met. Hannah's anxiety subsided. 'Seriously though, we are here for you, for babysitting. Go and have some fun! Don't worry about a bit of interest from the locals; they are harmless.'

Hannah thought of John, Lola, and the two friends in Ruby and Martine she had made here. As they dragged her over and involved her in the singsong, she relaxed and chatted with the other mums. Soon, they were all laughing and playing with their kids, all awkward questions forgotten for the moment.

She was walking through the park later on, Ava in her pram, when she sat down on the bench to text Brody. He was back on a big case, pulling lots of overtime in when necessary, so they had only had a few texts between them for the last week or so. He always checked in with her, and always asked about Ava. It made her think that perhaps she should make a bit of an effort, cheer him up.

Playgroup went well. Gossip mill is still grinding. Hope you and Bullet are not too fed up.

He texted back within seconds.

Bullet is bored in the car, and I'm trying to eat my lunch without his dog breath over my shoulder. You two girls made any friends?

Ava loved the toys more than the other kids to be honest. Nice people there. She had made some friends, and some of the mums had babies the same age. They would all be going up into school together, and it was weird to think that Ava might have some of her future best friends in this room. It made her heart glad to think of it. Bit by bit, Hannah's friends had fallen away when they'd had enough of Victor, who made it his mission to make them feel uncomfortable. Like they were in the way. He was perfectly cordial, friendly even, but getting to go on nights out was hard, and then impossible. Having no real family to speak of, it had made her world small. Smaller than it was now. Aside from missing Kate, she was really glad she'd taken the plunge today.

Independent lady eh? What are you up to tonight? I was thinking I might cook for you. At my house.

Hannah silenced a wailing Ava by passing her a juice box. Her little cheeks were sweaty from her exertions at group, and she was getting tired and irritable. Hannah read the text over and over. She found herself curious, but she knew it wasn't going to happen. Lola and John were great looking after Ava, but she didn't want

141

to put on them too much. They had enough of their own going on, and she valued their friendship.

No sitter, sorry. Another time?

Bring Ava with you. You can both stay over. I have a spare room, remember?

Shit. What was she going to say now?

Don't overthink this, Hannah. I will only seduce you with my cordon bleu skills, I promise. Say six o'clock, before Ava goes to bed?

Ava chose that moment to wang her empty juice box onto the grass, already crushed by her little fists. Hannah laughed, leaning in close to her daughter's face.

'What are you doing, litter bug?' Her eyes fell on the little dog toy that Ava had kept by her side since Brody had left it for her. 'What do you think, shall we go and see Bullet tonight? Have a sleepover?'

Ava babbled away back at her, and she took that as a yes. She was here to have a life after all. What was the alternative, sitting at home alone like so many other nights? Not a chance.

Do you want me to bring anything?

Just what you need for the night. The food is on me. See you later.

Putting her phone away, she took the pram handles in her hands and floated all the way home. She had a bit of packing to do.

See you soon x

She'd put a kiss at the end of her text, and Brody's heart leaped. She was in.

'Well, that was easier than I thought.' He spoke to Bullet, who was sitting next to him as they waited to be called. They were on duty with the drug task force, working on a small operation in Leeds. Another one of Big Phil's legacies getting ripped apart. 'Looks like we have some houseguests for the evening. You had better be on your best behaviour.'

Bullet huffed in his throat. Brody gave him a warning look in between quick bites of his lunch.

'I mean it. No bachelor pad moves. No licking your junk in public. No farting.'

Bullet let out a low howl, making Brody laugh.

'Listen, we need this to work. I need a wingman. You in, or you spending the night in the kennel?'

Bullet turned his head to one side, as though weighing his options up. When Brody held his fist out, Bullet bumped it with his paw.

'Good man.' He saw the signal from the officers outside, and his heart thumped with adrenaline. 'Time to go to work. We need to get off shift on time for once. It's go time, Bullet.'

He opened the doors, and the two of them headed out, all attention turned to the job in hand. As Bullet signalled he'd found something on the second floor they'd searched, Brody couldn't believe his luck. 'Good boy, Bullet! That's the spirit.' It looked like his wingman was on the same page, and he couldn't wait to see Hannah. The two of them cracked on, the adrenaline fuelling their urgency.

Walking down her street, pram and bags in tow, Hannah's heart beat a little faster with every step closer to Brody. The evening air was brisk, but not too cold, the heat of the sun slowly fading from the air around her. It was wonderful not to have the dark nights anymore, but she was aware that she was in full view of the house windows she passed. She wondered what she looked like to her unseen neighbours. Did she look like a woman in control? She found herself wishing she was a different person again. She often did it. The What-If game. *What if I'd been a better girlfriend? Wife? Mother? What if I'd have said no, all those times Victor chased me for a date. What if I'd just run the other way. What if. What if. Fucking what if. What if he hadn't been a total bastard. What if she'd realised he was in the wrong, and it was nothing she'd done or said, or didn't do. What if indeed.* What if Brody was different, like she thought? Like everyone around her seemed to believe about him, about them. Hell, about this place.

She caught sight of her side profile as she passed a parked car, and she realised something. She wasn't about what-ifs tonight. She was doing it. It bolstered her steps down the street. She was a free woman tonight. The what-ifs were up to her, and she shoved them aside.

Ava was wide awake but settled enough, dressed in a pair of fresh pyjamas after her bath. She was wide-eyed, looking all around her at everything her little eyes could take in. Hannah had brushed her tufts of hair back off her face, made sure she was warm enough for the short walk in the evening air. Her hair was starting to grow long enough to tie back, and Hannah had an abstract vision of her float into her head. Ava, more grown than she was right now. Long-haired, laughing. Dressed in school uniform, leaving her hand behind and heading into the school gates. She was growing fast, becoming more of her own person and less of a reminder of him as time went on. She saw her own parents in her child's face sometimes, the odd look that her dad would have given. The little dainty hand movements Ava made that made her think of her mother's, always soft and gentle.

She pushed away the pang every time that they never got the chance to see her, even once. She was glad that they were spared from the rest. It might have been different then though and, given her current destination, she couldn't quite bring herself to dwell on the pointless what-ifs. She shook her styled red hair out and focused on the night ahead.

Her steps gave her away as she trudged along the silent street, the odd bark or clang of a bin showing that rural civilisation was still ticking away around her. The methodical squeak of the pram wheel. As Brody's house came up overhead, Hannah's steps quickened. It looked different to what she remembered, although it was just the outside of a house. It wasn't about to

144

have a big blue flashing light on the top or look like a monster's mansion. Monsters lived behind all kinds of doors, but his house was homely. The garden was neat, a couple of dog toys scattered on the short grass. The porch light was on, and she could see that the bay window curtains were open. There was an unlit lamp in the corner of the room, the walls painted dove grey.

She took in everything she could before she got to the gate, distracting herself from her nerves. She'd spent two nights here. It wasn't the house; it was the night ahead. Her stomach was full of butterflies. She heard the front door open as she looked down to put the brake on.

'Hi.' His voice, as deep and sexy as ever.

He jogged down the path, a waft of aftershave floating past her in his wake and making her want to lean in closer for a better sniff test. Opening the gate, he took the bag from her arm and putting one hand on the pram, they both walked up the path together. She wasn't small by any means, but she always found herself taking in his size when they met. Sometimes, just for a second, it still unnerved her. It was getting less and less the more she was around him. She was curious about his body much more than she feared it for those split seconds of time. That was just a remnant of the old her.

'You okay?' he asked, and she felt his eyes on hers. 'And how about you, Miss Ava? How are you feeling tonight?'

Ava babbled away back to him, reaching out for her chubby fingers to get to him. He held out his hand palm up, and she placed her little hand in his. He pretended to shake her hand gently, and Ava laughed at him hysterically. 'Pleased to formally meet you both for dinner this evening. We trust our accommodations will be to your liking, Princess.' As he spoke, he projected in a funny voice, like a posh butler, and pulled theatrical Jim Carrey faces at her. Ava thought the whole thing was very entertaining, and she was still cackling with high-pitched, adorable laughter as he lifted her pram and ushered them both into his home. Bullet was nowhere to be seen, but she could hear an exuberant bark, followed by some pitiful whining.

'Bullet,' Brody shushed him with one word. A gentle word, for Ava's ears, but spoken with the authority he commanded to all those around him. Hannah was standing there in his hallway, wondering what the hell she'd just witnessed. As he took no time in putting the bag down, and fussing around Ava, she thought that her daughter might have just been charmed by this man. Just as charmed as she was.

'I'm glad you came.' He was in front of her now, Ava putty in his arms, the pram folded away and put in a hall closet by Brody. They both had daft grins on their faces, but his face fell as soon as he saw Hannah's. 'What's wrong? You okay?' He looked to Ava, as if to check her for sudden injuries or upset, and back at her. 'Sorry. Did I overstep?' He held Ava out to her. She took her from him, much to Ava's chagrin, and reached to take his hand in hers.

'No, you didn't. I just . . . that was nice. Thanks for the help.'

He pulled her in close, wrapping his arms around them both. Ava laughed, reaching for his face and giving his dark hair a good yank. He took it in his stride, pulling a funny face at her before pulling Hannah just that little bit closer.

'Come on then,' he said, leading the way down the hallway. 'I've set the spare room up for you both.' There was a series of muted thuds coming from the back of the house, and Brody rolled his eyes. 'And Bullet wants to say hello. That okay?'

'I think Ava would insist too.'

He walked into the kitchen, and Hannah noticed for the first time how welcoming it was. A modern, light kitchen like she recalled, with the smell of garlic and herbs wafting around her. On the kitchen island, there were two plates set, complete with wine glasses, napkins, the works. It looked like a photoshoot compared to her mismatched second-hand crockery and dated kitchen.

'Wow, this looks nice.' Nice was an understatement. It looked

146

so lovely, so romantic. She didn't quite know where to put herself. 'You didn't have to go to so much trouble.'

'It's nothing, really. I like to cook, but there's never that much point just for me. It's only lasagne and salad. Ready soon. I thought you might like to put Ava down first.' He opened the back door, and Bullet was sitting there waiting. 'Come on then, boy. Careful now.' He pointed to Ava, as though warning the dog that they had a child in the house. He needn't have worried of course. As soon as Ava clapped eyes on the hound she went nuts in Hannah's arms. The four of them played in the kitchen for a while, laughing at Ava's infectious giggle every time Bullet did something to make her laugh. For a highly trained animal, he was quite easy to wrap round Ava's fingers. He followed her around the kitchen from a distance when she started walking clumsily around.

'She's walking now? No way!'

Brody was clapping for Ava as she crawled towards him, Bullet in tow. When she got to him he picked her up and held her high in the air, twirling her around and telling her how clever she was. Hannah once again found herself watching this little family tableau, wondering to herself how this had happened. When she'd pictured her new life, she'd imagined just raising her daughter, scraping by to get her daughter through the early years. Hiding, and spending her life alone, just the two of them. Now, she felt like she'd found a home. It scared the shit out of her.

Looking at Brody, who was now chatting away to her daughter as he carried her around the kitchen, checking on the food, her heart felt like it was going to explode. *Was this what other families had every day?* She'd never really had it before. It made her heart hurt and pump with joy at the same time. Luckily, Ava soon showed signs of being tired, rubbing her eyes and yawning. She was knackered already from her day. Hannah felt a bit mean for feeling grateful, but then she stopped herself. She was a good mum, and she deserved to have a nice meal with adult company. She stopped the familiar voice in her head from speaking at all. She was about done listening. She wouldn't entertain it tonight. She could shut it out for one night.

'She's getting tired.'

Brody got up from the floor and nodded towards the staircase.

'I'll show you to the room. Dinner will be ready when you are.'

She followed him up the stairs, passing his bedroom and into the spare room. On the other side of the landing was another bedroom and a large bathroom. It was all neat as usual, nicely decorated in homely tones. It screamed of Brody. There were photos on the wall of him with his friends, his sister, but mostly they were of him and Bullet. On the wall in the spare room was a photo of the pair of them dressed as clowns, Bullet clutching a charity bucket in his mouth. She'd looked at them when she'd looked after him. She liked the feel of his house. It wasn't showy, or too masculine. She looked at the clown photo. She liked this one the best. It showed his fun side, the one he usually kept hidden behind his persona to many. He caught her eyeing it and blushed.

'It was a charity drive for the local children's centre.'

Hannah nodded at him, an amused expression playing across her features.

'I really like the red nose.'

'Sexy, eh?'

He blushed again.

'Yes, oddly,' she countered, her eyes on him. Ava squirmed in her arms, half drowsy with sleep, and the moment was gone. He reached under the bed and pulled out a travel cot. When she looked at him aghast, he shrugged.

'I borrowed it from John. I was a bit worried about her falling out of bed.'

Hannah had been wondering about that herself, now that Ava was even more mobile than the last time they'd stayed. Worrying that she couldn't be contained by a pillow barricade anymore. The memory of her sleeping on blankets on the floor when they'd first arrived in Leadsham was still a fresh wound. *This isn't like that. That won't happen again.*

'You didn't have to do that. But thanks.' She was half choked from speaking. It was so thoughtful.

'Of course I did. I'll leave you to it.' He leaned down closer and Hannah stopped breathing. His face was so close to hers, closer . . . closer. She could smell his aftershave, and it didn't do anything to quell the butterflies somersaulting around in her gut. He dropped a kiss on Ava's forehead. 'Night, little one. Sweet dreams.' He pulled away and smiled at Hannah. A real panty dropper of a smile that had her watching him as he padded down the stairs in his socked feet. For such a big man, he really was the gentlest person she'd met. She thought again of the phrase 'gentle giant' that she'd read about so much in books. It had left her cold before, and often mad at the authors. The giant she'd known before, though not as big as Brody, was anything but gentle. Bullish at best. Hellish at worst. *Stop comparing. There is no comparison.*

Once the travel cot was up and she was snuggled in, Ava was out like a light. When Hannah had made up the cot, she'd noticed that the sheet, which was wrapped in a plastic covering, had a receipt stuck to the back. Bought that very afternoon. Hannah was about to hide the receipt under the cot, pretend she hadn't seen it, but she picked it up to take it downstairs instead. Little lies turned into big ones. What would be the point? Did she want him to know she knew? That she wasn't dumb, or blindly trusting? Jesus, this wasn't her. She shook off the dusty thoughts. He'd done a kind thing for his guest and her daughter. She'd already sentenced him for being modest. Understated in his help, like always. She needed to lighten up. She laughed under her breath. Ava snored at that moment, a little contented shuddery snuffle. She smiled and headed down to him.

'So, John had the travel cot ready for the baby? That was lucky, on such short notice.'

149

He was sitting at the island, backwards on the stool. He had a bottle of beer in his hand, his long-sleeved navy-blue T-shirt rolled up his arms. His forearm went taut as he lifted the bottle to his lips. He took a long swallow. Bullet's head whipped to one side, an 'errr' sound erupting from his snout.

'I know, I'm answering.' He side-eyed the dog, and stood up, walking over to Hannah. 'He took your side. Rat.' He scowled comically at Bullet, who countered with a short bark and a paw over one eye. Brody chuckled, and turning back to her. He stopped. His eyes were straight on hers, and she noticed how long and dark his lashes were. A girl would kill for lashes like those. They looked good on him. They softened the harder planes. His expression was serious now, and she was about to ask him what he was thinking, when he leaned in. Just that little bit closer, and he brushed his lips over hers. From side to side, the barest little touches across her skin. Her lips parted, and he closed the distance between them. He kissed her softly, drawing his arms around her.

The beer bottle brushed down her arm, sending a chill through her as he held her tighter to him. She was in the air then, twirling around. He set her down on the stool without breaking any contact between their lips. Once he was satisfied that she was settled safely, he pulled away. 'Sorry, but I had to do that. I've been waiting too long between kisses.' She smirked, pleased he felt that way. 'Plus, I didn't want you to freak out. I bought the stuff for Ava today. I wanted her to be comfortable. I'm not presuming anything, but I thought you might . . .'

'Freak out on you? I might, if that's what you'll do to stop it.'

His jaw flexed, just for a second. His lips were on hers again now, more fervent this time. She kissed him right back, and she felt his muscles, tight. He was tensed up, and she wanted to stop whatever it was. He pulled away again, and took a seat next to her, moving her to face him.

'You can freak out on me as much as you want, I'm not going anywhere. I just didn't want you to think I was presuming anything, about you or Ava, or us. I just wanted you both to feel at home.' His jaw flexed again. 'Not that I'm saying it's your home, well . . . of course I want you to feel at home, but I'm not implying—'

She kissed him this time. To silence him. For a man she once thought rather sullen and burly, he was jabbering away like a schoolboy talking to a first crush. He was a daft idiot when he was like this, and she loved it.

She reached for his hands, which were now cupped around her face, and took them in hers.

'That was to shut you up and say thank you.'

His smile told her that she was welcome. 'It was nothing, really. The opposite of that kiss.' She blushed, but she didn't look away.

'I don't think we know what we're getting into here.'

'I do.'

'You don't,' she warned.

'Well, I know what you want me to know. The rest doesn't matter.'

'It will one day.'

'Perhaps, but I could get hit by a bus tomorrow.'

'Well, that's comforting to hear.'

He laughed. 'I just mean I'm not about to start worrying about something that might happen. If it does, nothing changes between us, unless you want it to.' He suddenly stood up, running to the oven. 'Shit! The lasagne!'

Chapter 19

Hannah hadn't said a word since he'd made a prat of himself, running around like a headless chicken, trying not to wake Ava up while saving their dinner. Luckily, though the cheese crust was a little overdone in places, it was still good. She was pushing a last little bit of lettuce around on her plate, and he was sitting there trying to fathom what she was thinking about. Bullet was fast asleep in his bed in the lounge. They'd eaten in companiable silence side by side, but she might as well be miles away. It was like she felt guilty for having fun or something. Another thing he was determined to make her see for herself.

'Tell me,' he said finally. 'If you're worrying about what I don't know is going to keep coming up, between us, tell me. Either way, I like you, Hannah. A lot. I don't date lots of women. I'm not a bad guy. I just want the chance to date you, whatever that means to you. But this barrier, it's hurting you. I don't like that part of it. It's not about me.'

He had expected the usual protests, or silence, but she looked at her wine glass instead.

'I'll need more wine.'

His lounge was twice the size of her cosy sitting room, and he saw her looking around with interest. She did that a lot, he noticed. She was always hyper aware of her surroundings. At the shop, at hers, here. She noticed everything. His sitting room was comfy. He'd made it that way to have something to look forward to at the end of a long shift. Pre-Hannah.

There was a large fabric corner sofa, a large dog bed in the same colour where Bullet was currently snoozing. It was neat like the rest of the house, the usual bachelor pad electronics and a large TV mounted on the wall. It didn't look quite lived in, like the rest of the house. Which was true, he supposed. Till Hannah and Ava had stayed those two nights. He'd missed them ever since.

Seeing her standing there in his house again, willingly too and not as a reluctant, skittish nurse determined to not owe him a thing, was still quite weird for him. He really liked it. They took the wine to the sofa, and when she sat down, he reached over and pulled her closer to him. He lifted his arm for her to tuck in underneath, but she pulled back.

'I have to tell you something first. I need to get this out. You might not want me near you once I've finished.' He was about to protest. He even laughed a little at the thought. He couldn't imagine walking away from either of them. Her words came first.

He heard what she said next, but it took him several rewinds in his mind to fully process what it meant. His arm had dropped to his side in shock.

'Andrew? I'm sorry for just blurting it out, but—'

He lifted his arm again, and she went to him this time. He held her close, and they both sat there for a second.

'You're not Hannah White?'

Chapter 20

'No. I'm Erin. Erin Nuffield.'

'Nuffield?'

'My married name.' Brody reeled inside as if someone had shot him, but his body was still. He still had her in his arms, and he didn't want to let her go. He knew that, as much as what she was telling him was blowing his mind. He'd been kissing a woman who didn't exist. He felt a twist in his gut as he thought of what that meant. Her changing her name and running meant she'd probably been through hell. He'd been on cases on the force. He knew how bad it could get.

'You're married?' he repeated. 'Ava's father?'

She nodded at the side of him. 'I can't get divorced – he'll find me. That's how they do it. I'd have to attend court for Ava. He'd fight me for her. I can't lose her. I live like a ghost. I don't use ID much; I use my new name to everyone apart from officials. I only use cash. He has access to the joint account.' Brody didn't tell her that he'd already picked up on the cash. John kept an eye on her at the shop. Once a cop, always a cop. Between the two of them, not much went unnoticed. Or they had thought not. He was kicking himself now for not connecting more of the bloody dots.

'I need to protect Ava from him.'

'You won't lose her. It won't happen. We'll figure it out.'

She shook her head. 'I just wanted you to know that whatever this is, it can't be more than this.'

'Whatever this is?' Brody shook his head. 'I'm pretty sure we both know what this is.'

'Yeah?' Hannah tried to pull out of his arms. He let her go immediately.

'Please, don't pull away. Talk to me. This is not "whatever" to me.'

'It's not to me either, but it needs to be. What about your job?'

'This is not about my job. I told you that before. I want to know what you think "whatever" is.'

'I like it when we're like this. Not fighting but . . . I don't know. You calm me. I trust you. I just . . . I like it when we're like this.'

'So do I, but that's not the answer.'

'He hasn't gone to the police; we would have known. The police would have checked my records. Found me. He'll be worried about raising attention. Which means he's looking for me. For us. To take us back. Lie to people about where I went. He's good at convincing people.'

'What about other people? Haven't they reported you missing?'

Hannah laughed then, but it was a hollow, choked effort that made Brody's heart break. 'I have Kate, my friend. My parents are dead, I left my job when I got pregnant. He never liked me working really. He got rid of my friends too, over time. No one to sound the alarm yet.'

Brody normally wouldn't stop thinking about the repercussions of all this, and what it meant. His trained brain would be flying through all the scenarios, the systems in place that could be accessed to help them. But that wasn't what he was focusing on. He was just pulling Hannah closer to him and holding her as she spoke. Telling him how isolated she'd been, and how she'd planned her escape and run for her freedom in the middle of the night. Not once, but twice. He felt nothing but awe for her strength, and he couldn't believe his own damn luck that Bullet had dragged him to the park to piss on trees that day. She'd literally landed in his life, and he'd known it was for a reason.

He'd seen the fight in her that day as she wrestled the mugger for the pram, and he felt it now in her voice. She wasn't crying, just finally telling someone in her new life about her old one. He was meant to find her that day because she was his. No, she didn't belong to him; she was her own person. That way of thinking was for the likes of her husband. They were just two people who belonged together. He would rather die than hurt her. He sat there holding her, listening. It was what he was good at.

Brody hadn't said anything for a long time, but Hannah had finally finished her story. He'd never let his body be out of touch with hers, not once. She'd seen the look of disbelief on his face when she'd blurted out her real name. It had soon given way to understanding though, a sobering look. He knew what it meant now. How difficult and impossible it would be for them to be together. She needed him to understand that; because she didn't want him to get hurt. And she knew she would not survive hurting him. She liked him too much. As daft as that was so soon, it felt right. She'd had a hard enough time letting him in, and now she had, and she feared the worst.

She was enveloped in his broad arms, and she loved every second of being there. He was too still for her liking now though. Frozen by the side of her. Was he realising that she wasn't worth the hassle? That she was too damaged for him to want now? She pushed herself off the sofa quickly.

'I'll just check on Ava.'

She didn't look back, but she heard him moving plates in the kitchen when she was in Ava's room. Ava was sleeping soundly, looking comfy. She leaned down and dropped a kiss on her head before heading into the bathroom across the hall. She used the toilet and freshened up, looking at her rather pale features in the mirror. *Well, that's it. He knows. You told him. He'll probably run for the hills, but at least he knows. You wanted him to wise up, walk away. Didn't you?*

She pulled a face at herself in the mirror, telling the voices in the back of her mind to shut the hell up. She was in charge now. She'd spoken her truth, and she was still standing. It felt bloody good. She could hear him letting Bullet out, and the back door closing again.

When she opened the bathroom door, Brody was standing at the bottom of the stairs. She stopped and, looking down at him, she went with the feeling in her gut and beckoned for him to come upstairs. He raised his brows but padded up the stairs to meet her.

'Everything okay?' he asked, but his eyes were focused on her lips. She reached up to run her fingers across his jawline. He made a noise at the back of his throat, and she reached up to kiss him. Just before their lips touched, she slowed.

'Will you stay with me tonight?' She knew what she was asking him. She'd just told him all her secrets and told him that there was no future. As confusing and rather brazen signals went, this was a strong contender. 'I don't really want to leave you.' It wasn't much, but it was true. She was telling him the truth, just like he asked. She didn't want to be alone. Not after opening that little box in her mind: her past. She didn't exactly want to spend the evening alone in a strange house, watching the shadows dance across the darkened room.

'I don't want to leave you either,' he breathed. 'I can sleep on the floor.'

He saw her frown before she could catch it.

'Okay.' She said it flatly, and her heart pumped wildly in her chest. Relief? Disappointment. 'If you want to. I meant together, in bed. Too much?' She'd gone bright red now, matching her hair. 'I'd like you to hold me.'

He shook his head. 'Not too much. Sounds good.'

157

He let her use the main bathroom, him using his en suite. He slipped on the shorts and a V-neck black T-shirt he'd brought to the bathroom, while she got ready elsewhere. He felt sick with nerves, and he was a little bit worried about sharing a bed with her. Being a man, if she got close, he knew his interest in her would be a bit harder than usual to hide. He usually just slept in a pair of boxers or nude, but that was out of the question. He heard her enter the bedroom. After brushing his teeth and checking out his face in the mirror, he opened the door to join her. She was already in his bed. *Wow.* It was a sight that knocked the wind out of him.

'You need anything?'

She shook her head. 'Thanks for tonight. It was lovely.'

'You're welcome,' he said back, slipping into bed beside her. He kept his distance, pulling the covers over him and making sure he hadn't hogged them. He felt a bit clumsy, oafish at the side of her. He felt like he was too big for the bed, now that there were two of them in it.

He stayed on his own side of the bed. It was strange to share with anyone that wasn't Ava again, but she liked the look of him as he came out of the bathroom. His legs were thick, muscular. She could see the thick set of his arms through his T-shirt, and she wished she could push the sleeves up, just to see more. His broad shoulders. He was absolutely gorgeous, and it hit her like a thunderbolt. He'd stood there in the doorway for what seemed like hours, but mere seconds had passed. Long seconds of her thoroughly checking him out and liking what she saw.

She couldn't read his face, which was gradually less baffling to her the more she knew him. She was learning to read him more day by day. He gave away more than he thought without words too. You just had to look – that was another thing she'd learnt. She felt a burst of pride that she was here, in his house. She was stronger than she'd ever been. She just needed to keep her resolve tonight. She'd only wanted comfort, but now they were here, it was . . . charged.

'Light on or off?' he asked softly, putting his phone on charge on his bedside table. The bedroom door was ajar, light from the landing a strip across the carpet.

'Off, please.' She wasn't afraid of the dark here. The thought thrilled her. She settled down under the covers, looking up at the ceiling. When she glanced across at him, he was eye level, on his back. Looking right at her.

'You comfy?' he asked awkwardly, and the pair of them burst into laughter. 'Sorry. That was lame.'

She giggled again. 'It really was! I'm sorry, I know this is weird, but—'

'It's not weird.' He turned on his side towards her, and her body followed his as if pulled by an invisible string. 'We're dating, and you were sleeping over anyway. I'm weird.' He dropped his gaze, but then his jaw clenched and his eyes were on hers. 'I want you here. Both of you. I know that this is new, and you have things to deal with, but I'm not going anywhere, Hannah.' He paused for a moment. 'Erin is you, and you are Hannah, and I like every part of you. I know you have Ava, and she comes first, but all I'm saying is you have me too. I really like you, and I don't say that lightly.'

'You don't say anything, from what I hear,' she quipped, and he rolled his eyes.

'I've spoken more to you than I have to anyone, apart from John. Believe me. He keeps ribbing me about the change in me.'

Hannah grinned then, thinking of their friends, always conspiring in corners and laughing with each other. They always wanted to spread the happiness.

'He's here for you too.'

'Does he know?' She froze, suddenly horrified that they'd been discussing her. Had Lola said something? She'd seen Hannah's ID – she needed it for her employment. When she took in the

159

name, she never said a thing. Hannah got paid in cash every week, a taxpayer. Erin got paid for Hannah's work, so to speak. She had nothing else. She would have to contact more people, risk more. Child benefit, for a start. Not that she had access to that right now. It went into the joint account.

'You can trust John. I won't tell him anything you don't want me to, but he's an ex-copper. A bloody good one at that. He approached me, mentioned some things. The cash. How nervous you get sometimes.'

Hannah sighed, but she said nothing. She trusted John and Lola, and they still employed her. They didn't ask her any questions. They'd been so welcoming to her when she'd first arrived, and she had to admit, she knew that Brody had told her about the job knowing that they would take her in. It didn't take a genius to work that out, and she didn't miss a trick these days. She couldn't afford to.

Brody had protected her from the minute she'd met him, but he never made her feel weak, or pathetic. He gave her time to think about things. There were no games or hidden meanings. He was unlike any other man she'd met. Not that she'd met that many, but the old cliché still screamed at her. The way he was around Ava, and the kids at the library. She took Ava now when he did his little shows, and she loved it. Bullet was like her very own bodyguard too. She had a vision of the pair of them walking towards the school gates, Bullet on the lead and Ava in tow. Her daydreams were expanding, and she didn't exactly hate it. It wasn't real though. This was what they had, but only till Victor found her. Even if she could stay, it would never look like her dreams. That would be too easy, too Hallmark for reality.

'What are you thinking?' he asked.

'That sometimes things don't turn out the way you want them to.'

He moved an inch closer, his hand reaching for hers. 'Given that this evening was a date I planned, and you're now lying here looking absolutely beautiful in my bed, that stung.' He squeezed her hand gently, bringing it to his mouth and dropping a kiss onto it. 'But I know what you mean. I have a bit of a different philosophy to life. I think that good things happen to bad people, just as much as the other way. I think that there's not much in life – nothing permanent – that can't be changed. It's not over, Hannah. Not by a long shot.'

She didn't say anything then, but she knew he wasn't going to let this drop. The full truth about her past hadn't come between them, but it would soon enough. Looking at him now, she knew that she had to make the most of just being here. She shuffled closer still and felt him freeze. 'Sorry.' She went to move backwards, but his hand was on her back.

'Don't be, I'm not.' He shot her a wolfish grin, and then they had the giggles again.

Chapter 21

Hannah woke up in his arms the next morning and floated to work. She left before Brody, eager to get to the childminders' and get an early start. Before the rest of the village woke up and watched her do the walk of shame out of his house. It wouldn't be that shameful of course. They'd kissed, but nothing more. He'd touched her skin in all the safe places, but she'd still really enjoyed his touch. She woken up more than a little frustrated, and as she woke up as the little spoon, she got the distinct impression that he'd been feeling the same. It hadn't been awkward, though. Ava had woken them up, having been a perfect angel and slept straight through the night. They'd just started their day together easily, and she'd left him eating toast that he'd made for them both, sipping his tea with his dog at his feet.

The second she got into the bookshop, Lola was on her. She took the decaf iced coffee from the cardboard tray that Hannah had brought with her, taking a big gulp and crunching on the ice. 'Oh God, that's better than sex.'

'I heard that,' John replied from the corner of the stockroom.

'I meant you to.' Lola called back in a singsong voice. 'I would make love to this drink in front of you both, right now.' She took another gulp, and then eyed Hannah as she sat down on one of the office chairs. 'Now, I have my beverage. Give me the details.'

'I'm in here!' John called again.

'Then leave!' Lola laughed, batting him away when he came out and tried to take a swig of her drink. 'Touch it, and I will never forgive you.'

John went in for a kiss instead and headed out into the shop.

'You would forgive me anything, darlin'.' He tipped an imaginary hat in her direction to match his faux cowboy drawl. 'I'll just be out here, earning my keep. You ladies put your feet up.' He winked at them both and shut the door behind him.

'God he's annoying, and gorgeous, all at the same time. The pregnancy hormones are fun, aren't they?'

Hannah laughed. 'Oh yes, I remember. Thrilling.'

'Speaking of thrilling,' Lola said. Hannah was drinking her caramel latte and she was grateful for the second to brace herself for the question. 'How was the date?'

'Good, thanks.' Hannah teased her, taking another swig and relishing the taste. She was having a fantastic morning. She was positively skipping, but questions made her think. 'He's lovely.'

Lola beamed. 'How lovely?' She waggled her eyebrows theatrically.

'Lola! We've only been on a couple of dates.'

'Yeah, a lot more than three, I think. I was just asking you know, in my hormonal state.' She let her voice trail off, but Hannah knew what she was doing.

'Stop bullshitting me! You want details!'

Lola made a vomit sound. 'Not too many. Brody's like a brother.' Then her face dropped with shock. 'So there *are* details! Spill!'

'We kissed.'

'I knew that.'

'Again I mean. We cuddled.'

'I cuddle my nana. Is that it?'

'We slept in his bed. Like I said, we kissed, and it was nice.' They'd done a little more than pecking. They'd really kissed, with

163

tongues, and teeth, and lips. He'd held her all night long. His body wrapped around hers. It was a hell of a date. 'It was great actually.' She bit her lip. 'I really like him, but it's just dating. Nothing heavy.'

She didn't miss Lola's frown, but she stood up to get to work not long after.

Three hours into her shift, the pocket of her work apron vibrated. She kept her phone on and with her these days. For Ava, Martine and Ruby. And Brody. She read the message as soon as she could, and it was him.

How's your day? I can't stop thinking about you.

Funny, I was just thinking about you. Pretty good. Lola and John are on top form. She knew he would groan when he read this.

I can only imagine. What are you up to tonight?

She thought of her night. She had Ava to pick up, some laundry to do. Other than that she was, as usual, quite free. She'd been reading loads, reviewing books for the shop, escaping for an hour into the pages of a happy story, on an evening once Ava was down. She'd got the television now, but it was barely on. Reading distracted her far more than the TV could. It wasn't her main distraction though. That was Andrew sexpot Brody.

She couldn't stop thinking about him, and after last night, she knew that they were getting closer. Very close. Too close. It was getting harder and harder to deny her feelings for him. The way he made her feel when she was with him. Victor tainted everything, and she feared for the relationship she was too afraid to properly start. She just couldn't stop though. He was in her head, her heart. Brody was part of her life now, and she couldn't imagine changing that. She pushed her fears away. It was just dating. He knew what the score was. She still found her stomach flipping as she tapped out a reply.

Nothing. You?

* * *

164

Hannah felt Brody approach the shop door. It didn't make any sense to her, but she knew he was coming. She was used to watching a man, sensing his moods, his presence. This was different. It was like her nerve endings woke up and signalled to her that he was there. She felt like an excited spaniel, frantically happy at the sound of the key in the front door.

A second later, the shop bell rang and he was standing in the doorway. He wasn't in uniform, and she could tell from his still slightly damp hair that he'd just showered. He'd only finished work an hour ago – she knew his shift patterns now. She was dealing with a couple of customers, a father with his little boy. He was looking at the comic books, and his dad was trying to steer him to the football annuals. She'd spent the best part of half an hour talking to them in the children's section, and she was just ringing up their numerous purchases. The father did a pretend gasp when she told him the total, and his son giggled at the side of him.

'It's a good job you're worth it,' he said, giving his son a nudge and getting one back. Hannah was smiling at them both, when she saw Brody's face, and her smile disappeared. He kept his distance till they had left, the brown paper bag full of books swinging from the young lad's side. Brody said goodbye to them, but when they were through the door and down the street, he turned the open sign to closed, and clicked the lock shut.

'We need to talk,' he said, a stricken look on his face. When she went to walk over to him, he pulled a sheet of paper out of his pocket. He pushed it into her hands. 'John?' he called out. 'You there?'

Hannah looked at him, but he was already striding into the back. Something was off with him. He was all business, his back ramrod straight. He barely looked at her, but when he did, his eyes were cold. Swallowing, she looked at the paper in her hands. She didn't read the headline of the poster, or the words. She just saw her face. Erin's face.

* * *

165

The four of them sat in the back office, Lola drinking from a bottle of water, the rest with a stiff whisky in their hands from John's office stash. Hannah had gulped the whole thing down, relishing the burn it ignited in her throat. She looked for the bottle, and Brody was there, sitting next to her, refilling her glass. She noticed he filled his again too.

'Who else knows?' John asked, his face as dark as his former partner's. Lola wasn't saying much, just cradling her belly, one hand wrapped around her water bottle. Hannah looked at Brody.

'My friend Kate, I rented the house from one of her friends. She knows where I am, but she won't tell. He's already tried to talk to her. She said she'd not heard from me. He doesn't know what good friends we were. Are. He must have found something that led him to her. She was my midwife.' *He didn't know because she'd kept it from him. Just like everything else she wanted to cherish.*

Brody's eyebrows lifted. Erin Nuffield. Missing person. The flyers were posted up in Leadsham's outskirts, Brody having seen one on a lamppost. He'd driven past it while on the job. The fact it had been ripped in half wasn't lost on her, and looking at him now, she could see how unhappy he was. The whole room was filled with sombre faces, and she hated herself for coming here. For bouncing into their lives and putting them at risk. Brody. John and Lola had a baby coming in mere weeks, and now they had all this on their doorstep. John nodded at her, but he was looking at Brody. She realised that he hadn't been talking to her at all. Brody looked at her, but she looked away.

'I haven't told anyone at the station. Yet.'

Hannah stood up from her chair. 'I have to go, now. I'm late for Ava.'

She needed to get out of there; she couldn't look any of them in the eye. Brody's hand was around her arm in seconds.

'I already rang Ruby. Told them I wanted to take you out. They offered to have her for the night. I said you would ring them when you got a chance. Let them know your plans.'

166

Another pair of people she cared about who were now involved in her deception.

'Why did you do that? I still need to pick her up!'

Brody pushed her gently back into her seat. 'Ava doesn't need to see you like this. She's safe there. I'll take you to pick her up after if you like. I'm not trying to muscle in or take charge, but we need to get in front of this, Hannah.'

'I agree.' John's words were like steel. 'We need to go to the force, get them involved.'

Hannah laughed, but it was a bitter, hollow sound. 'I went to them before, but they didn't do anything. He convinced them it was just me, being dramatic, and they believed him, told me they couldn't do anything. They made it worse, not better. I didn't have Ava then either. I won't let him have her. If I go to the police, I'll be arrested.'

'Bastard,' Lola piped up.

'That's why the flyers are there. Don't you think he would have reported his wife and child missing if he could? Dragged me back, kicking and screaming? Got Ava taken away from me? He wants this kept quiet. I'm not missed, Andrew; my social circle wasn't exactly massive. I can drift right out of my old life, if he'd let me. But if he gets me back there, I'll never get out again.'

'It doesn't mention Ava at all,' Brody confirmed, nodding to the torn pieces of paper. 'The photo doesn't even look like you.'

'Haircut,' she ventured. 'Plus, I'm not permanently terrified like I was in the photo.'

'It's more than a bit of a different hairstyle.' His words were clipped, and when she looked at him his jaw was clenched so tight she feared he'd crack it in half. 'It doesn't look like you at all.' Their eyes met, and she finally saw it. He wasn't just angry, he was incensed. 'The way you look, your expression, everything. It's not you.'

'It's an old photo.' She looked again at the flyer, at herself. It didn't look like her. Not the Hannah that she was now. She was so close to happy, and the picture reminded her just why she left.

The woman in the photo looked haunted. 'It was taken a while ago.' It felt like forever.

'I prefer your hair now,' Lola said, nodding to the photo. Hannah heard Brody mutter 'agreed' under his breath. 'What are we going to do then?'

'I'm going to leave,' Hannah said, once again trying to get up. Brody and John stood with her.

'No, Hannah, you're not going anywhere.' But Brody didn't block her, and when she grabbed her bag and went to leave, he didn't stop her. She heard him call her name, but she wrestled with shaky hands on the main shop door, crying now with fear and frustration.

'For God's sake, just open!' She grabbed the handle, rattling the door hard against the lock. 'Damn you!' She tried again, this time unclicking the lock and wrenching the wood out of the frame. She was halfway down the street, when Brody's voice was there again. It was well after shift now, the ending of the day's heat already making its presence known. She tried to get her phone out of her bag, to call Ruby, a taxi, but her hands were so shaky she could barely open the zip.

'Hannah, wait!'

She felt her fingers close around the phone, but she decided to keep walking instead. She wouldn't make sense if she spoke to Ruby right now.

'Hannah, stop! Please!'

She heard his footsteps behind her and turned to face him.

'Where are you going? I told you, Martine and Ruby have Ava. She's fine.'

'I need to get her. I need to go home.'

'I'll take you; you're in no fit state to go alone.' He paused, taking in her shaking body. 'Leave Ava where she is tonight. She'll be nearly asleep now anyway.'

She knew he was right. He knew Ava's routine. He paid attention, but that just seemed to scare her further. Ava knew him now; he was in their lives. *All your fault. I told you, you can't do this alone.*

'I can't wait, I have to go. Tonight.' She half screamed her words, drowning out the blasted voice in her head. She didn't want those voices back in her life. She wasn't that person now. She wouldn't be again. She had to keep running.

She went to move, but Brody's hand stopped her in its tracks. She rounded on him, trying to pull his arm away.

'Let me go!'

'You're really leaving?' His voice was bleak, as if he couldn't quite believe what he was hearing.

'I have no choice! He's getting closer. I am not going back to him, and he will try to take Ava. Don't you get it? He'll never let me go!'

'Neither will I.' He put his hand on hers, taking her bag gently from her hand. 'You've been drinking – you can't go to Ruby's in this state. Ava is fine, I promise. We need to stick together on this. John said—'

'I am not involving John and Lola. I've already caused enough trouble, and I don't want any of you dragging yourselves into this.'

'We want to help. They're your friends, and I—'

'I can't involve you either. Not anymore. I don't want this to affect your life.'

'What life?' he asked, suddenly furious. 'What life, Han? Before you, I had work, and friends, and Bullet. That was it. I thought it was enough, but it's not now. It's never going to be enough now. You can't leave. You would be leaving me, and I won't give up on this.' He leaned in, taking her face in his hands. 'I'm falling for you, Hannah. I've fallen. You didn't see me when I saw that poster. I was at work, and all I wanted to do was to get here, to you. I don't want you to run. Not ever again. Please, stay here. Stay with us.' He stabbed the air behind him. 'Stay with me.' He reached for her hands, and clasped them in his, over his heart. 'Stay and be with me. I'll keep you safe; I'll help you to fight.'

169

As he wiped her tears away, she finally calmed down. Her heart stopped feeling like it was going to explode out of her chest, and her shaking lessened.

'I don't want to be someone who needs to be saved. Ever again.'

'I never said you did.' His lips twitched into a smile. 'You gave the mugger a good go.'

She laughed, thinking about how determined she'd been not to let go, how hard she'd fought. That was her. 'I was terrified.'

'I know, but you did it. You protected yourself and Ava. More than once. Let me help you keep doing that.' He wrapped his arms around her, and she went willingly, kissing him before he could say anything else. Anything that he said would make it harder for her to walk away from everything. Harder to walk away from him. He kissed her again, but it was much more than before. He was showing her everything he wanted to show her about who he was, and she wondered again to herself how the hell she'd shared a bed with him the night before. If they were in bed right now, she knew she would never stop kissing him. And she wouldn't stop there.

'Move in with me,' he said, pulling away only enough to get his words out. He still had her bag in his hand. 'You've only got a bit left on your lease. Wait till it's done if you want. If you need time. Give up the house and move in with me.'

Hannah felt her heart stutter in her chest. Live with another man? Give up her little house?

'I know.' He grimaced. 'It's a lot, but honestly, Han, it's not about your situation. Well . . .' He bit his lip. 'It helps the situation we're in, but it's not that. I want you with me. Since you stayed over those nights, I missed you. Both of you. It felt right. No pressure. You are your own person, Hannah. I just want to be in your life, and if I can make it that bit easier for you, it's a bonus.'

170

Chapter 22

He'd driven her and Ava home that night, parking the car right outside her house without a word. He was different now; his easy smile wasn't as visible. He'd asked her to stay over at his again, given that he had Bullet to get back to, but she'd sent him home. He'd walked back, leaving his car where it was.

She couldn't think when he was there, wanting to know what she was thinking and feeling. She couldn't just move in with him – that was madness. She wanted to give him the chance to take it back. It was far too soon. Even with the feelings they had for each other. The whole of Leadsham could see it. She'd had feelings like this before though, and imagined a rosy life. Victor had given her that in the beginning. No red flags. Sure, he had a quick temper sometimes. He got a bit grumpy when he was tired. Or hungry. Things build up. No one expected to leap from the frying pan into the fire, but the saying didn't exist without a reason. She didn't think that Andrew would ever hit her, but people broke up. They grew apart. Even without the stress she and Brody had looming. If they broke up she'd have to leave, and she liked it here. She didn't want to uproot again.

Some of the customers were friends to her, and she realised that while she often felt alone, she never really was. She could be the real her, and people liked her. After those first few weeks in the house, just her and Ava, she thought that that would be her life. Alone. She'd accepted it readily, but now she had the flyer in her purse, reminding her of the threat posed to her, she didn't just feel scared. She felt out of control again, like someone had reattached the strings to her puppet body when she wasn't looking.

It wasn't so much that she was scared to see her husband. She was, but she was more terrified of losing her new life. As Hannah, she felt more like herself. She'd been lost before, but now she realised *how* lost she had been. She wanted that full life. She wanted Kate to visit, to meet everyone, to see her, laugh with her again. Spend time with Ava. They'd barely seen each other before, and she loved her. She wanted to be able to have this life, and more. She didn't want to run, she realised. As she checked the locks on her house one more time before going to bed that night, she thought about Brody. He'd been so serious when he'd asked her, but not like it was a surprise to him. She knew from his face that it was the truth. This wasn't something he'd only just considered.

This only confused her answer even more. It was hardly for the right reasons. So fast. It could just be lust he felt; the feelings might wane with the pressure. Was it pity even? She didn't that from anyone, let alone him. If she thought anything was from pity, she would leave and never go back. She couldn't bear it, not from those around her.

He said he was ready for this, but was she? If it didn't work, it would be awkward. She'd be right back where she'd begun. Homeless, needing a new start. She worked with his friends, lived around the corner. Heck, if she and Ava lived with him it would be even worse. She thought about what to do for the best and settled under the covers. She wasn't following her gut, she realised. She thought back to how she'd felt when he'd asked her. It was more than shock she'd felt. Reaching over in the near darkness for her phone, she checked the time. It was a little after ten. She brought up their messages, reading his last few to her. He hadn't been in contact with her since he'd left, and she respected him for giving her space. But she realised she didn't want space anymore. She wanted to live her new life.

You awake?

It was a good ten minutes before he answered.

Yeah, you okay?

I wanted to ask you something.

Ask me anything.

She laughed at his familiar shorthand. Frowning, she pushed all thoughts of her past from her mind and went with what she wanted for her and Ava.

Would you really have asked me to move in this fast if we didn't have this issue?

His reply came back in seconds.

In all honesty? No, not quite yet. I've thought about it a million times. I would have wanted to, but I wouldn't have wanted to rush you. It is what I want though, long term and now. Issue or not.

Would we share a room?

Up to you. Ava can have the spare room either way. I can even sleep on the couch if you want, downstairs.

She didn't want to think of him on the couch and thinking of him next to her night after night, she suddenly had a realisation. To do this was a huge risk. Once she gave up the house, she wouldn't get the same deal again. She'd lose the last few months she had to save. If she relaxed, she'd lose her urgency. Her savings weren't enough to make her feel comfortable. She only just had enough to live on, and her lease was running out fast. She needed to know that this would work. For all of their sakes. She didn't want to explode another life. Holding her breath, she typed out her message.

I have another question, and it's a big one.

Try me.

I think we should sleep over again, before I decide.

Nothing. No telling sign on the screen that he was typing a reply. Or typing and deleting several replies.

'Oh God, you've scared him off. He's changed his mind.' She groaned, hiding her head in the pillow and screaming into it. She pulled her face out of the pillow and replaced it with her fist. She pounded it a couple of times, and then her phone beeped. 'Shit.' She dived for it on the bed, dreading and desperate to read the reply.

Will have to be at mine. Pack some overnight clothes. Bullet and I are coming to pick you both up in ten.

She read it three times before she squealed in shock.

'Oh my God!' she screeched. 'Oh my God.' She looked at herself in the mirror. She was still in her jogger bottoms and an Aerosmith T-shirt. She jumped out of bed, running to grab her holdall.

He'd taken her bag and her hand, and they'd walked back to his house, barely speaking. Pram wheel squeaking the whole way up the street. Ava had transferred like a cute little sleeping burrito. Once they were inside, he'd locked up, and then turned to her with an intent gaze.

'Thinking about my offer, aren't you?'

'Yes,' she told him. She didn't want him to take it back, but she needed to be there with him. To spend time with him, to give him the chance to really consider his offer. She wanted him to be sure, and not just reacting to save her. She would rather never see him again than that. 'You? It's a lot, Andrew. We're still so new. I think we should find out how compatible we are before we live together, threat or not. Having a baby live with you full-time is an adjustment in itself, without the rest. I thought a sleepover might help.'

'I agree.'

'There's still time to back out.'

'Don't need it.' He was up close to her. 'Can I kiss you now?' Ava was sleeping in a travel cot, settled in the spare room.

'Do you have anything to ask first?'

'We've kissed before. I know what's what.'

She laughed, and his grin widened.

'I didn't mean that.'

'I know. I like you, Hannah. We're together, aren't we? I want this to work. It's soon, yes, but I don't do things I don't mean. You and Ava are part of my life now, and this is the next logical step.' His brows shot up. 'The moving in, I mean. The sleepover is a nice surprise.'

'Logical step?'

'Yeah.' His brows furrowed. 'No. It is logical, but that's not why I asked, Han. I really think this could work between us.'

'Okay.' She swallowed nervously. 'We're on the same page then.'

'Yep.' He kissed her, and she relaxed a little. She was going to live with this man. The thought danced around her head. The voices stayed silent. She knew it as much as they did. She and Brody fit together. He was so calm, so kind. He knew her, and she loved how he handled himself. Watching him with Ava was mesmerising, as much as he was by everything she did. She trusted all of that.

'Brody?' she said softly to him.

'Andrew.' He scowled a little. 'To you, I'm Andrew.'

'Andrew,' she breathed, and he kissed her that bit more fervently. 'How do we do this?'

His brow raised, and she laughed at his expression. 'This, this? Or moving in together, this?'

'Moving in together.' She laughed. 'Do you have a plan?'

'I'll show you,' he teased, giving her the filthiest grin she'd even seen on him. He looked at her lips, his smile turning rueful. 'I just want to hold you tonight, Hannah. There's no rush for the rest. We have no need for a plan tonight.' His kiss was so soft, so sincere. She couldn't help feeling a little disappointed.

'Are you sure?' she asked. He groaned, kissing her forehead.

'I just want you to relax. Spend time with me. No rush for the rest if you're not ready, okay?'

His jaw dropped.

'I meant the talking. The ex stuff. Not . . . that.' He kept his gaze steady. 'No rush for anything.'

She pouted without realising, but he spotted it. 'Hey, trust me. I would like nothing better than to be really, truly close to you.' He took in her form then, his words giving out. She heard him swallow. 'You dressed in my sweats is something else.'

That released a grin from her lips so wide she thought her face might crack. He laughed at her delight. 'I just want you here. We've got time. That's enough for me.'

The way he'd led her up the stairs and held her close had told her everything she needed to know. She was going to be moving in. *Rebound, mistake.* The words had flicked across her brain, but she refused to listen. She went with what she felt. 'Okay, we can try living together.' He descended on her again, kissing her hungrily.

'Really? You want to?'

'Sure, let's see what happens.'

He has curls, Hannah thought to herself as she reached for one, rubbing it gently between her fingers. The light was dim through the closed curtains. She could see the sun was barely rousing. He stirred as she ran her fingers lower along his neck. Across his broad shoulders she teased, her fingertips tracing a soft line right to the end.

'That's nice,' he rumbled. He reached his arm back under the duvet, wrapping it around her as he turned. She ended up in the nook of his arm, and her fingers started to chase along his muscular chest. He was fit, in every sense of the word. When she thought of the way he'd looked at her when he stood on her doorstep the night before, Bullet next to him, her tummy flipped.

'What time is it?' she asked him. He glanced at his watch, pulling her closer for a squeeze before heading to the bathroom. She watched him walk around the bed half naked, till he caught her.

'It's six a.m., perv. I thought you were asleep.'

She threw a pillow at him. 'Am not!'

'I saw you looking, and not just today.' He waggled his eyebrows at her, and she glowered at his laughter behind the en-suite door.

'Oh yeah?'

'Yep,' he called. 'You only want me for my truncheon.' He laughed again, and she smirked as she got out of bed. She had the day off, John and Lola not taking any arguments to the contrary, but she wanted to get up and go get Ava from the spare room. She'd missed her, like she often did when she'd been asleep.

Ava was still fast asleep, so she left the door ajar and let her sleep a little longer. She dressed and headed down the stairs, flicking the kettle on to make them a coffee. The letterbox clanged, and she jumped. Padding into the hall, she saw the local paper sticking out of the slot. She took it to read with her coffee. There was nothing out of the ordinary. Her face wasn't on the front page, and there was no mention of her. She shook her head, feeling ridiculous all of a sudden. She folded the paper in half and slung it on the kitchen worktop.

'That bad?'

He was dressed in sweats and a tank top, and she marvelled to herself at the sight of him again. It was corny, but they were still so new. She still appreciated different things about him when he walked into a room. Right now she was just replaying the highlight reel from last night in her head. The kissing. The way he'd held her. They'd laughed in bed too, about silly things. It was such a revelation to feel so happy. What had happened to get them here, deciding to trial living together, was the last nail in the coffin of her marriage – not that it needed one. She saw it as a huge leap for freedom. A very enjoyable one at that. With more to come. She walked to him, and he wrapped her into his arms without hesitation.

'You smell nice. Ava having a lie-in, eh?'

She inhaled his scent. He smelled of the shower. Soap, shampoo. Spicy. 'Yeah, I thought I'd let her sleep a bit longer. You got time for breakfast?'

He shook his head. 'No, I'd better go get ready. Sorry I have to work today, but I'll call when I can. I'll have to be fast.' He pulled a face. 'I snoozed my alarm, didn't want to leave my bed this morning.'

She grinned as he pulled her in for a long kiss. 'Ring me anytime if you need me, or the station. Or John. Have a good day.'

She kissed him again, not wanting to say goodbye just yet. She loved how he didn't smother her, but she could see from his tight expression that he was worried. He'd called out her name in his sleep. Just the once, but he'd been tossing and turning, and she didn't like that this was affecting him so much. John and Lola too, and with the baby coming. She was lying to people, had always been lying to people. Now people knew, and they were worrying too. She couldn't bear that and the fear together. She had to pick one life, and fully live it. She didn't want to drag anyone into her trouble, but she wasn't going back.

Ruby answered their front door with a full dinosaur head on, complemented by indigo blue dungarees and a top so bright it made a rainbow look like a streak of mud.

'Morning! Come on in.' She pulled her head off, brushing her hair out of her eyes.

'Sorry about last night.' Hannah hovered on the doorway, Ava in her arms.

'Don't be daft. Listen, come through. Martine's okay at the minute. The chaos hasn't started yet. Ava can play with the others, eh?' She sang the last sentence to her daughter, taking her from her arms, and the bag, and disappearing behind the door of the chaotic, child-filled room. Before Hannah knew it, she was back and ushering her into the kitchen.

'Now, about last night?' Hannah looked at Ruby, wondering what she knew.

'Yes, I know, I—'

'Brody asked us to babysit.'

Hannah dreaded the next question. She hated lying. 'What's up, Ruby?'

Ruby looked at her as if she was being stupid.

'What's up?' She started laughing. 'Tell me about the date!'

'He never said that!' Hannah barely got to tell her about Brody's offer before she erupted into shocked, delighted gasps.

Her response wasn't unexpected. It made Hannah laugh. Ruby had obviously wanted to quiz her since she'd shown up to collect Ava the night before, Brody in tow. He was trying to be chilled about everything, she knew. He was hiding his concern for her. Very badly. She could see right through him, but she liked him all the more for it. He really was a teddy bear, with a gruff grizzly coat.

'Shhh! I don't want everyone knowing.' She spooned another half teaspoon of coffee into her cup, groaning as Martine came running over. Ellie from the village had arrived for her shift. They were so busy at the minute they'd taken on more trained staff, who were currently giving the children breakfast. 'Please, keep it quiet,' she whispered in vain.

Ruby bounced on the spot, clenching her fists. 'This will kill me though! When you came round last night, I thought something was wrong you know. The looks on your faces!' She leaned in closer. 'Kept you up, did he? Need the caffeine?'

Martine jabbed her in the ribs. 'Give up with her!'

'You haven't heard what she said yet!' Another jab in the ribs from Martine. 'Ooow!'

'Oh come on, no one's listening here. We won't tell anyone.' Martine was watching Hannah with a very different expression from Ruby's. She'd been the same the night before. She caught Hannah looking at her and busied herself with making some juice and milk pitchers up for the toddlers. 'Can I tell Martine?' Ruby half begged.

Hannah rolled her eyes, but they would know soon enough. If she did decide to move in with Brody wouldn't that draw more attention to herself? The rumour mill would be in overdrive. She looked at the two women. 'Listen, I'm a very private person. I really don't want people knowing, but I trust you two. Do you understand?' She wanted to trust them. She'd come today to show she was fine, to assuage any ideas of something being wrong in Camp Hannah. They had to know Ava's correct address anyway – she would have had to tell them eventually. It was Leadsham, after all. For a woman hiding herself for so long, it was a freeing feeling. Now she wanted to spill her guts about her news. Friends told friends things like this, right?

Ruby looked excited, her face full of joy. Martine took a minute to smile, as though something had passed between them that Hannah didn't understand. She put her hand on Ruby's shoulder. 'Hannah, I promise you we won't tell anyone a thing about you, or Ava. Friends never tell.'

Hannah smiled at them both. 'Okay, well . . .'

Chapter 23

The two women led her back through the hallway, into the large open-plan dining room and kitchen. It served as a great play area for the kids and went into the garden too. Ava was sitting at a highchair, enjoying a second breakfast by the look of things.

'Mama!' she said, clear as day.

'Oh my God!' the women behind her said together. They held each other, jumping on the spot.

'Has she said that before?' Hannah asked, desperate for the answer to be no.

'No! I swear, that was the first time! Clever girl, Ava!' Hannah gave Ava a huge hug, Ruby holding her fist out. Ava formed a podgy fist and touched it to Ruby's. Ruby turned round and beamed.

'I DID teach her that though. She said mama! That's amazing.' Her face frowned a little. 'Oh damn, we didn't get to video it.' She looked at Hannah who was looking at Ava with tears streaming down her face. 'Oh love, bless ya!' She reached for a hankie from the dispenser on the sideboard, and Hannah took it.

'She said mama, not dada. I thought babies usually said dada first.' He'd gloated when she'd told him that from the pregnancy books. She shouldn't have told him, of course. She learnt what to hide eventually. He was so excited to be a father to everyone on

181

the outside, looking in. He made all the right noises, but barely bothered in reality. When the novelty was bright and shiny. Since Ava had started babbling and trying to make sounds, Hannah realised now she'd been dreading the word the whole time.

'Well,' Ruby said, moving to sit both of them down. Hannah sat down without complaint, and Ruby put her arm around her. Ava was busy spooning porridge into her mouth, with mixed success. 'Not always. My first word was "bubble", apparently.' She grinned when Hannah laughed. 'I know, I was ahead of the curve, even then. She saw you, and the word came to her. It's as simple as that.' She pointed at Ava, who was now repeating her new word and showing her teeth as she laughed at herself. 'Look at her, Hannah. She's thriving, she's happy. You're her world, and that's why she said mama. Now.' Hannah felt Ruby's fingers on her arm. 'Are you going to tell us what's going on?'

Hannah looked at her daughter, laughing and enjoying the moment, safe and happy. This is who she was in Leadsham. She was mama, and she was here to stay.

'I need your help,' Hannah said. 'I have things to tell you, things you might not like. If you don't want to get involved, I won't say a word against you. I just think it's time you knew.'

Ruby shook her head, and Hannah's heart dropped into her boots.

But Ruby said, 'You're a friend, this is what friends do. Tell us.'

Reaching into her bag for the item she'd gone home for before bringing Ava here, Hannah passed it to Ruby.

'This is mine. Was mine. In another life.'

Ruby opened the purse and saw the driving licence registered to Erin Nuffield. With Hannah White's face. At the side of her, Martine didn't look shocked. 'Fuck. I knew it,' she muttered. 'You really are one of us.'

When Hannah looked at Martine, the look between the two women before her made everything click. Martine wasn't surprised; she was remembering. Ruby pulled her close.

'I got away too,' Martine said. 'Before Ruby, I was with a man.' She clenched her fist over her heart. 'You won't have to do this alone. Not on our watch.'

The three women embraced, and Hannah wondered just how many people had their own pain, behind the smiles. She hated Victor all the more for being part of the problem.

'Thank you,' Hannah said, and held her friends tight.

At six o'clock that night, Hannah walked into Leadsham Police Station, Ava in her pram. She pushed it right up to the desk, grateful that the small waiting room was empty. It wasn't the biggest police station, and she felt a little less intimidated. She waited until the female officer behind the counter had finished typing on her computer screen before speaking.

'How can I help you?' The officer smiled, and it gave Hannah the impetus to speak.

'I need to report my husband,' she said, as clear as a bell. She clenched her fist and pulled the flyer out of her pocket. 'I left my husband due to him beating me, controlling me, not allowing me to work, and threatening our child.' She put the flyer down in front of the officer. 'I ran away from him, and I took my daughter. I have evidence to prove my story.' The officer didn't say anything, and Hannah could barely catch her breath. Her heart felt like it was trying to bounce out of her body, and her head was full of screaming voices, all telling her different things. *Run.*

Leave and run. Don't ever stop.

She won't help me.

Please help me. I deserve my own life.

'He's after me,' she pushed out of her mouth. 'The flyer is from him. He hasn't been to the police, because he knows that I already did. Before.' She had records on him after all, from reporting him in the past. 'I ran away. It was wrong, but I don't deserve this.' She pulled her daughter back, so the officer could see her. 'I did this for her. So I know you asked if you could help me, but was that just what they teach you to trot out?' She could feel her fear turning into anger now, her past visits to other officers coming to mind. They had tried to help, she supposed, but the law was the law. 'Or can you actually help us to get out of all this?'

The officer licked her lips, rubbing them against each other before replying.

'Yes, I can help you. Come through.' She buzzed the door next to her, and they opened automatically. The officer was standing there, and she held up a finger as she spoke into the radio.

She asked for another officer to return to base, and then turned back to Hannah.

'Let's go find a room. Are you safe right now?' she asked.

Hannah looked her over before answering. 'For now.' She nodded, and the officer nodded back, a determined look on her face.

'Good, my colleague is something of an expert in these cases. He's on his way back in now.' She looked down at Ava and opened a door behind her. Inside was a comfortable-looking family room. Couches and a small toy area. Secluded from view, with tempered glass and low blinds.

'In here?' Hannah asked. She had been thinking of some grotty interview room.

'Yes. You'll be fine here.' The officer showed her where everything was. 'Right, drink?'

Hannah nodded. 'Er, yes. Please.'

'We have some juice for the little one, in the fridge over there. Won't be long.' She closed the door after her, and Hannah felt herself relax a little. She wasn't in handcuffs quite yet then, for kidnapping her own child and living under a fake name. That might still come, she knew. She'd read enough news stories to know that the abused didn't always have the law on their side. The kidnapping was true anyway. She'd not given a false name on anything official. She'd been careful. He'd told her enough times what he'd do if she tried to get away. He'd get her sectioned, or declared unfit, then take her daughter. She would rather die than let him take Ava. He would rather kill her than let her live without him. Then what would happen to Ava? It would be too much to ask of Kate, and so his parents would raise her. They saw no wrong in him, or if they did, they never acknowledged it. If Victor even went to prison. If not, it would probably end up being him bringing Ava up . . .

Forty long minutes later, the officer returned with a colleague, and coffee. They all sat down, and Hannah started to tell her story.

It was late when she finally returned home. Ava was fast asleep in her car seat. Brody had driven to pick them up. He pulled straight up to his house, and she let him take them and their gear inside. She felt like she was on autopilot. Her legs worked, but she was bone-tired, and she had spoken so much that she felt like she didn't have any words left. She felt dirty and cleansed at the same time.

Ava was changed and settled straight back to sleep. As soon as her eyes closed, Brody took Hannah straight to the en suite.

'Ruby and Martine got some of your stuff from your house. I thought it would be better than me going through your knicker drawer. I put some bits in here for you, something to wear.' She nodded at him dumbly, and he leaned in. Lifting his hand, he hooked his finger and put it under her chin. Tilting her to meet his eyes. 'What can I do?'

He sounded so earnest, so desperate, she kissed him. He stilled, pulling back. 'Hannah?'

'You're already doing everything. Just hold me.'

He held her tight, and when she kissed him again, he didn't pull back.

When they were showered, fed, and lying in bed, she told him about what had happened. The police had been helpful, and would be on the lookout for any suspicious activity. They'd verified her ID, and advised her to seek legal advice when she could, to start divorce proceedings and custody agreements. They'd spoken with her new GP, who had verified the child's reason for visiting, and the healthy wellbeing of the child and mother. With the fact that Brody had told his chief about their relationship the same day, telling them of their intention to live together, they seemingly had nothing to worry about with his job either. The fact of their relationship would be kept from Victor, and Brody would be firmly off the case.

They seemed far more concerned with finding Victor on their patch than dealing with Hannah, or Erin as she was. After all, no charges had been filed by Victor. The flyer was with them now, and Hannah felt better not having it with her. She'd been surprised it hadn't burnt through the cheap lining of her bag.

Brody listened without speaking, just holding her as the little spoon as they lay under the covers. It was easy to tell him things without looking at him, and not seeing his reactions. When she was finished, he turned her to him.

'Well, tomorrow morning the four of us can get away if you like. I have some time off work arranged, and Lola's mother is going to be in town for a while, so she is going to help in the shop. No pressure, but I have already done a little bit of packing. Don't freak out on me, okay? It's not set in stone.'

She didn't speak for a full minute, and he didn't flinch.

'How much packing?' she asked with an arched brow. She caught his smile, pulling him in for a kiss. 'Where are we going to go?'

The relief on his face was obvious. 'The beach. I have a friend with good contacts too. Private. We don't have to go, but I did have leave. I thought it would be a good time to get out of Leadsham for a while. Nothing's booked that can't be cancelled. A mate owed me a favour.'

Hannah did what she relied on. She answered with her gut. 'The beach sounds good right about now. A trial extension, eh? A holiday, with a one-year-old? Good luck,' she teased.

Brody grinned. 'No freak-outs. That's a good sign. It's going to be just the ticket. Trust me.'

'I do.' She pulled him close once more. 'I really do.'

Chapter 24

The second they'd seen the Leadsham exit sign in Brody's rear-view mirror, Hannah started to focus on the trip ahead.

'So, what are we doing to do there?'

'What aren't we going to do! Crabbing on the docks, walking on the beach, making sandcastles with Ava.' He looked in the rear-view mirror. 'Hot dogs.'

'Woof!' Bullet agreed.

'I can go stock up; we can get the barbecue going on a night. It's going to be good.'

'Sounds like a pretty packed weekend,' Hannah mused.

Brody replied without missing a beat. 'I took a week off; we don't have to rush.'

Hannah gawked at him. 'A week, I can't! Lola's due to pop soon, and the shop?'

'Her mother is in town from today, and if you met her mother you would know that everything is in her capable hands. That woman makes Mary Poppins look like a slacker.'

'What about John?'

'Luckily, she adores John. Absolutely loves the man, so he'll be happy she's there too. We're not going to the moon. If you want to go back, we'll just go back.'

'No.' She shook her head quickly, laughing off her worries. She'd taken off into the big blue yonder before, but this time she actually felt good. Like she was heading to some fun. Ava was chattering away in the back, making them laugh when she danced to the music. She had learnt the word 'dog' now, and so Bullet was now just 'dog' to her. He was sitting in the back, chipping in now and again. Mostly he just sat and watched the cars. Ever on duty, Brody would tell her. She noticed that his eyes constantly searched too. When they'd hit the motorway, his shoulders had sagged with unmistakable relief.

Where they headed, near Bempton Cliffs, was a small place. A few holiday homes, each with their own enclosed gardens and play areas. Close to the shops, but even closer to the beach. They only had to open their back gate, and they didn't have far to walk till they felt the sand on their toes.

'This place is great!' Hannah said as Brody opened the front door. There was already a suitcase there sitting in the hall. One she didn't recognise. 'Who . . . ?' They were standing in the hallway, Bullet in the back of the car. Ava was in Brody's arms, asking for Bullet and reaching for the front door. 'Dog! Dog-og!'

'Hi, Erin.'

A voice behind her made her want to run.

'Kate! How!' She turned around, but Brody held up one of Ava's hands with his. 'How did you—'

'Not guilty. It was Lola.'

Lola. She really was a force of nature, that one, just like Kate. She was going to regret ever giving Lola her number for Kate, in case of emergencies. In case he came. She had evidence. Photos, medical records. Things Hannah had managed to sneak to her. Nasty little notes he left her at home. Proof of the bastard he was. She knew the score. If Hannah went missing, or shit went south with the police, Kate would take everything she had to the authorities, shout it from the rooftops if needed.

'Well, thank God for Lola!' She went to throw her arms around her friend, and Kate pulled her close.

'I'm so glad to see you,' Kate whispered into her ear as the two women cried together. 'I'm so glad you're both okay.'

'So, what's going to happen?'

Kate was cradling a glass tumbler of wine in her hands as they sat together on the couch much later. Ava had eventually tired herself out, so excited to see her auntie Kate that she'd burned through her energy even after napping in the car.

'I don't know. The police said that they would be looking out for him. They can't exactly contact him without tipping him off. Since all he did was put up a flyer, they can't arrest him. I'm lucky that they didn't arrest me, I think, for taking Ava. I think Andrew and his friends must have intervened on my behalf. I never used the Hannah White name for anything official. I just took Ava from him for her own good.'

'Using a fake name isn't the worst thing in the world, and they can see that Ava is cared for. Did you give them my details? I already told you I can testify, Rin.' She'd always called her Rin back then. She had had the best midwife known to woman. Thank God for her. Ava was the reason they'd met. A midwife seeing the bruises of an expectant mother and not turning a blind eye. A real friend, by the end.

Hannah nodded. 'Andrew said that they'd try to keep you out of it as much as they could. How did you get away from work, with your shifts? I didn't have a clue you were coming.' She wondered once more at just how much Brody did without even saying a word. It wasn't all down to Lola. 'How bad has it been?'

Kate looked across at Brody, who was busy indoors shuffling bags and boxes around in the kitchen. He'd been unusually quiet since they'd arrived. It unnerved Hannah. It was quiet even for him. Whenever she caught his eye, he had such a strange expression on his features. She didn't understand it, but he looked like something was eating him up.

'What did Brody tell you?'

Hannah's eyes were back on Kate's now. 'What do you mean?' 'He followed you?'

'Don't freak out.' Kate was sitting next to her, and Hannah was sitting on the couch trying to catch her breath.

'How did he know where you were? Who you were?'

'He followed me from work. I've had a few hang-up calls. Heavy breathers on a withheld number. He must have dug something out, I don't know. I got the security guards to flag his plates and keep a log. I'm safe. He knew we got on well that first meeting; the son of a bitch must have worked it out. It's okay; they challenged him last week, and he hasn't been back since. He doesn't know anything. It was just a hunch I think, on his part.'

Hannah smiled ruefully.

'It wasn't hard. I was on my own and he knew it.'

Brody walked back in, a plate of snacky bits in his hands.

'Sorry.' He put the plate down. 'Didn't want to interrupt.'

Kate yawned theatrically. 'Well, I need to get to bed anyway. I have to get back tomorrow. I just wanted to see you both.' She beamed at her friend. 'You look great. Ava is doing so well.'

'Thanks.'

'Rin, I mean it. She's good.' She looked across at Brody, and when she looked back, she waggled her eyebrows and stuck the tip of her tongue out at Hannah. 'You both are, by the looks of it. I'll be on the road early, so I have to sleep.' She looked a little sad. 'Keep going, okay? Ring me when you can.'

She said her goodbyes, smushing Hannah in a tight hug. As she did, she whispered, 'He's great, Rin,' in her ear, and when she caught Kate's expression, she could tell it was nothing but approval she felt. Relief perhaps. She'd been scared for them both, angry at the need for her to run at all. Railing against the system. 'Keep in touch. I meant what I said about the witness statement, and I'm not the only one in your corner now.' She winked at her.

'Be careful,' she urged her. 'Call the police if he shows up again.'

Kate nodded, and as she passed Brody, she reached up and hugged him too. Brody looked surprised, and his eyes searched for Hannah's. She was smiling her head off.

'Well done, big guy,' Kate said, tapping him on the back as she left. 'Night, you two. I'm in with my niece by the way, so night duty is on me.'

Brody came to sit down next to her, and she fit perfectly into the nook of his arm as always. With her hand on his chest, she could feel his heart beating in the quiet of the room. 'Does that mean she approves?'

Hannah laughed softly, enjoying the feeling of being close to him again. It was a cliché, she knew, but she really did feel safe in his arms. Like she could sleep, and nothing would even get close enough to touch her dreams.

'Shall we go to bed?'

'I can take the couch.'

She raised her brows at him.

'This little couch?' She smirked when he registered the size of it. 'Well . . .'

'Come on, you daft bugger.' She stood up, taking his arms with her. Of course, he was so bulky that the second she tried to yank him up out of his seat, she pinged straight back onto his lap. He laughed, catching her.

'Okay, I'm coming.' He suddenly rose to his feet with her in his arms, putting her neatly down before him. 'Lead the way.' She could barely find her feet after that. Such power. It was as though she were a pillow, not a full-grown person. It made her coil up. Just for a second, when he'd moved so fast, so easily. It had scared her. Just for that second, before her brain registered she wasn't back in a situation that might hurt her. She didn't say anything as she took his hand and led him upstairs. They got into the bedroom, and Hannah noticed that the other bedroom door was shut tight. *Kate.* She laughed in her head. Brody closed the door behind them, but he didn't move any further. When she turned to look at him, the room still dark and only lit by the last of the daylight between the open curtains, he looked upset.

'What's wrong?'

'I was going to ask you the same thing. Did I scare you, just before?'

She closed the distance between them, and her hands were on his chest once more. His heart was racing – she could feel it under her fingertips.

'Not at all. It wasn't that. I just didn't realise your strength.' From the look on his face, she could tell she hadn't explained herself enough. He didn't look happy. He looked gutted. 'I don't mean like that. I know you, and your job, your training. I know how strong you are, but you are so gentle with me, it was just a surprise when you moved so quick. Not a bad one either.' She reached up and brushed her fingers down the length of his face. He relaxed a little, his shoulders not quite reaching the ceiling now. 'I'm not made of glass, Andrew. That's all I'm saying. I'm not broken. I won't break.' And she knew that she wouldn't. Nothing would take her down; she wouldn't let it. She hated that her past was always there, between them. 'I wish I'd met you sooner.' He took her into his arms then. 'I wouldn't swap Ava for anything, but I wish . . . I don't know.'

'Hey,' he shushed her. 'You're here now – that's what matters. We have the rest of the week to ourselves.'

'Now that sounds good. Are you sure it's not putting people out, though? What about your job?'

Brody chuckled, taking off his clothes slowly as he spoke. 'The guys are sick of seeing me. Normally my boss has to force me to take my leave. Trust me, everything is in hand. We can forget the world here.'

193

She knew what he said made sense, and she wanted that. To be here, spending time with the pair of them without the rest of it, but she still had screaming doubts in her mind about the whole thing. She'd tried to hide in a distant corner of the earth and get through the next few years alone. Now, she seemingly had a whole village of people willing to fight her corner within months. It wasn't just her and Ava anymore.

As she undressed and slipped under the covers beside Brody, who took her in his arms the instant she got close, she knew that she couldn't give any of this up. She had a life now, one she actually wanted. No one was going to take that from her without a fight. She even thought that this week would be a real test for her and Brody too. One of those tests would be not succumbing to sleeping with him. She had been keeping him at arm's length, nothing more than kissing and touches of her skin that made her want to jump his bones. He was patient, never pushing. Making love felt weird to even think about, but she kept coming back to those words. *Making love.* That's what it would be. And quite possibly sexy as hell and wild as well. It was going to be a hard week of nights at the beach.

Kate had gone by the time they got up, wanting to drive home when the roads were quieter. She'd left a note saying goodbye, telling Hannah to stop stressing and enjoy the break. Ava had woken with the dawn, and Hannah had padded through into the other room and collected her. The two of them were sitting having breakfast when Brody came into the room, wearing a low-slung pair of grey jogging bottoms, pulling on a black T-shirt.

'Good morning, ladies,' he said jovially. Bullet barked at him from his place under the stove. 'Bullet. No bacon for you, big guy.' The dog whined in response, and Brody gave him a look. 'Nope.'

He went to kiss Ava on the forehead, coming away with a bit of cereal on his chin. He flicked it off, laughing. Ava went to give him some on her spoon, and he sat next to her in her highchair, pretending to eat what she gave him and making the funniest little noises. Ava was delighted, squealing with laughter. Every now and again she'd waggle her spoon in excitement, sending more bits of sticky globs flying around the room. He didn't bat an eyelid. Hannah watched the pair of them, absorbed in their game and each other. He was so gentle with her, so patient. A huge lug of a man with a big scary-looking dog, and the pair of them were wrapped around Ava's little finger.

She had a sudden flashback to her old life. It burst into her head, and she tried to block it out, but snapshots kept coming. Flashes of feeling afraid, unsafe in her own home. A place that should be a comfort but felt like a gilded prison. Of being shouted at to "shut the kid up" because he couldn't hear the TV, or him moaning about Ava spitting up on his favourite shirt. She felt her breathing get heavier, so it was harder for her to take a solid breath at all. There was an invisible malevolent force, pushing on her chest and cutting off her air supply. She drew in a gasp, and Brody's eyes flicked to hers. He moved his chair closer to hers, putting his free hand on her lap and giving her leg a comforting squeeze. She reached for it with both hands, gripping it for dear life, and he leaned in further. She felt the hardness of his body against hers, a solid rock to lean on while she weathered the storm swirling around her. She leaned into him closer, feeling the warmth of him envelop her.

'I don't want to be like this anymore,' she heard herself utter. 'I don't want to run. I want a divorce. I want us to be like this. All the time.'

Brody's eyes were on hers, and he wrapped his hand around hers. 'Then don't run. Don't freak out. Freak out on me, but not without me by your side. Let me be something to lean on while you fight this fucker.' He said it with a steely glint to his words, like he'd been waiting for her to tell him as much. 'Stay, in Leadsham. With me, and Ava and Bullet.' Bullet barked at the side of him. 'I won't let you go through this on your own.'

She leaned in and pressed her lips to his. Right in front of her daughter for the first time. He jumped, his head turning to look at Ava, who was watching the pair of them with a big sticky smile on her features. Hannah cupped his stubbly chin between her hands and kissed him again. 'She knows who you are to me, Andrew.'

He smiled, wrapping her into him as Ava laughed at them both, still banging her spoon away on her tray. 'Good,' was all he said. 'Whatever you want to do, I'm ready.'

They spent the rest of the days at the beach in a blissful bubble of solitude, and they were the best few days of Hannah's new life. Brody knew this because she kept telling him, over and over as they spent time together. They were like a little family, him and his dog, and Hannah and her daughter. Brody loved them both fiercely, and he knew Bullet felt the same. It was scary and exhilarating all at the time same, but Brody knew what he wanted. He'd known it since that day in the park, and being here now, seeing her laugh and smile, he knew that he wanted this forever.

Hannah was different here, he realised. This week had been another revelation. She'd shown him so much more. Still on edge, at times, but she was more relaxed. More of Erin made herself known, but it was still his Hannah. Just . . . amplified. Gloriously sexy and amplified. He could see it in the way she walked on the beach, not caring that she was barefoot, her long trailing skirt wet from the sea spray and little clumps of sand. She'd carried Ava right up to the water, leaning down so that her child could stick out her pudgy little hands and touch the sea for the first time. It had taken his breath away, watching the two of them together. He'd held back, way back on the sand, his dog at his feet, and observed them. He felt like he didn't want to encroach on their little moment of freedom. The freedom he knew that Hannah was feeling every bit of in that moment.

He took a couple of photos on his phone, wanting to keep the memory for them all, but mostly for him. So that he could remember how she was, if she changed on their return to Leadsham. So that he could remind her of that feeling, of how good being on that beach without a care in the world had felt.

'You ready?' He'd been up with the lark that morning, taking his coffee outside and watching the sun rise on their last day away. He'd felt rather than heard her at the side of him. She watched the morning with him for a moment, and then they headed inside.

'I think so.'

He passed across his coffee mug, and she took it with a smile. Raising his arm, he waited till she was tucked into his side before he spoke again.

'Are you really ready for this? We can do other things you know; we could move . . . I could put in for a transfer . . .'

Bullet barked at the side of him, but Brody shot him a warning look. He didn't want to leave, of course not, but he would for her. For them, to keep them safe. For her to stay that woman on the beach.

'I don't think Bullet's quite on board.' She brushed him away with her words, but he shook his head.

'It doesn't matter, it's just . . . stuff, Hannah. I don't think you get it.'

'I get that I came crashing into all your lives, with my moods and my secrets, and now everything's tense and difficult. Lola's pregnant, John's got his own stuff to sort through, and you . . .'

Brody laughed then, and it came out a little hollow. Hannah was wiping Ava down after her breakfast, and he waited till she was sitting on the play mat a little way away before he spoke again.

'I wasn't . . . anything, before you two arrived. I went to work, I had my friends, my routine. That day in the park, you blew me away. The minute I laid eyes on you, I just had this feeling that you were meant to be there. I can't explain it, and I don't think I need to.' She was busying herself with the dishes, picking things up, taking them to the sink. Methodically, like a robot. Like she did when they'd first met. He turned in his seat, and she finally stopped.

'Can you put that plate down, and come talk to me? Don't let this week get spoiled. Don't hide from me now. Please.'

She looked down at the plate in her hands, as though she'd not even realised that she'd been holding it.

'Sorry,' she said to the plate. She worked it through her hands, like an eager learner driver. *Never cross your hands. Nine and three. Ten and two. Why am I thinking about that right now?* He waited, giving her time and space to work it out. She wasn't fully in the room, and they both knew it.

'No need to be sorry, Han. Will you come sit with me?'

She put the plate down on the side, before picking it right back up again and putting it away with the others in the cupboard. She came to stand at the back of the chair she'd just vacated, but instead she turned, and slowly sank onto his lap. Brody took the weight of her easily, pulling her closer to him and stroking her hair back from her face.

'You're so beautiful,' he whispered to her. *I love you. Please don't shut down.* It hurt to keep all of the things he wanted to say to her in his mouth, in his head. He had never been so full of words before. She'd brought him back to life, and she didn't even see that.

She rolled her eyes, breaking into the little embarrassed smile she sported that always made her look so cute. She never rated herself, and one day he wanted her to see the woman he saw. The woman who had blossomed these last few months, all on her own.

'You're not so bad yourself,' she said back to him. 'It's been so nice, being here with you.' She looked at Ava, who was busily banging one block against the other with a very determined look on her face. 'All four of us, it just works, doesn't it? I . . . we never really had that before.' She sounded happy about it, but her face told a different tale.

'And you don't trust it,' he offered. He caught himself thinking the same sometimes, but for a different reason. He couldn't believe he had them in his life, and she didn't trust that he would stay.

If he could really show her how he felt, she would never worry about him leaving her or letting her down. The irony was, if he told her *how much* he felt, she would probably run a mile, and he couldn't risk her upping and leaving. The thought of her rocking up to a different town, struggling on her own with Ava, it was one of the two scenarios that kept him up most nights. When he wasn't sound asleep with her in his arms. 'I get that. We don't really know each other that well. It's been fast.'

'I know you better than I know most people,' she retorted. 'It's not you, Andrew. Really it's not – I just don't want to be a burden, and I don't want any trouble around anyone I care about. I don't want to lose my life, or you. He'll try his best to smash everything. I know it. He won't stop. When we go back to Leadsham, it's not going to stop. He will find us, and spread his lies, and I'll have to leave again or stand and fight. I'm trying, but I can't even face going back in the car. Leaving here.' She choked back a sob. 'You don't know him. I feel like I'm destroying you.'

Brody felt his jaw clench, but she didn't notice. Instead of clenching his fists, he held her a little tighter instead. 'The only thing that would destroy me is you two not being with me. You're not a burden to anyone.'

'I know, but I feel like one, and that matters. I don't want to live like this anymore. I just don't. It was always going to come to this. I needed to come out and speak, but I still have a lot to do. I don't know why you'd want that in your life.'

Brody felt stricken, but he didn't utter a word. She didn't get it. He was in. He couldn't have gotten any of the words he wanted to say out of his chest. They congested there, burning him from the inside out. She took her face in his, moving closer onto his lap. 'I'm saying I'm going to fight. I'm going to go home, and fight like hell. I'm going to fight for my life, our life. I just want you to know it won't be easy.'

'I don't scare easy. Get ready to be picked up, okay?'

Brody had picked her up off the chair without registering the motion, and he spun her in the air. She giggled her head off, stopping abruptly as his hands froze in mid-air. Lowering her face to his, he kissed her till she ran out of breath entirely. When they came up for air, giggling like a pair of idiots, they knew that it wouldn't be a picnic. They clung to each other at every opportunity as they packed up the car, checked over the property and settled Ava and Bullet into the car. They drove the long way home, stopping for a lazy lunch in a country pub off the beaten track. Ava ate like a champ, and the owners were only too happy to feed a very well-behaved and well-admired police service dog too. They ate their hearts out, talking about what came next, and when the time came to travel the last leg, Ava fell asleep as soon as they hit the road, and the pair of them held hands the whole way home. He pulled up outside his house, the question of where they were going to sleep never addressed. They walked out of that car as a family, a very united and determined fledging.

The whole way home, the words he'd whispered in her ear after her speech played over and over.

'Hannah, I thought you were leaving me. Nothing will scare me like that again.'

Hannah heard the bang of a pan and stirred from her slumber. Turning over in bed, she saw that Brody's side was empty, and cold. She laid back, running her hand over the pillow he'd slept on the night before. They'd stayed up talking long after they'd locked up for the night. Finally, she'd not been able to keep her eyes open a moment longer. *Ava.* Ava was quiet. She jumped out of bed, jabbing her toe into the side of the frame.

'Arrggh, shit!' she exclaimed, before walking straight into Brody in the doorway.

'Whoa, here's Mum!' Ava was in his arms, looking like a tiny doll as always, nestled against his huge frame. She was already dressed in a really cute outfit she recognised from their holiday purchases, and she had a face full of red sticky jam. 'We just had breakfast,' he said with a rueful smile. 'Heard you crashing about.' He looked theatrically around him, as if the house was falling down behind her. 'Panic, did you?'

She rolled her eyes at him. 'Maybe. You should have woken me.'

'And miss breakfast with this one? To be honest, I was awake anyway, and Bullet was cross-legged. You got work today?'

Hannah shook her head. 'Nope, free as a bird, thanks to Lola's mother, but I do have something to take care of, so I might take Ava to the bookshop anyway. What about you?'

'Ah well.' He nodded to Bullet, who was sitting by the door. 'I have to nip into work, get some paperwork done before my shifts start again. Do you fancy meeting up later?'

'Come to mine?' She leaned up for a kiss to distract him. 'I should get my post, check the place over. I think the new tenants are due soon.' The owner of the house had even offered to refund some of the rent since she was leaving early, but she'd refused. She could never repay him for what he did for her. She was glad he'd found a new tenant so quickly.

'Text me a time, I'll be there. Have a good day, ladies.' He kissed them both, and he was on his way out of the door minutes later. Hannah looked around for something to clean, but the house was as neat as ever. The man obviously hadn't slept much at all. She got Ava ready to go out and headed out of the door to the bookshop. She thought she heard footsteps behind her a couple of times, and she turned to look a couple of times more. She didn't see anything but the trees blowing in the wind, the odd passer-by she recognised as a regular. Her grip tightened on the handles of Ava's pushchair, but she managed to will her feet to take a normal pace, and not break out into a run. Progress, yet again.

She heard the footsteps again just as the bookshop came into view, but she didn't trust herself to look again till she was inside the place with the pushchair she'd bought on payday. She'd sold the pram and made a bit of a profit. It had been top of the line. Victor would be livid, and she liked the thrill of that.

Whoever the walker was, they were a passing dark shadow at the window now, still heading up the street. She couldn't see them clearly through the panes, but they had their hood up against the wind in any event. She was still staring when she heard Lola's voice behind her.

'Hiya! How was the holiday? Any gossip?'

Hannah took two steps to the door, wanting to stick her head out into the street and check for the man, but she turned instead with a smile. *It was just a man, Hannah. Get over it.*

'Well, it was pretty great.' She motioned down to Ava. 'I'm sorry to ask this after everything lately, but could you watch Ava, just for a little while? I need to make a call.'

Hannah walked out to the little crop of trees, just off the parade of shops. Lola had waved her off with a slightly worried look on her face, when she'd told her what she needed a babysitter for. She'd not said a word though, she just smiled and took Ava from her. Her mother was busy running the shop like a tight ship. She looked just like Lola, and was just as nice. A maternal type Hannah couldn't help but warm to immediately. She'd melted like a puddle at the sight of Ava. She was a very eager nana.

She'd left them reading a book, snuggled on the beanbags in the kids' corner. John was in the kitchen, but he'd stayed out of the way. She could hear him though, singing to the radio and clanging the odd utensil around from time to time. She'd once caught him playing the drums with some wooden spoons, singing an Oasis song at the top of his lungs as he toasted paninis on the grill. He was at home in his kitchen. From what she'd learnt about him, which wasn't much as he was quite tight-lipped, was that he was damaged too. From a case similar to her own. And healing, like she was. In different ways she knew both her and John saw the bookstore as a lifeline. A cosy place of escapism that was much needed given their realities. The ones they'd escaped from. He was happy in his kitchen, his pregnant wife nearby, his old station and his colleagues close. She knew he would be the first running up the road if anyone ever needed him. That was John, and Brody.

Andrew Brody was surreal. She often found herself looking at him, wishing she could meet his parents, see him as a child. Work out how this big, brutish-looking hunk of a man was so kind, so gentle, and so honest. He was an angel sent from heaven, her mother would have told her. If she had been that kind of mother. She'd never really known her. Hannah had always just kind of imagined the types of things that mothers said. She read about it in books, watched it in films. Her own mother had done her best, but it had been a rough ride growing up. She'd never been the hands-on type, not the mother Hannah wanted to be for Ava. She'd repeated the patterns of her mother in some ways, sure – picking the wrong man – but she'd broken the cycle too. She'd left, and now she was going to stand her ground.

Taking her phone out of her pocket, a new throwaway SIM card installed for the purpose, she slowly sank down to the grass, laying her coat under her as best she could to avoid staining her clothes on the soft ground beneath her feet. She needed to do this and be able to walk back into that bookstore and hold her daughter without breaking down. Without feeling she was running for her life, terror-stricken and traumatised once more. She crossed her legs, and after dialling a familiar number she despised, she held her free hand into a tight fist, enjoying the sting of her nails in her skin as the number rang out. Once. Twice. The line clicked open, and she held her breath.

'Hello?'

She didn't say anything.

'Erin? Is that you?' He sounded panicked, heartbroken, but she felt nothing but icy dread. She knew him too well. He was simmering. She could feel the crackle down the line. He was playing a part. What a shame for him she knew he was a crap actor.

'No,' she replied, blinking back a hot tear and keeping her voice steady. Deep. 'Erin is gone.'

'Gone,' he stated, his voice a little flatter now. 'Where did she go, eh?' She heard the click of a lighter and closed her eyes. Him and his fucking flip lighter. She hated the sound of it. 'Erin, talk to me.'

'Erin is dead,' Hannah forced out, her voice taking on a flicker of anger of its own. 'You killed her.'

Chapter 25

'I killed her, eh? What is this game you're playing, Erin?'

'No games,' she spat back. 'I told you, Erin Nuffield is gone, and she's never coming back.'

'Your name is my name, Erin. You're married to me. Ring a bell does it? You took my baby. You ran off, and took our daughter. Our daughter, Erin. OUR DAUGHTER. What the hell is going on?'

'You know what's going on. We left because of you. I changed our names. We have a new life now, and I'm ringing to tell you that you need to stay the fuck out of it. You will never hear from me again.' The tears came now, but her voice didn't shake once. She clenched her fist tighter, to take the edge off her panic, but then stopped herself. She was hurting again, for him. No more. Her tears stopped.

'That's what you have to say to me? Who the hell do you think you're talking to? Tell me where you are, Erin. I'm already looking.'

'Oh yeah, what did the police say?' She put her hand down on the grass, grabbing at tufts and pulling them from the earth. 'Did they put out a missing person's report?'

'Don't push it, Erin. Tell me where you are, right now.'

'No! This is not how this works. You will not see us, not like that, ever again. We are not coming home. I'm going to fight you, every step of the way. So tell me, what did the police say?'

'You fucking bitch.'

There it was. She'd poked the beast good and proper now. She swallowed hard but kept it up.

'I didn't think the nice act would take long. I've been to the police, Victor, and they know all about you, and our horror show of a marriage. Stay away from us, I mean it.'

'Or what? Who do you think you are?'

'Or the police will come for you, and I'll go to court—'

'You ran off with my kid and didn't tell me whether you were alive or dead. I know your mother was a bit of a scatty bint, but I thought you were better.'

'You leave my mother out of this. You're not father of the year.'

'Shut up!' he boomed down the line. 'I love Ava. Tell me where you are now!'

'You love Ava? Really??' She threw a huge clod of grass at the tree stump in front of her. 'You could have fooled me.'

'I did though, didn't I? For long enough? We have a kid together, Erin.'

'Don't you even say my name.'

'You belong with me, and I'll call you what I like, Erin. You need to stop this and come home. This is going to get bad if you don't. I'm closer than you think.'

She felt her heart stutter to a stop and didn't reply. 'It doesn't matter how close you are, Victor. What was before will never happen again. Don't come near us. Leave this alone. Goodbye.'

She heard the rage of him, shouting down the line, but she ended the call, and when he rang back a moment later she turned the thing off and smashed the SIM card to pieces. Leaning back against the biggest of the trees, she processed the call. Replayed every detail in her head. He could be close. She wasn't stupid – she knew he was rather adept at this. She had hoped to gain something from the call. An idea of his state of mind. What he knew. Where he was. It was easy to read his moods, with the amount of practice she'd had.

From early on in their relationship, his attentiveness was nice. He'd really noticed her; he took an interest. After her upbringing, being first on someone's list was something she'd never experienced before, and for a time she'd loved it. Till it got a little awkward. Him turning up to her nights out with friends, getting her to come home early. One time he'd even caused a huge scene because she'd been chatting to a male friend. Someone from her old neighbourhood, who she'd bonded with over their equally shitty upbringings. That night had been the first time she'd looked at Victor and seen who he really was, but by then it was too late. Their lives were linked, and when Ava came, her world got smaller and then shrank altogether. Till it was just her and Ava.

She knew that she'd incensed him, and she hadn't done it to be cocky, or to make things worse. She'd needed information. She wouldn't be able to contact him. Once he was arrested, it would be through a wall of people. She needed to read his state of mind. How close he might be. She'd needed to tell him how she felt. For her own sanity. A tick of the checklist back to sanity. Back to herself, and her future.

She'd felt those words inside her for so long. Saying them to Victor now felt good. She'd longed to say them to him. To be able to tell him that they were gone and never coming back. Keeping what she wanted to say to him close to her chest a minute longer was unbearable. She'd needed him to know that the Erin who left was dead. She'd died in that house, on that bedroom floor. It had been Hannah who had scooped Ava up, got her bag and walked right out of the door with her. Fleeing to Kate's where her stashed stuff was waiting. To a new life, with friends, and a job. Independence. Poverty at times, fear ever there. A man in her life who had helped her grasp her future.

But the fear wasn't there now, she realised with a smile. She'd told him, she'd *showed* him that she wasn't going to just keep taking his shit over and over. She wiggled her toes, checking her nervous system wasn't tricking her, but she was here, and feeling freer than she had in a long time. After putting her old SIM back into her phone, she half skipped to the shop, and didn't see the observer, watching her from the shadows in the car at the top of the street. She was far too happy to care right now, and she couldn't wait to tell Brody.

Brody grabbed a large ham and cheese baguette from the display cabinet, rolling his eyes at Officer Reymond as he asked for a salad bowl. He knew he'd be hungry again in an hour and moaning on their shift.

'You sure that's going to fill you?'

Peter Reymond shrugged him off, picking up the dressing sachet from his plate and drizzling the oily contents over his large salad. The whole thing would be about fifty calories, and Brody knew he was going to regret his choices.

'Yeah, I had a big belly buster this morning at the greasy spoon, don't tell Angie.' His wife Angie worked in the control room, and she was like an all-seeing eye. She knew everything about everyone, and she wasn't afraid to say it either. 'She's got me on this health kick. We had tofu burgers last night.' The face he pulled told Brody that he didn't approve.

'Ah well, she's doing it for your own good.'

Peter had had a heart attack the year before – too many quick lunches out on the job. It was easy to grab a microwave hot dog from a petrol station, but they added up with the long hours and odd eating times. Brody had seen a few men arrive with six-packs and see their waistlines expand. The job took its toll. Luckily he had Bullet to run around with, and he kept himself fit. Lately, with the sleepless nights and the white-hot sexual frustration of being so close to Hannah and not yet making love, he'd been hitting the gym a fair bit too. He didn't want to cross that last line, not when she was going through so much. He wanted her head to be clear when it finally happened. All two and a half seconds of it. He frowned at his own bad joke.

'I know, but seriously, mate, some of the stuff.' Peter patted his belly as if he was apologising to it. 'It just don't agree with me. I'm losing weight, but I'm not sure it isn't just the crapper talking.'

'Nice.' Brody winced. 'Listen, not to change the subject, but I wanted to ask a hypothetical.'

'Oh yeah, is this with my internal nose, or my copper nose?' Peter knew the law and the police handbook, and he would know what to do. ''Cos I have been apprised of your situation. Off the record, of course.'

'John Tucker called you,' Brody said with the lift of a brow.

'Tucker called me. He's not doing that well with being off the case, so to speak.'

'We don't want another loss.' Peter nodded with him. Brody knew he remembered the case too, the one that had caused John to give in his badge. The domestic violence case that kept occurring. They'd both tried everything to get the victim out of the situation, but she was so fearful, so controlled by a man who played the law like a fiddle. One night, they had been called again, and it was over. Having to tell her family and see the case through had taken a lot out of their community, and the officers involved. It was the kind of thing that didn't happen in places like Leadsham, and the villagers had had a rude awakening to the real world when it had. They were healing now, but he knew that there were many Hannahs out there, and not all of them were free. 'Work know about us, but what if he shows up? She had to file a report, right?'

'Right, for the child especially. Taking off with his child does complicate things, but proving why she ran – she has that?'

Brody nodded, not wanting to say anything that she wouldn't want spoken to a stranger. 'She left with what she could get.'

Peter tapped him on the arm, a meaty slapping sound as he connected. 'We've got your back, lad. Eat up.' He nodded to the baguette and speared a piece of lettuce with his fork. 'And get me a sausage roll before we go, I'll eat it outside.'

Brody nodded, and the two men ate. As he headed back on shift, his phone buzzed. Hannah had text him.

I called him. I know you said not to, but I had to say it to him. Before he gets caught. I told him I'm going to fight. See you at mine, 6 p.m.? Brody tapped a reply back, telling her he couldn't wait. He didn't want to comment on the other thing, not by text. He didn't want to put his stamp on what she was going through. She'd changed since they'd met, and he needed her to feel that independence. It wasn't the best move, but it was done. He was strictly hands-off on the case. He'd already got her living with him, and he knew she wasn't entirely happy about it. The circumstances at least. The swift nature of it. He didn't tell her that really he was glad that she was doing it so quick. He didn't want to be that guy; it felt like he was preying on her situation almost. He didn't want to be a person who made her feel like that in any way. She was her own person, and he loved her for that.

'It looks like things are in motion,' he told Peter as they got into the van, ready to go search a housing estate where some of the minor players had been scouted. A couple of the residents had been supplying bits of information, and they were about to take down three of the properties in one swoop. John always called it a 'shakedown' because when they hit, everything was taken into custody, be it evidence from the places or the people who scattered when they came knocking.

The rest of the afternoon was hectic, and Bullet was on the ball as usual, helping to bring in a big haul for their afternoon's work. There was a lot of paperwork to be done, but the empire was crashing down around Big Phil's ears. It was a thing of beauty for the officers and their months of hard work, but Brody was more looking forward to getting home that night and seeing Hannah.

* * *

When Brody arrived at her old bolthole, Hannah was already sitting and waiting for him, on the couch playing with Ava. The rest of her possessions were in a couple of bags next to the pram. He must have walked over from his house. She never heard a car, but she knew his big strides by heart.

'Good day?' she asked as he sat down next to them. Ava immediately went to him, and he tickled her till she belly-laughed.

'Yeah, it was as it goes. You okay?' He looked flushed, so she knew he'd had a good day at work. He shone on the good days, like the sense of achievement was fuelling him.

'Good. I called Victor, like I said. He didn't like it, but I told him what I needed to.'

He kissed Ava's fingers, and she dropped her little head of hair onto his chest. He covered her with his left hand, stroking her back and took Hannah's hand in his.

'She's getting tired.'

He stood up, lifting Ava on him without moving her an inch. 'Come on then, let's walk home. I left Bullet there.'

He put Ava into her pushchair and took all the bags from Hannah as she locked up for the last time. She had no further link to this house, but she couldn't help but feel thankful, and a little sad. The charity shop was taking back what she didn't take with her. The manager had taken her to one side.

'We're still here, remember. And we'll donate what you gave us.' Her brows had raised in question. He'd patted her hand. 'For the next brave woman in need.' She'd hugged him tight before leaving. She'd go back there, she resolved. Help give back. They'd helped make her rented little house into a home. It had been Ava and Hannah's first home, the first one that mattered.

She turned the key in the lock, but she didn't take it out.

'When we first moved here, you know, I was a wreck.' She reached out and touched the wood panel with her palm. 'It was cold, and the heater wasn't great. We had nowhere to sleep, so we slept on the floor. I had to haggle in charity shops to buy

211

furniture. No one would hire me.' She could hear Brody putting the bags down, and she wanted to turn to face him. She wanted to post the keys through the door like she'd promised the landlord and walk away. To Brody's house, Brody's bed. She wanted to hop, skip and jump right into her new life. She just couldn't take the key out of the lock – not yet.

'Do you need time?' Brody was standing with his hands by his sides when she turned to face him. 'Oh God. Han, I knew I'd rushed it. If you need more time, I can get a patrol car to come by once in a while.'

Ava was busy trying to pull apart her picture book, not bothered by the scene one bit. Hannah watched her as he spoke. She knew that her child wouldn't remember this, any of it, and she was grateful. For the most part. If she remembered anything from the time in this house, it was more than being scared. 'I can wait, Hannah. I feel like I pushed you—'

Her hand left the door handle. 'Don't you ever think that. You did nothing but give me time. I'm not scared to leave. I'm grateful to this house. It wasn't all bad. This was our home.' She kissed him on the lips, slow and soft. 'I was just reflecting. That's all. I'm not the same woman who slept on that floor. It's time to go.'

'You sure you're ready?' He chewed his lip as he looked from her to the door. 'Shit, Hannah, I feel like I'm making things worse. If you need to stay at the house, I can . . .'

'Brody.' She stopped him. 'No patrol cars, I told you. No panic alarms. No pepper spray. I was just saying goodbye to an old friend, that's all.' She pulled him close to her, taking the key out of the lock for the last time. 'I'm ready for what comes next, believe me.'

'Have you not dropped that kid yet?' Mrs Barclay, one of the bookshop café's loyal customers, was always to the point. It was lucky Lola's mother Peggy had gone home. Lola had insisted, because her mother's mothering had driven her pottier than the lack of coffee did. Lola managed to keep her cool at the rather awkward and personal statement of her current distress by the woman before her.

Despite this, Hannah loved Mrs Barclay. She planned to be a version of her when she was older. She never kept the truth in, and tact wasn't much something that she was concerned with.

'You must be fed up to the back teeth.'

Lola, who was currently sitting in one of the comfy chairs in the corner, huffed back at her. 'No, I'm fine. Just a few days overdue – nothing major.' She was sitting and sipping a raspberry-leaf tea, looking like she wanted to take the belly off like an itchy cardigan. It was a warm day in early summer, and the open windows were doing little to dampen down the humidity. Mrs Barclay shot a knowing look at Hannah before leaving with a fresh cream cake and half a dozen of her favourite crime reads. The second the door closed, leaving the two women alone, Lola continued, replying, 'Except for the fact that she doesn't want to come out.' She scratched at her bump, moving the elasticated waistband of her trousers into a comfier position. 'I farted on John last night. Not near him, but on him.'

Hannah pushed a copy of *Pride and Prejudice* back into place on the shelf and tried not to laugh. 'So? You're married! That's allowed.'

'Not in my house it's not.' She looked mortified. 'I've never done it.'

'You must have!' The irony of shelving Austen whilst arguing the merits of marital flatulence only served to fuel her amusement. She was still buzzing after the night before. Every night she'd been at Brody's, she'd slept like a log and waking up wrapped in his arms was the icing on the cake. It was proving harder and harder to play down her feelings for him. Or her lust. Their abstinence was becoming almost Austenian in itself. Still, even if he farted, she wouldn't mind. Oh God, she had it bad. Victor being quiet again had allowed her to enjoy her cohabitation. She couldn't wait till they finally had sex. She knew he was feeling the strain. He was at the gym a lot for a man who didn't need to work out so much. She focused back on Lola, who'd huffed to get her attention in the first place.

'Come on, you're pregnant. He'll understand. It's John – you couldn't meet a nicer bloke. Apart from his friend, of course.'

Lola made a sick motion with her finger in her mouth, but she nodded along too. 'True, we have a couple of good ones, but that's not the point. When I'm in bed, I'm like a bloody beached whale, honest to Christ. Last night was so sticky, the fan was on but I was baking. Poor John was trying his best to keep me cool, but I was just miserable. I got up to spend a penny, and I let rip. I mean, it was bad, and with my pickled onion craving . . .'

'Please don't tell me you shat yourself, Lola.'

'No, but it was still like a pickled onion factory like there for at least two hours. There was no air. I think I'll just divorce him, start a new life.'

'I wouldn't recommend it – you love John.'

Lola's face dropped, and Hannah wanted to bite her tongue off. 'Oh God, that was a joke. I'm fine, really. I didn't mean it to be snippy. I am glad I left, believe me.' Lola moved in her chair, trying to get comfortable but looking like she'd failed. Hannah walked over to the customer fridge and paid for two cans of cold, caffeine-free cola. She passed one to her boss and took a seat next to her. John was out running errands and doing local deliveries, and they were usually quiet till lunchtime. Especially when the heat meant that many were out in the sunshine, mostly in their gardens or in the pub beer garden.

Lola took a deep sip and smiled for the first time that morning. 'Ahh, thanks. I know you didn't mean it nastily; I just feel so proud of you. And a little scared, sometimes. I can't help it. John worries too. I just want you to know that we are here, one hundred per cent for you and Ava. Brody loves you – err, to bits, you and Ava.'

'I love him too.'

214

Lola's smile widened. 'You do?'

'God yes. It scares the shit out of me though, and I kept expecting him to wake up, or find someone better, or get fed up . . .'

She'd seen him some days after a bad shift, seen his haunted, tired features. He'd always played with Ava though and been nothing but attentive to the pair of them. It was when Ava was asleep, and things were quiet when he'd change. Never to anger, or frustration. Just being a little quiet, hugging her a little bit tighter on the sofa. Wanting to hear about Hannah's day and giving minimal detail back about his. She knew him on his bad days, and they were still some of the best days she'd had with him. With anyone. Ava too. He channelled his bad days into good and gave back to his community. He was a literal hunk. She didn't want to cause him pain.

'I just think that it's still quite new, under this pressure, and a bit too good to be true.' She couldn't look Lola in the eye, so she took a long drink before adding, 'He's too good to be true, right?' She looked to Lola and realised that she did need an answer, because she didn't understand it herself. 'And if he's real, this super guy with his super dog, all burly and quiet, and loving, if he's real? Then I don't get it.' She slapped her hand against her forehead. 'Because a guy like that should not want a bundle of trouble like me. The whole ex thing. The police issues. Ava. And, I mean, he's highly trained. I work in a bookshop . . .'

Jesus, the moods were obviously preying on her mind more than she thought. It was like a torrent coming out of her.

'Hey!' Lola objected, banging her fist down on the chair arm. 'Stop spiralling. And also, objection, it's a very nice bookshop. That pays well.'

'True, and I didn't mean it like that, but after childcare, and stuff for Ava, and me? I'm not flush, and I can't just live with Brody forever. It's his house.'

'Yes you can, and that will be fine with Brody.'

'But that's a negative, Lola.'

'Why? He has that big house, he pays his way, you pay your way. You are both nuts for each other.'

'He loves Hannah though, and I'm Erin, remember?'

'I never met Erin, I would have liked her I'm sure. I do know Hannah though, and she loves Andrew Brody. She's tough as old boots and is shacked up with my copper mate and everything. At it like rabbits they are.'

'We are not.'

'You are!'

'Nope. He's loving, he's close, but that's it. It's starting to get a bit weird when we first get into bed, but he's been tired lately anyway. He wants to wait till things calm down, but we're just waiting for things to move along. He wants to wait till my head's clear I think. He's being patient, but . . .' She bit her lip. Bedding Brody wouldn't affect clearing her head, because she was worrying about Victor anyway. And the fact was, even in her situation, with all the worry, she wanted to. She was dying to take things further with her boyfriend. She cared for him. Every night in his bed was getting harder, in more ways than one. 'He's been working later since we got back, some big job he can't talk about, but it's been bothering him.'

John came through the door then, and Lola shot up to meet him. Well, she got out of the chair after a couple of failed attempts, and then needed a wee, but before too long they were both in the kitchen dealing with the lunch rush. Hannah ran the bookshop counter, and whenever she caught a glimpse of them together they were deep in conversation. And avoiding her eye. She tried to push the feelings of fear she felt flickering around her, and she rang Ruby the minute she got a free moment. She always checked in on Ava.

'Hey, love, everything okay?' Ruby was as cheery as ever, and she could hear the kids laughing in the background. 'We've got them all under the air conditioning in the living room. *Toy Story* and ice pops are going down a treat.'

'Oh good, Ava doing okay?'

'She's as happy as Larry, love. Just let me go into the office.' The noise dimmed down after Hannah heard the click of a door. 'Are you sure you're okay?'

'Yeah, I just wanted to remind you to be careful, okay? Keep your eyes open.'

'Love, it's so hot at the minute that the kids are happy with shade, ice-pops and the paddling pool. We've been changing our routine lately, staying closer to home. Don't worry, we have the doorbell cameras, and the house alarms. We lock the electric gates at the front.'

Hannah knew the house was a nice detached that also had a kiddy-proof garden and electric entrance gates. The cars were kept separate from the house by a wall, and the whole place had CCTV. Ruby was a dab hand with tech, and she had their house all wired up and modern as could be. It was like a nursery in a private home, and she knew she could trust them with Ava.

'Sorry, I know I'm being a pain.'

'You're ringing to check on your daughter, and the rest of us. Nothing wrong with that, and besides, Brody has already been to check out the place.'

'What?' He'd never mentioned it.

'Yeah, the other night. He came over when the kids had gone home, helped me adjust the cameras so we could cover optimum ground, checked the fences. He even sent a buddy of his from the fire station over to check the smoke detectors and exits. The kids loved Reggie the fireman that day. Anyway, like I said, we're like Fort Knox here, love. You go enjoy your day, and we'll see you later.'

'Thanks. See you soon.' Hannah put down the phone, bewildered. *The other night.* He'd said he was working late, but she wondered whether he had been working on cases or working behind the scenes to protect her. Calling in favours at work, other services. She gnawed at her lip. It had started already, and Victor hadn't even shown his face yet. Her name was out there now, on court documents and at her local doctors. Ava was registered too. She'd even applied for the money due to her daughter, a bank account. Things were easing.

She pocketed her phone in her work apron and threw herself back into work. When five o'clock came, and Brody pulled up, she still didn't know how she was going to act around him. She decided to focus on cleaning the till area instead, dragging her heels even though they had to go collect Ava and get on with feeding her, bathtime, the little routine they'd got into lately. Brody had offered to collect them both that night, and she felt awkward when the shop bell went.

'Hi.' She tried to keep a straight face as she cleaned a teeny speck of dirt off the screen of the till. 'I won't be a minute. Did you have a good day?'

'That depends.'

He fell silent, and she finished her task in silence. When she'd done, she had no choice but to look at him. 'On what.'

'On how mad you are that I went to Ruby's house.' He rubbed his shoe on the floor in the pose of a regretful teenager. 'She called to tell me, thought she'd upset you.'

'So is everyone in on this then? Do we have cameras, at our house?'

'No!' Brody looked appalled and she swore under her breath. 'Not at our home.'

'Sorry, that was wrong. And cheap.'

'No, it's a fair question, and no, other than the doorbell camera and the camera on the dog pen for Bullet, that's it, and you've seen those, and the security system.' She'd set the house alarm herself that morning. 'If you want any more security, we can look at that together. I just figured that with the kids being there, it wouldn't hurt to prepare them, check things over. Ava loves it there, doesn't she?'

'Yes, and thank you, but you should have told me.'

'Yes, and I also should have told you that I've been looking for him, for the poster of the flyers, but I didn't, because I did it off duty and I didn't want to scare you. We had a sighting, so I drove up there one night. It went cold, I didn't find much, but the description fit his profile.'

'And if you'd have found him?'

'I would have notified my colleagues and driven home to you.'

'Nothing else?'

'Nothing else. I have nothing to say to that man. Ever. My only thought was for you.'

'What about your job?'

'My job is what I do, not what I am, and I did nothing wrong. I am looking for a person of interest – that's all – and the case led that way. I documented my findings to my superiors and I'm already stood down from the case.'

'You have that speech prepared?'

'It's not a speech, and that's the way I talk at work.' He looked stern when he'd been speaking, professional, but his eyebrows waggled at her now, and he was her Andrew again. 'Just because you turned me into a sissy, doesn't mean people have to know. I was keeping you safe, and I knew you wouldn't like it. I messed up, and I'm admitting it.'

She folded the cleaning cloth in front of her, sticking it into her cleaning caddy and shoved it under the counter.

'Okay, well help me lock up and you're forgiven.' She picked up her bag and shop keys and, after walking over to him, she dropped the keys into his outstretched hand. 'Thank you for protecting me, but I can do this, you know. I don't want anyone else to get dragged in.'

His hand tightened around the keys, and they headed out into the street. He locked the doors swiftly and tucked her into his arms as they headed out to the car. Hannah was just leaning in closer to Brody, when she caught a movement in the corner of her eye. Turning, she looked straight into Victor's eyes, and she froze in place. Brody clicked open the car, opening the door for her, and she thought for a moment that he hadn't noticed. She didn't know where to run to. That was her first thought. She would have run back into the shop, but Brody had the keys. The door was locked. Brody's car door was open right at the side of her, the passenger seat looking so normal, she wanted to laugh. It would be so easy just to get into the car and drive to collect Ava. Go and buy some things to cook together later, before bathing Ava and finding some film on the box to watch. Maybe tonight they would have made love.

That was gone now, and she couldn't believe how she was feeling. Anger. She was scared, but she was feeling anger more. At the fact he was here, and that she wasn't ready. She hadn't had nearly enough time.

'Just get in the car,' Brody said, in a low, easy voice. He smiled at her and nodded his head ever so slightly in Victor's direction. 'It's okay.'

She looked from him, back to Victor, and he was standing there next to his car, plain as day. He looked tired, jowls filled with stubble. He'd put on weight; he looked stooped somehow. She couldn't work out why he looked so different, but when she met his eyes again, he was right in front of her. She took a step forward, towards Victor, and then another. She crossed her arms, feeling her fingers close around the strap of her bag. Coiling herself instinctively. Two more steps, and then he took a step, and she shouted, 'Stop!' His leg faltered, but then he took the step. She felt her anger flicker, but he didn't lift his other foot.

'We need to talk, ERIN!' He shouted her name for Brody to hear, but he hadn't moved an inch. She could hear him watching them, but she knew he hadn't moved a muscle.

'I said everything I had to say to you on the phone. Leave. I'm calling the police.'

She pulled her phone out of her bag and unlocked it with a

shaky hand. She glared at her hand for a second, willing it to stop, and started to dial.

'We need to talk, alone. Ava doesn't deserve this.'

'Don't talk to me about Ava. You never gave a shiny shit before.'

'Woo! That mouth! You've gone a bit country girl, haven't you? Living up here, with the farmers.' He nodded his head sharply in Brody's direction, and she heard him take a step closer to her.

'Put the phone down, get in the car. We'll talk,' Victor said.

'That's the only car I'm getting into.' She pointed at Brody's vehicle as she dialled the final nine, putting her phone to her ear and hoping to God he didn't rush at her. 'Yes, police please. My estranged husband is here, and I fear for my safety. I have a court case pending. I have a restraining order against him.'

Victor snorted at her, laughing the way he always did. Like a rabid hyena. Brody was closer now. She heard him mutter, 'This guy?' under his breath, and she was laughing before she could stop herself. That shut Victor up. She knew he hadn't heard Brody. She gave out the location of the bookshop, knowing that the police were literally on the street already. She wondered whether Victor knew that. He didn't show an ounce of being rattled.

'I'm glad you find this funny, but you won't for long. Kidnapping our daughter, leaving me to run the house, and the business? You know your place is back at home, looking after all that. Running off, coming here?' His eyes darkened, and she fought the urge to cry. 'You know how it went last time you left. I got you back.'

'Yeah.' She nodded, her face curling with anger. 'And I paid for it.' The last time he'd found her, before she got pregnant, he'd dragged her home. She hadn't gone back to the library after that. Not working was her punishment. One of them. 'I'm never coming back.'

'We're leaving,' Brody said behind her, and she felt his hand close around hers. He didn't move her, just held her hand, and she pulled him closer, towards the car.

'That's my wife you have there, Big'un.' Victor couldn't leave it. Nothing had changed. 'I'll be wanting you out of the picture. This is a family matter.'

Brody waited till Hannah was in the car, and he walked around to his side at the front of the car. He never turned his back to Victor, but he took his time. When he came to sit next to her, she reached for his hand and gripped it tight. His face looked relaxed, but she knew she must look terrified. She felt it.

'He won't leave. How the hell did he find me?'

'He's been close for a while. Small town.' He didn't look happy about that this time. Before they knew it, a police car pulled up at the side of Victor, and Brody pulled out on to the street, heading in the opposite direction. He drove a different route to collect Ava, and once Hannah had her, he drove them straight home. No supermarket shopping for them tonight. He was on the phone when she got out of the shower, Ava having crashed out without a murmur of dismay. She'd had a busy time in the paddling pool, playing in the sun with her little friends, and had worn herself out.

'The station dropped him back off at his car, he's been warned not to contact you again. He's claiming he hasn't been served.'

'I'll check tomorrow, with my solicitor. See what's next. They have the proof.' Hannah tried to talk about the injunction, but her words came out in a garble. She was trying to pull a jumper on over her sweats, feeling ice cold, but her arms were refusing to work, and she ended up in a mess of clothes and arms.

Brody sat by her until she calmed down. Eventually, she was dressed and breathing normally. Sitting side by side, backs against the wall, she turned to look at him.

'You know, this night would be a lot better if you took your clothes off.'

'God, you kill me when you say things like that.' He kissed her. 'We'll have our time, once things settle down. There's no rush, baby.'

His laugh was the only thing she got, but he didn't take his body an inch away from hers the whole night. Bullet slept at the top of the landing, between both bedrooms, a new basket beneath him.

Chapter 26

Brody was distracted for the next week. His operation was winding up, the person who assaulted him due in court. He'd been called to give evidence in court, and the news had not been welcome.

'I can try to get it rearranged,' he said doubtfully over coffee that Thursday morning. Hannah had the day off and was looking forward to taking Ava to the toddler group to see the girls. Since that day outside the shop, Victor had not been seen. The police had warned him off contacting her again, and her solicitor confirmed that he had dodged the servers. They'd posted it through his door, their old front door. He was denying receipt of anything. Her solicitor was ploughing on regardless, trying to get Hannah, Erin as was, her life back. She didn't want a penny from him, though her solicitor had strongly advised against it. Brody had backed her all the way, giving her support. They were decorating Ava's room together. Brody was excited about it. He'd picked out some samples from the local DIY shop, asking her to pick what colours she wanted. 'I can try and pull some strings, get it vacated for a bit.'

Hannah was already shaking her head. 'No way. You got hurt by that arsehole, you need to be there to tell the truth. You've both worked too hard on this.' She stroked the scruff of Bullet's neck as she passed him, putting the breakfast things away. Ava was talking more and more. Dog. Mama. The other night, she'd looked straight at Brody and said, 'Dada.' They'd both pretended not to hear it, but she saw the look on Brody's face. He lit up from the inside, and Hannah didn't want to contradict her daughter. So she ignored it. She was a pro at that now. He was more of a father than her real dad was; it was only natural. 'Besides, we're fine. I'll be busy at work; Lola is desperate to start her maternity leave. She's done in but she wants to be near John too so the café is the best place.' Hannah had extra hours planned at the shop, and given the last few weeks, she wasn't about to let John and Lola down. Plus the money would help. Solicitors weren't free, and she wanted to maintain her own money and independence.

'I know, John's eager for her to rest too.' Brody spoke in sullen tones, and she went to sit on his lap.

'Andrew, I'm fine. We have to live our lives, remember? Now, you go to court, and kick some arse.' She straightened his dark grey tie, smoothing down his crisp white shirt and taking in the contours of him. 'I'm going to get ready, go see the girls.' He opened his mouth again, and she pushed her index finger against his lips. 'Shush. I'll take my phone. Martine and Ruby will be there, and I'll come home straight after. Okay?'

She could tell he wasn't comforted much, but she kissed him by way of distraction. 'And if you have a bad day, when you come home I can do this . . .' She ran her fingers down the side of his neck, making him groan. 'And this . . .' She undid one of his shirt buttons and pushed her fingertips inside, running them down the length of his chest. He sighed heavily, squirming in his seat under her.

'Distracting me won't work, Han,' he said between gritted teeth.

She smiled knowingly. 'Oh really?' She blew on his ear, and he looked across at Ava. She was oblivious, playing with one of her toys in the corner. Bullet was following her around as usual. Best buds. 'I think it might.'

He groaned again, pulling her closer for a quick and very deep kiss, before lifting her off his lap. He adjusted his trousers, and she smirked at him.

'It's not funny,' he grumbled, but she caught his sexy smile. 'You're killing me here.'

'Your ban, not mine,' she sang back at him. 'I'm ready when you are.'

His eyes widened, and she laughed again. She loved to tease him. She did hope he would cave eventually though. It was getting far too steamy in their bedroom; it was affecting her sleep more than the worry.

'Tonight,' he said gruffly. 'I might just cave with a little persuasion.' His lip twitched in the adorable way she liked. 'I just want it to be right. For both of us.'

Hannah's stomach flipped. 'It will.' She whispered the last part into his delectable ear. 'I know how right it will be, trust me.' The answering groan he gave made her wish the whole day away.

She kissed him again, giving him something to think about while he was sat in that courtroom. She wished she could go, see him up there, but she had a feeling it wouldn't be the best move. Too risky. Too close to home too. Her day in court was coming, and she would have to get through that. 'Now go to work; get those bad guys.'

He left begrudgingly, gathering her to him at the front door and kissing her breath away before heading out with Bullet. He was due at the station to go on another job with another handler whilst Brody was in court. Another reason for Brody's distracted mood this morning. He didn't like Bullet out without him, and it was well known at the station that Bullet had the same opinion. He worked well with others, being the professional hound he was, but Brody and Bullet were as close as two partners could be. The whole station could see that. Hell, the whole village.

* * *

226

She watched them drive away and finished up with breakfast. She cleaned everything up, packing up some snacks to take to the group. She went to get ready, noticing the time on the clock. She often went a little earlier, to help Ruby and Martine set up. She was halfway up the stairs, Ava in her arms, when there was a soft knock on the front door. Frowning, she turned to see a dark shadow in the glass and froze.

It wasn't Brody. Brody wouldn't knock, and the shadow was too small. The knock came again, the shadow moving lower. A second later, the letterbox flap flipped up, and she ran up the stairs out of sight. Ava was chatting away, and she shushed her. Hands shaking, she put Ava into her cot in her room, shutting the curtains quickly and passing her a few toys.

'I know you're there, Erin. I could see you. Open the door. Now.'

Victor's voice stopped her in her tracks. At the sound, Ava looked up and started to cry. Her face was fearful. *Did she remember him? Or is she reacting to me?* Hannah gathered her breath and tried to think. Victor banged again. Not enough to draw attention she noticed. The neighbours would all be at work by now. She was due to meet the girls. *The girls!*

'Erin, open the door. It's time to come home. Stop all this shit. You're costing me money!'

She pushed Ava's bedroom door to, hugging a crying Ava to her behind the door. Every hard knock he made cut into her. Shaking, she felt something dig into her hip from her pocket, and Hannah came bursting out of her. It was as though Erin was there for a second, holding her daughter to her body tight and wishing she could disappear forever. To escape the inescapable.

'Get up,' she growled at herself, and Ava stopped crying. She stood up, grabbing for the mobile she'd shoved in her pocket on her way up the stairs. She dialled 999. When the operator connected, asking which service she required in a thick Yorkshire accent, someone spoke. They asked for the police, citing that they were in danger. A woman and child. The voice rattled off the address, their names, the details of the restraining order. All while downstairs, Victor talked through the letterbox. He was getting louder now, having heard Ava. *How the fuck did he find us here? He must have waited for Andrew to leave. Bastard.* The operator took the details down, assuring her officers were on the way. To keep calm, to lock themselves away, hide till the cavalry arrived. The operator was still speaking to her, but she ended the call. Trying Brody with frantic fingers, she got his voicemail. *Shit. He was due in court, he'd probably had to turn his phone off.* She went to dial John, but then thought of Lola and dialled Martine instead.

'Hi, love, you running late?'

Hannah burst into tears at the sounds she could hear on the line. On a normal Thursday off from work, she would be there now. Having a coffee using the cups she could hear tinkling in the background. She knew that Martine would be able to hear the noises around her too.

'No. Victor's here. I've rung the police, but Andrew's in court.' She realised then that the voice on the 999 call had been her. She'd done it. She'd parroted off that information. She brushed her tears away angrily, peeping out of the bedroom window. She couldn't see anything. No people.

'Open this fucking door now! Erin, this is your last warning!'

She could hear Martine in her ear, telling her it would be okay, shouting things at Ruby so fast she couldn't understand what she was saying. Ava wailed again, and was repeating 'mama, mama, mama' over and over. The occasional shuddering 'dog-gie' breaking her heart. God, she wished Bullet was here. She could hear Victor at the back of the house now, banging the fence, shouting her name. She listened on the line to her friend, back behind the door.

Martine sounded like she was running a marathon, the shock making her words come out thick, heavy. Weighted with the panic woven within them.

'We're with you, Hannah. Stay hidden, help is coming. Okay, keep talking.'

The thick wooden cricket bat she'd bought and stashed in Ava's room when they moved in sat at her side now, pulled from the back of the wardrobe where she'd stashed it from even Brody's eyes.

'It's okay,' she whispered to Ava, who was settling down on her chest. The occasional jump of her little body as her father made more noise, going crazy outside her home. 'It's okay.' She could hear Martine breathing heavily, Ruby shouting something indistinct. Voices around them. It didn't sound like the community centre. She listened to her friends' panicked movements, her daughter's unsettled shrieks and sobs, her own heartbeat. The sound of the back of the house being torn apart by the wolf she'd feared forever. She heard a smash of glass, and Ava whimpered.

'It's okay, Ava. We're safe.' Half the police station would be giving evidence today, it was a big week. The rest would be covering the day-to-day work. She couldn't hear the sirens yet. *When were they going to come? Trust him to wait till I'm weak. Alone. Cowering.*

'I can't do this,' she whispered to herself, shutting her eyes tight. She heard Martine in her ear then, as clear as a bell.

'Yes you bloody can. I did it once. Ruby knows. You can do this. Ruby, get the key out! I can't see anything, quickly! Hannah, get off the floor now. You have to get out. We're coming to get you.' A second later, she heard a commotion at the front door, just as a loud smash and shattering of glass pervaded the back. The front door opened, and she was on her feet, hand on the door handle. She had Ava gripped to her, the bat in her hand, heavy. Her other hand shook on the handle. The phone was shoved in her back pocket, and she heard the line drop out just as she heard her friends.

'Hannah!'

229

She opened the door, and Martine was halfway up the stairs. There was a deafening thud from the kitchen, a wrenching sound. The back door was toast, Hannah knew. Ruby was standing in the doorway, sweating and wild-eyed as she looked down the hall towards the kitchen. She raised her hand, and Hannah thought how long it looked, eerily alien. Then she realised it was a rolling pin, taken from the community kitchens. These women had raced across the village to help her. She felt Erin within her, nod at Hannah in agreement. *We can do this. Move!*

Then there was a loud smash, and Victor was there in the kitchen doorway as they were halfway down the stairs. He looked at them, Martine on the stairs, looking at Ruby in fear. She was prone in front of him, right in front of the doorway.

'Run, Ruby!' Hannah shouted, and she heard Victor laugh. She hated the sound to the very pit of her soul. Ava started to cry again. Ruby, rolling pin still raised high, didn't move. She didn't take her eyes from Victor. 'Martine, take her!' Hannah turned and shoved Ava into Martine's arms, and Victor tried to grab at her through the banister. 'Bitch!'

She kicked out at him before he could get her. She shoved Martine up the stairs. 'Lock yourself in the bathroom!'

She could hear Victor coming, and Ruby was right there. She wouldn't let her get hurt. She couldn't. She felt the bat in her hands as she took the stairs two at a time, getting in front of Ruby just before her nemesis. The anger in his features was so familiar to her, it nearly took her off her feet. She pushed Ruby back out of the door, trying to block the stairs and protect the others, and she saw Victor's fist fly back, the angle of his feet change. *No. NO. Never again.* Erin and Hannah said that together, and finally, they were one again. 'NO VICTOR!' She raised the bat with everything she could and brought it down on him as he reached for her throat. 'NOOOOO!' she screamed! 'Never again!'

She went to raise the bat again, waiting for his fingers to curl at her throat, but there was nothing. She looked around, and he was on the floor. Ruby took the bat from her, crossing it in her arms with her rolling pin.

'Now that,' she said, panting. 'Was pretty damn Hannah.'

Chapter 27

Officer Brody's house was now officially a crime scene. Hannah had heard one of the other officers say it over the radio. It wasn't gossip, just plain facts. She was sitting in the back of one of the police cars when he found her, and she couldn't look him in the eye.

'You shouldn't be in here,' he said angrily as he slipped into the seat next to her. The other officers were all talking to Ruby, who was speaking animatedly and miming wielding a bat with gusto. The officers were taking notes, nodding occasionally. From her view out of the open window, she could feel the sun. She also saw Martine rolling her eyes at Ruby as she walked around in small circles with Ava. They'd all been checked over by the paramedic. The police had arrived minutes after, finding all three women and a baby outside, and Victor tied up and coming to. The police had bundled him off to the hospital cuffed to an officer. Brody was pressing charges against him. Everyone was. 'Are you okay? I saw Ava.'

He'd checked on her. The thought warmed her a little, through the numbness. 'We're fine, and they have to check the house out. It's wrecked. It's going to cost a fortune.'

Brody reached for her hand, taking it in his and rubbing it. 'You're cold. Sod the money. I'm insured. We can redecorate the whole place together.' He frowned, and she wanted to rub it out of his skin. 'Or move. I'm so sorry I wasn't here. When I got off the stand, the lads came and got me but . . .' She saw the fingers on his other hand clench, just for a second, but then he relaxed. 'Anyway, it seems the local toddler group had things covered.' He pulled her close then, as if he'd been holding back. She ended up half in his lap, wrapping herself around him.

'Er, Hannah . . .'

'Sorry, I'm just very glad you're here.'

'Yeah, well I love you, Hannah. Not the time I know, but after today I'm not holding words back anymore. I love you, and I am so proud of you. I was terrified. I thought you were both . . . Never mind what I thought – you defended each other. John is mad by the way. You owe him a call.'

She couldn't take everything he said in after proud. 'Proud of me? I panicked. It was awful, I—'

Brody stopped her in her tracks. 'You were amazing. You defended yourself, your friends, and your daughter. You got help here. You were calm on the phone. I heard. Victor is done now. After this, the witnesses. You're safe, Hannah. We can shut this down.'

She hugged him tight. 'We? You're off the case, remember.' She pulled back and looked into his eyes. 'No more time spent on him. Ever.'

Brody took her in, dropping a long kiss on her lips before he answered. 'Anything you want. I prefer the question game anyway.' His devilish smirk made her wish they were on their sofa at home. Then she remembered the police cars, the forensics, everything. The car fell silent. 'We need to go get Ava, sort this mess out.' He nodded, preparing to get out. She pushed her hands onto his chest, stilling him.

'Before I say this, I want you to know that the thing I like most about you is the way you let me be. You let me find my feet.'

'You already had them.' Ever the gent. Never the one to take credit. 'It was all you.'

'Yeah, well thank you. I love you, Andrew Brody. For so many reasons, including that.' She looked around at them. 'The uniform's a bonus.'

'You do? Hannah, I didn't say it to—'

'Stop.' She laughed. Another piece of numbness fell away. 'Andrew, I love you. I've been trying to sleep with you for weeks. I love our life.' She bit her lip. 'I'm just sorry the way it happened, what happened here. Not where I am now. I belong here, with you. I chose to be with you, Officer Brody.'

'Call me Andrew,' he teased as he pulled her closer.

After they'd kissed as long as they dared leave Ava for, which wasn't long, they headed back to reality. Brody's strong hands never left hers as they collected Ava, spoke to the girls, said their goodbyes to the cavalry as they finished their various tasks. Brody spoke in hushed tones to many people, and she knew he was piecing the scene together in his mind. They might need to redecorate after all, just to please him. She knew he was thinking the same.

Before too long, it was just the three of them. The women in the community centre had taken Ruby and Martine's kids, all the mums in the villages seamlessly making it work like a superwoman phone tree. They had to get back now though. They'd done so much. Hannah had thanked them over and over, and Brody had hugged each woman so tight they'd both blushed furiously.

They sat in the living room, Ava sitting on Brody's knee. The fuss she'd had since the incident had made her ecstatic, but it would be a long time before Hannah would be fully sure that Ava wasn't traumatised. She knew the signs, and her daughter had her, and their new pack. The wolf was dead.

'When I came here,' she said as they sat and took in the events of the day, in their mess of a home, 'I was Hannah, and Erin was just locked away. She was sick and tired of fighting. I really think I split myself in half.' He listened as always, her rock to lean on when she needed it. 'You saw both in me, and I think that's one of the things I was the most scared of. I never thought I'd find someone like you.'

'You have no idea how much I feel that about you.' His goofy grin told her how much.

'I've decided to keep my name, change it officially. I meant what I said to Victor: Erin is dead. She's part of me, but I'm Hannah here, at home. What do you think?'

Brody grinned, and she kissed him again. Ava made mwah noises at him, pushing her palm to her face. Brody did it back to her. Thick as thieves as ever. Bullet was snoozing by his feet. He'd done nothing but sniff when he'd got back. Brody had had to make him stop looking for Victor. Hannah was going to sneak him a prime steak when Brody wasn't looking. He was a good dog.

'I think I love you all. Hannah.' He dropped a kiss onto her lips. 'My Hannah.'

Two years later

'It's Facebook official! Hannah White is in the building!'

She burst through the door, her change of name deed in one hand, her divorce papers in the other. Brody had booked the day off to take her out for the occasion; Ava was at Martine and Ruby's. She was currently into drum kits and singing every Disney song known to man in her squeaky cute little voice. A day off from that wouldn't hurt their ears. She was doing well. Victor had no contact now, and he hadn't tried since the attack either. It had been about control, not love. It had been from the start.

'Are you ready to wine and dine a free and single woman?'

Bullet was at the door to the kitchen, sitting like a sentry. She could see something flickering in the gap in the doorway.

'Hey, boy, where's Brody, eh?' She always called him Brody when addressing the dog. They were work colleagues, after all. He slowly moved aside, and she noticed he had something stuck in his collar.

'What's this?' She pulled a rolled-up piece of paper out.

Bullet nudged the door open, going to sit at Brody's side. He was sitting at the island. She always found him so sexy sitting there. They'd updated the kitchen, well the whole house really. They'd had a lot of naked painting fun, she recalled with a blush every time she saw the happy yellow walls in the kitchen. He was dressed to match her, her smart dress complementing his smart suit. The flickering was from the candles on the countertop, two filled glasses of champagne next to an ice bucket.

'I thought we could celebrate in style; we have time before our reservation.' She went to sit on the stool next to him, and he pulled it closer to his. 'How do you feel?' His eyes searched hers, but she felt nothing but relief. Happiness. Life was good.

'Free,' she said simply. 'Happy. I love you.'

He grinned, looking a bit sheepish. 'Good, then you won't freak out when you read the note.' She remembered the rolled-up paper in her hands, and went to open it. His hand hovered over it. 'Hannah, I mean it.' She looked up at him, intrigued now. His eyes locked onto hers, as they always did. 'No freak-outs. It's just the question game.'

She opened the note as the cogs turned in her head. When she read the words, the yes was out of her lips a second after. Pushed out with her heart and her gut. By Hannah, and Erin – the two halves of her who loved him to distraction.

The note said: *Will you do me the honour of becoming Mrs Hannah Brody?*

Of all the things she'd done in her life, she knew she could live the rest of it quite happily playing the question game. Of their lives. Just like that.

A Letter from Rachel Dove

Thank you so much for choosing to read *Someone Like You*. I hope you enjoyed it! If you did and would like to be the first to know about my new releases, you can follow me on Twitter/Facebook/Instagram/Tiktok below.

Domestic violence affects people all around the world and is still rather a taboo subject even in these modern times. During the pandemic, with the cases rising, services being stretched, court systems closed down, I felt driven to write a book to reflect these issues, in a realistic way. I hope I have given Hannah the voice that she deserves, and you take something away from her story. As with all my books, the characters are at the heart of my stories, and I firmly believe that above all, love wins. Look after each other, till the next time we go on a fictional adventure.

I hope you loved *Someone Like You* and if you did I would be so grateful if you would leave a review. I always love to hear what readers thought, and it helps new readers discover my books too.

Thanks,

Rachel Dove

Instagram: https://www.instagram.com/writerdove/
Twitter: https://twitter.com/WriterDove
Facebook: https://www.facebook.com/RachelDoveauthor/
TikTok: https://www.tiktok.com/search?q=writerdove&t=165703
7378922

The Forever House

**Escape with a feel-good romance
that will warm your heart this summer!**

Emily Hendrickson is tired of being the wedding guest and never the bride. Working at her local paper as a wedding columnist, she can't wait to write her own happy-ever-after.

When she bumps into her childhood sweetheart, **Calvin Albright**, her world is knocked off balance. Calvin has returned to the quiet town of Hebblestone desperate for a fresh start. After his wife tragically died two years ago, he wants nothing more than to find a new home and settle down with his son, **Isaac**.

Isaac can see how lonely his dad is – he's determined to help him find love again and complete their family . . .

After uploading a video to his blog in search of a new girl-friend for his dad, he convinces Emily to use the local paper to make the video viral and sift through the potential candidates.

But as the letters to Calvin begin to flood in, could the promise of love be closer to home than they think?

The Second Chance Hotel

April Statham had it all – until her husband left her for a blonde ten years her junior. Now she's thirty-five, single, and starting again. So she does what anyone in her position would do: she impulsively invests her life savings in the chalet park she used to visit as a child, on the beautiful Cornish Coast.

The Shady Pines Chalet Park is . . . ramshackle. But it has one big advantage – it is as far as physically possible from April's ex, his new fiancée, and her old life. With gorgeous handyman **Cillian O'Leary**, April is looking forward to the challenge.

As visitors arrive, April realises that Shady Pines isn't just a second chance for her, it gives Cillian another shot at happiness too.

But when he moves into the chalet next door, April's painful past starts to catch up with her, and she struggles to reconcile her feelings for Cillian.

Is April's new beginning destined to end in failure – or will she find new friends, a new life and new love at her second chance hotel?

Fans of Jenny Colgan, Emma Davies and Debbie Johnson will love Rachel Dove!

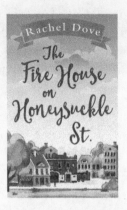

The Fire House on Honeysuckle Street

Lucy is looking for a fresh start. Sam is in search of his past. But what they both need most might turn out to be each other . . .

The picturesque village of Westfield is about to welcome some new residents.

Sam has transferred from London to the local Fire Brigade, but his move has more to it than a desire to escape city life. There are answers Sam needs to find and the village is the place to look.

Lucy is at the end of her tether. Between her marriage falling apart and single-handedly dealing with her son's special needs, Lucy knows something needs to change. Could Westfield be the new beginning she needs?

A heart-warming, laugh-out-loud romantic comedy, perfect for fans of Cathy Bramley and Heidi Swain!

Acknowledgements

With every book I forget just how much work (and snacks, crying, punching a pillow, research, and procrastination) goes into creating one. From a nugget of an idea, a headline, or a character whispering in my head – a story is born.

Writing is a solitary beast most of the time, but there is a whole camp of people who are involved in the process, and that's before it gets to you lovely readers, bloggers and reviewers!

Massive shout out to my readers, book lovers, my fellow writers/bloggers in the book community, including to name but a few:

Mary Jayne Baker, Lucy Keeling, Vikkie Wakeham, All at Squadpod, Rachel Burton, Lynda Stacey, Victoria Cooke, Kate Beeden, Rachael Stewart, and many more. I love you all! Thanks for keeping me sane and being as nutty as I am.

To Wakefield Libraries and the folks at Stanley Library, who big me up all the time and are amazing supporters of community, caring and fiction in general.

Huge thanks to Belinda Toor and Abigail Fenton and the team at HQ for their support, encouragement and patience. I wrote this book suffering from bereavement, covid, and then long covid, and whilst I despaired it would never be completed, and my brain was in fact mush, they never wavered or lost faith. It's been a journey, ladies. Thank you.

Huge gratitude to my lovely friends and family for supporting me, putting up with my clacking away on the keyboard, forgetting dinnertime, and muttering to myself as I committed Hannah's story to the page.

Thanks to my two teens, J and N, for draining our bank account daily, allowing me to wash your daily wardrobe changes (Lady Gaga changes her outfit less than you two!) and mud-filled kits.

Thanks for making me drive you everywhere you want to go at the drop of a hat, while picking up enough mates to fill a football field. All while groaning at my music choices and telling me to park MILES away from anyone you know. Your dad is a die-hard Ed Sheeran fan, just be grateful I introduced you to good music too. (No offence, Ed. I actually love you as well.)

Thanks for being so full in heart that we always get told how amazing you are. We have always known this, but it's good to hear anyway.

Thank you for always making me laugh, showing me that the world is not all doom and gloom, and for rolling your eyes when I try to be cool on TikTok. Don't worry, I will NEVER stop being embarrassing, but your mates think I'm cool, so there. Once I perfect the dancing, it will only get worse.

And finally, to my husband, Peter. Thank you for being you. You are my best friend and I love you completely. You are always the hero in my storybook and the sparkle in my eye. I weave you into every book boyfriend, immortalised forever for everyone to love, but I get to keep you.

Dear Reader,

We hope you enjoyed reading this book. If you did, we'd be so appreciative if you left a review. It really helps us and the author to bring more books like this to you.

Here at HQ Digital we are dedicated to publishing fiction that will keep you turning the pages into the early hours. Don't want to miss a thing? To find out more about our books, promotions, discover exclusive content and enter competitions you can keep in touch in the following ways:

JOIN OUR COMMUNITY:

Sign up to our new email newsletter: http://smarturl.it/SignUpHQ

Read our new blog www.hqstories.co.uk

🐦 : https://twitter.com/HQStories

f : www.facebook.com/HQStories

BUDDING WRITER?

We're also looking for authors to join the HQ Digital family! Find out more here:

https://www.hqstories.co.uk/want-to-write-for-us/

Thanks for reading, from the HQ Digital team